THE
SEVENTH
COMMANDMENT

THE
SEVENTH
COMMANDMENT

LAWRENCE
SANDERS

G. P. PUTNAM'S SONS
New York

G. P. Putnam's Sons
Publishers Since 1838
200 Madison Avenue
New York, NY 10016

Library of Congress Cataloging-in-Publication Data

Sanders, Lawrence, date.
The seventh commandment / Lawrence Sanders.
p.   cm.
I. Title.
PS3569.A5125S48   1991   90–43225 CIP
813'.54—dc20
ISBN   0-399-13611-8

Printed in the United States of America
1   2   3   4   5   6   7   8   9   10

This book is printed on acid-free paper.
∞

THE
SEVENTH
COMMANDMENT

1

It was a swell year.

In January, her boss, Mike Trevalyan, sent Dora up to Boston to look into a claim on a homeowners' policy. This yuppie couple had gone to New York for the weekend and returned Sunday night to find their condo looted. They said. All their furniture and paintings had disappeared. They had made a videotape to record their possessions, and wanted the Company to fork over the full face value of the policy: $50,000.

It took her two days to discover that the yuppies were bubbleheads with a fondness for funny cigarettes. Every piece of furniture in their pad, every painting, had been leased; they didn't own a stick. They thought all they'd have to do was take out an insurance policy, pay the first year's premium, sell off their rented furnishings, and file a claim. Hah!

In February, Dora went to Portland to investigate a claim on a quilt factory that had been totaled by an early-morning fire. The local fire laddies couldn't find any obvious evidence of arson, but the quilt company was having trouble paying its bills, and that two-mil casualty policy the owner carried must have looked mighty sweet.

It took her a week to figure out how it had been done. The boss had pulled a wooden table directly under a low-hanging light bulb. He had heaped the table with cotton batting. Then he had draped the 150-watt bulb with gauze, switched on the light, and strolled away, humming "Blue Skies." The heat of the bulb ignited the gauze, which fell onto the batting, and eventually the whole factory was torched.

In April, she went to Stamford to look into a claim for the theft of a Picasso pencil sketch from a posh art gallery. The drawing was valued at $100,000. She was in Stamford less than a day when the Company got a phone call from a man claiming to be the thief and offering to sell the artwork back for twenty-five grand. Trevalyan called Dora and told her to liaise with the FBI.

After several phone calls, she set up a meet with the crook in a shopping mall parking lot. She handed over the marked cash, received the drawing, and the FBI moved in. The artwork turned out to be a fake, and the "thief" turned out to be the lover of the art gallery owner who had filed the claim. He had engineered the whole deal and had the real Picasso sketch in his safe deposit box.

In May and June, every claim Dora investigated was apparently on the up-and-up. Everyone seemed to be honest, and it worried her; she feared she had overlooked something.

But things got back to normal in July.

It happened just outside of Providence at the summer home of a Wall Street investment banker. His wife said there had been a power failure shortly before midnight. The banker stumbled around in the darkness, found a flashlight, and started down the basement stairs to check the circuit breakers. The wife heard him shriek and the sound of his fall. A few moments later the lights came back on, and she had hurried to the basement to find her husband crumpled at the foot of the stairs. Broken neck. Very dead.

Dora got there a day after it happened, and the wife's story sounded fishy to her. It took on a more profound piscine scent when she noted, and pointed out to the investigating detectives, that although all the electric clocks in the house showed a loss of about twenty minutes, corroborating the wife's tale, the timing clock on their VCR hadn't been reset and showed the power had gone off at 9:30 P.M. that evening.

Questioning of neighborhood yentas suggested that the wife had been having a torrid affair with their part-time gardener, a husky youth who studied the martial arts and frequently competed in karate tournaments. The gardener might have been physically strong, but there was little between his ears. He broke first and admitted he had taken part in a murder plot devised by the wife.

She had smuggled him into the basement late that afternoon while her husband was out playing croquet. At 9:30 P.M., the lover cut the power at the main switch. The banker came cautiously down the basement stairs. The gardener caught his ankle and after he fell, broke his neck. Power was restored, and they let the electric clocks show a lapse of twenty minutes. But they forgot about the VCR timer. Their motive? The banker's life insurance, of course. And love, Dora supposed.

In September, she went to Manhattan where a local

politico claimed his Hatteras 37 Convertible had been stolen from the 79th Street boat basin. It took Dora less than a week to discover he had *given* the yacht to his ex-mistress, a vengeful woman who had threatened to talk to the tabloids about his bedroom peccadilloes. These included, she said, a fondness for wearing her lingerie—and she had the Polaroids to prove it.

Dora found the boat moored at City Island. The ex-mistress had changed the name on the transom from *Our Thing* to *My Thing*.

October was filled with a number of routine cases, but in November Dora investigated the claim of a wizened dealer in autographs and signed historical documents. He said the gems of his collection, several rather raunchy letters from Samuel Clemens to his brother, had been stolen from his shop. The Worcester police told Dora that the store showed every evidence of a break-in, but they couldn't understand why other valuable items on display hadn't been taken, unless it was a contract burglary: The thief had been paid to lift the Mark Twain items and none others.

Dora came close to okaying the claim until she noticed ("You're a pain in the ass," Mike Trevalyan had once told her, "but you're observant as hell") that the office walls in the dealer's musty shop had recently been repapered. It seemed strange that the dealer would spend money to brighten his private sanctum while the remainder of his store looked like the loo in the House of Usher.

She hired a local PI with more nerve than scruples, and one dark night they picked the front door lock of the dealer's shop. It took them less than a half-hour to find the Samuel Clemens letters, in plastic slips, concealed beneath the new wallpaper in the back office. It turned out that the dealer was suffering a bad case of the shorts, having conceived an unholy passion for a tootsie one-third his age whose motto was "No pay, no play."

Dora returned home to Hartford to find her husband, Mario Conti, planning their Thanksgiving Day dinner. He had been a long-haul trucker when she married him, but had since been promoted to dispatcher. However, his real kingdom was the kitchen. He loved to cook and had the talents of a cordon-bleu, which was why Dora, who stood five-three in her Peds, usually weighed 150 pounds (or 145 during semimonthly diets). But Mario had never called her "dumpling" or "butterball," the darling man.

"Tacchino di festa!" he cried, and showed his shopping list.

"Salami?" she said, reading. "And sweet sausage? With turkey?"

"For the stuffing," he explained. "Trust me."

"Okay," she said happily.

They invited twelve guests, family and friends, and the dining room of their snug cottage was crowded. But everyone praised the turkey as Mario's masterpiece, and the numerous side dishes and gallons of jug wine made for a real *festa*.

There was enough food left over, Dora figured, for two more dinners, but it was not to be. Trevalyan called on Friday morning, although it was supposed to be a holiday.

"Better pack," he said, "and get down to the office. I'll brief you here."

"Where am I going?" she asked.

"Manhattan."

"For how long?"

"As long as it takes."

"How much is involved?"

"Three million," he said. "Whole life."

"Whee!" Dora said. "Natural death?"

"Not very," Trevalyan said.

2

Helene Pierce watched him dress. He had a good body—
not great, but good. Flab was beginning to collect on his
abdomen and his ass was starting to sink, but for a guy of
forty-six, what did you expect?

"I wish you could stay," she said. "I could order up some
food. Maybe that chicken you like with rosemary and garlic."

He was standing before the long mirror on the bathroom
door, flipping his tie into a Windsor knot.

"No can do," Clayton Starrett said. "Eleanor wants me
home early. Another of her charity bashes."

"Where?"

"At the Plaza. For children with AIDS. I had to buy a
table."

"A party so soon after the funeral?"

He turned and shrugged into his vest. "You know Eleanor and her charity bashes. Besides, all the clichés are true:
Life really does go on. He's been dead—how long? A week

15

tomorrow. People used to mourn for a year. Women wore black. Or, if they were Italian, for the rest of their lives. No more. Now people mourn for a week."

"Or less," she said.

He stood before the mirror again, adjusting the hang of his jacket. Everything must be just so.

"Or less," he agreed. "You know who's taking it hardest?"

"Your sister?" Helene guessed.

He turned to look at her. "How did you know? Her eyes are still swollen. I've heard her crying in her room. I never would have thought it would hit her like that; Felicia is such a fruitcake."

"What about your mother?"

"You know her: strictly the 'God's-will-be-done' type. Since it happened, she's practically been living with that guru of hers. I'd love to know how much she's been paying him. Plenty, I bet. But that's her problem."

"Have the police discovered anything new?" Helene asked.

"If they have, they're not telling us. They still think it was a mugger. Probably a doper. Could be. Father was the kind of man who wouldn't hand over his wallet without a fight."

"Clay, he was seventy years old."

Starrett shook his head. "He could have been ninety, and he still would have put up a struggle. He was a mean, cantankerous old bastard, but he had balls."

He took up his velvet-collared chesterfield. He came over to sit on the edge of the bed. He stared down at her. She was still naked, and he put one hand lightly on her tawny thigh.

16

"What will you do tonight?" he asked.

"I'll call my brother and see if he's got anything planned. If not, maybe we'll have dinner together."

"Good. If you see him, tell him everything is going beautifully. No hitches."

"I'll tell him," she promised.

He leaned down to kiss a bare breast. She gasped.

"You're getting me horny again," she said.

He laughed, stood up, pulled on his topcoat. "Oh," he said, "I almost forgot." He fished into his jacket pocket, took out a small suede pouch closed with a drawstring. "Another bauble to add to your collection," he said. "Almost three carats. D color. Cushion cut. A nice little rock."

"Thank you, Clay," she said faintly.

He started to leave, then snapped his fingers and turned back.

"Something else," he said. "The claims adjuster on the life insurance policy is in town asking questions. A woman. I've already talked to her, and she's planning to see mother, Eleanor and Felicia. It's possible she may want to talk to our friends. If she looks you up, answer all her questions honestly but don't volunteer any information."

"I can handle it," Helene said. "What's her name?"

"Dora Conti."

"What's she like?"

"Red-haired. Short and plump. A real butterball."

"Doesn't sound like an insurance snoop."

"Don't let her looks fool you," he said. "I get the feeling she's a sharpie. Just watch what you say. I'll call you tomorrow."

She rose and followed him into the living room. She locked, bolted, and chained the door behind him. She brought the little suede pouch over to her corner desk and switched on the gooseneck lamp. She took a jeweler's loupe from the top drawer, opened the pouch, spilled the diamond onto the desk blotter.

She leaned close, loupe to her eye, and turned the stone this way and that. She couldn't spot a flaw, and it seemed to be an icy white. She held it up to the light and admired the gleam. Then she replaced the gem in the pouch and added it to a wooden cigar box, almost filled. Her treasures went into the bottom desk drawer.

She knew she should take the unset diamonds to her safe deposit box. She had been telling herself that for a year. But she could not do it, *could not.* She liked their sharp feel, their hard glitter. She liked to sit at her desk, heap up the shining stones, let them drift through her fingers.

She called Turner Pierce.

"He's left," she reported. "Going to a society bash at the Plaza with his wife. How about dinner?"

"Sure," he said. "But I'll have to split by ten. I'm meeting Ramon uptown at eleven."

"Plenty of time," she assured him. "Suppose I meet you at seven at that Italian place on Lex. The one with the double veal chops."

"Vito's," he said. "Sounds good to me. Don't get gussied up. I'm wearing black leather tonight."

"You would," she said, laughing.

They sat at a table in a dim corner, and three waiters fussed about them, knowing he tipped like a rajah. They both had Tanqueray vodka on ice with a lime wedge. Then they studied the menus.

"What did you get?" Turner asked in a low voice.

"Almost three carats," Helene said. "Icy white. Cushion cut."

"Nice," he said. "But you earned it."

"He said to tell you everything is going beautifully. No hitches."

"I'm glad he thinks so. I have a feeling Ramon isn't all that happy. I think he wants more action."

"I thought the idea was to go slowly at first, get everything set up and functioning, and then build up the gross gradually."

"That was the idea, but Ramon is getting antsy since his New Orleans contact was charged."

"Will he talk?"

"The New Orleans man? I doubt that very much. He had an accident."

"Oh? What happened?"

"His car exploded. He was in it."

She raised her head to stare at him. "Turner," she said, "watch your back with Ramon."

"I never drive my car to visit him," he said, grinning. "I always take a cab."

They had double veal chops, rare, and split orders of pasta all'olio and Caesar salad. They also shared a bottle of Pinot Grigio. They both had good appetites and finished everything.

"Not like Kansas City, is it?" Turner said, sitting back.

"Thank God," she said. "How many hamburgers can you eat? Listen, Clayton said there's an insurance claim adjuster in town asking questions. A woman named Dora Conti. He thinks she's a sharpie and says she may want to talk to Lewis Starrett's friends."

"No sweat," he said. "You know, I liked the old man. Well, maybe not liked, but I admired him. He inherited a little hole-in-the-wall store on West Forty-seventh Street, and he built it into Starrett Fine Jewelry. They may not be

Tiffany or Cartier, but they do all right. How many shops? Sixteen, I think. All over the world. Plenty of loot there."

"There was," Helene said, "until Clayton brought in those kooky designers. Then the ink turned red."

"That was last year," Turner said. "He's on the right track now. Let's have espresso and Frangelico at the bar; I've got time."

They sat close together, knees touching, at the little bar near the entrance.

"Felicia phoned me again," Turner said.

"Oh? What did she want?"

"You know."

"Clayton called her a fruitcake."

"That she is. In spades. But she could be a problem. So I'll play along."

"Dear," she said, putting a hand on his arm, "how long have we got? A year? Two? Three?"

"Three, I hope. Maybe two. I'll know when it's coming to a screeching halt."

"And then?"

"Off we go into the wild blue yonder. You know what my cut is. We'll have enough in one year, plenty in two, super plenty in three. And you'll have your rock collection. We deserve it; we're nice people."

She laughed, lifted his hand to her lips, kissed his knuckles. "Dangerous game," she observed.

He shrugged. "The first law of investing," he said. "The higher the return, the bigger the risk."

"Busy tomorrow?" she asked casually.

"I'm meeting Felicia for an early lunch. The afternoon's open."

"Sounds good to me," she said.

20

3

The Company kept a corporate suite at the Hotel Bedlington on Madison Avenue, and that's where Dora stayed. She called Mario to tell him about the sitting room with television set and fully equipped wet bar, the neat little pantry, and the two bedrooms, each with a king-size bed.

"Great for orgies," Dora told him.

Mario lapsed into trucker talk, and she giggled and hung up.

The hotel had a cocktail lounge off the lobby and, in the rear, a rather frowsty dining room that seemed to be patronized mostly by blue-haired women and epicene older men who carried handkerchiefs up their sleeve cuffs. The food was edible but tasteless; everything lacked seasoning. They needed a chef, Dora decided, who had Mario's faculty with herbs and spices.

But that's where she had lunch with Detective John Wenden, NYPD. They met in the lobby and examined each other's ID. Then he inspected her.

"You know," he said, "if you lost thirty pounds you'd be a very attractive woman."

"You know," she said, "if you were Robert Redford you'd be a very attractive man."

He laughed and held up his palms. "So-ree," he said. "It was a stupid thing to say, and I apologize. Okay?"

"Sure," she said. "Let's go eat."

"You got a swindle sheet?"

"Of course."

"Then I'll have a steak."

"Take my advice and use plenty of salt and pepper. The food is solid but has no flavor."

"Ketchup covers a multitude of sins," he said.

The ancient maître d' showed them to a table against the wall. Detective Wenden looked around at the oldsters working on their watercress sandwiches and chamomile tea.

"Think I could get a Geritol on the rocks?" he said.

"Whatever turns you on," Dora said.

But he ordered a light beer with his club steak. Dora also had a beer with her chef's salad.

"You married?" Wenden asked her.

"Yes," she said. "Happily. You?"

"Divorced," he said. "All New York cops are divorced— didn't you know? Occupational hazard. How much was the Starrett insurance?"

"Three million."

"That's sweet. Who gets it?"

"Thirds; equal shares to his wife, son, and daughter. Hey, I'm supposed to be asking the questions. That's why I'm buying you a steak—to pick your brain."

"Not much to pick." He paused while the creaking waiter served their beers. Then: "You read the clips?"

She nodded. "A lot of nothing."

"That's all we've got—nothing."

His steak was served. He cut off a corner and tasted it cautiously. "You're right," he said. "Cardboard." He sprinkled the meat heavily with salt and pepper as Dora dug into her salad.

"You can talk with your mouth full, you know," she said. "I won't be offended."

"Okay," he said equably, "let me give you a quick recap.

"The victim is Lewis Starrett, seventy, white male, retired president of Starrett Fine Jewelry, Inc. But he's still chairman and principal stockholder. Shows up every working day for a few hours at their flagship store on Park Avenue. Lives in an eighteen-room duplex on Fifth Avenue with his wife, daughter, son and son's wife. Also two live-in servants, a butler and a cook-housekeeper, a married couple. The deceased was supposed to be a nasty, opinionated old bastard but everyone agrees he was fearless. His first mistake; it doesn't pay to be fearless in this city.

"Every evening at nine o'clock, Lewis Starrett takes a stroll. His second mistake; you don't walk at night in this city unless you have to. He goes down Fifth to Fifty-ninth Street, east on Fifty-ninth to Lexington Avenue where he stops at a cigar store and buys the one daily cigar his doctor allows.

"Then he continues north on Lex to Eighty-third Street, smoking his cigar. West on Eighty-third Street to his apartment house on Fifth. They say you could set your watch by him. His third mistake; he never varied his route or time.

"On the fatal night, as the tabloids like to say, he starts his walk at the usual time, buys his cigar at the Lexington Avenue shop, lights up and starts home. But he never makes it. His body is found facedown on the sidewalk between Lex and Park. He's been stabbed once, practically between the shoulder blades. Instant blotto. No witnesses. And that's it."

Detective Wenden's timing was perfect; he finished his story at the same time he finished his lunch. He started to light a cigarette, but the maître d' came hobbling over to tell him the whole dining room was a no-smoking area.

"Unless you want dessert and coffee," Dora said, "let's go into the cocktail lounge and have another beer. We can smoke in there."

"You got a deal," he said.

They were the only customers in the bar. They sat on uncomfortable black vinyl chairs at a black Formica table, sipped their beers, smoked their cigarettes.

"Was he robbed?" Dora asked.

Wenden looked at her curiously. "Do you always go to this much trouble to check out an insurance claim?"

"Not usually," she admitted. "But this time we've got three million reasons. The Company wouldn't like it if someone profits illegally from Starrett's murder."

"You mean if one of the beneficiaries offed him?"

"That's what I mean." She repeated: "Was he robbed?"

"Negative," Wenden said. "He had all his credit cards and a wallet with about four hundred in cash. Also, he was wearing a gold Starrett watch worth fifteen grand and a man's Starrett diamond ring worth another thirty Gs."

"But you figure it was a bungled robbery?"

"Not necessarily. Maybe a coked-up panhandler asks for a buck. Starrett stiffs him, maybe curses him, and turns away. His family and friends say he was capable of doing that. Then the panhandler gets sore, pulls out a blade, lets him have it and takes off."

"Without pausing to lift his wallet or watch?"

"There were apparently no witnesses to the stabbing, but maybe the killer didn't want to push his luck by staying at the scene for even another minute. Someone might have come along."

"I don't know," Dora said doubtfully. "Seems to me there are a lot of maybes in your scenario."

The detective stirred restlessly. "Have you investigated many homicides?"

"A few."

"Then you know that even when they're solved there are always a lot of loose ends. I've never worked a case that was absolutely complete with everything explained and accounted for."

"Another beer?" she asked.

"Why not?" he said. "I've got nothing to do this afternoon but crack four other killings."

"That much on your plate?"

"It never ends," he said wearily. "There's a lot of dying going around these days."

Dora went to the bar and brought back two more cold bottles.

"Why do I get the feeling," she said, "that you don't totally believe your own story of the way it happened."

"It's the official line," he said.

"Screw the official line," she said angrily. "This is just between you and me, and I'm not about to run off at the mouth to the tabloids. What do *you* think?"

He sighed. "A couple of things bother me. You ever investigate a stabbing?"

"No."

"A professional knifer holds the blade like a door key, knuckles down. He uses an underhanded jab, comes in low, goes up high, usually around the belly or kidneys. It's soft there; no bones to snap the steel. The blow that killed Starrett started high and came down low into his back. An amateur did that, holding the knife handle in his fist, knuckles up. And it was amateur's luck that the blade didn't break on the spine or ribs. It sliced an artery and punctured the heart—more luck."

"For the killer, not Starrett."

"Yeah. Ordinarily one stab like that wouldn't kill instantly."

"Man or woman?"

"A man, I'd guess. That shiv went deep. Plenty of power there. It cut through overcoat, suit jacket, shirt, undershirt, skin, flesh, and into the heart."

"A long blade?"

"Had to be. You talk to any of the family yet?"

"The son," Dora said. "Clayton."

"What was your take on him?"

"I got the feeling he wasn't exactly out of his mind with grief."

Wenden nodded. "I thought he was controlling his sorrow very well. From what I've been able to pick up, he and his father didn't get along so great. Clayton became president and CEO of Starrett Jewelry when the old man retired, and I guess they didn't see eye-to-eye on a lot of business decisions. Plenty of screaming arguments, according to the office staff. But that's not unusual when a father gives up power and a son takes over. The heir usually wants to do things differently, try new things, prove his ability."

Dora sighed. "I hate these family affairs. They always turn out to be snarls of string. It's so sad. You'd think a family would try to get along."

The detective laughed. "Most homicides are committed by a family member or a close friend. You talk to the attorney yet?"

"No, not yet."

"A nice old guy. He was Lewis Starrett's lawyer from the beginning."

"Who inherits?" Dora asked.

"The wife," Wenden said. "For tax reasons. About eighty million."

"Wow! Nothing to the son or daughter?"

"Well, you say they'll each be getting a million in insurance money. And I guess Lewis figured Olivia would leave everything to the children when she shuffles off."

"What's she like?"

"Olivia?" He grinned. "I'll let you make up your own mind. The daughter, Felicia, is the one to look out for. She's off the wall."

"How so?"

"Crazy. Runs with a rough downtown crowd. But I'll say this for her: She seems to be taking her father's death harder than any of the others."

"What about Clayton's wife?"

"Eleanor? A social butterfly. She's on a zillion committees. Always planning a party for this charity or that. She loves it. Maybe because she can never wear the same dress twice. Listen, I've got to split. Where do you live?"

"Hartford."

"Going home for the weekend?"

"I doubt it. My husband may come down if he can get away."

"What does he do?"

"He's a dispatcher for a trucking company. Works crazy hours."

"Well, if he doesn't show up, maybe we can get together for a pizza."

She stared at him. "I told you I was happily married."

"And I heard you," the detective said. "What's that got to do with sharing a pizza?"

"Nothing," Dora said. "As long as we keep it on a professional level. Maybe we can compare notes and do each other some good."

"Sure we can," Wenden said. "Here's my card. If I'm not in, you can always leave a message. Thanks for the lunch."

"My pleasure," Dora said and watched him move away, thinking he was an okay guy but he really should get his suit pressed and his shoes shined. She knew he had to deal with a lot of scumbags, but he didn't have to dress like one.

4

The flagship store of Starrett Fine Jewelry, Inc., was located on Park Avenue just south of 57th Street. It occupied one of the few remaining town houses on the Avenue in midtown Manhattan, surrounded by steel and glass towers. The baroque six-story structure, built in 1896 as the family home of a shipping magnate, was designed by a student of Stanford White, and the exterior had been cited by the Landmarks Preservation Commission.

The jewelry selling area was on the ground level, with silverware, crystal, and china on the second. The third and fourth floors were designers' studios and shops for engraving and repairs. Executive offices filled the top two stories. Starrett's main workshop for the crafting of exclusive designs was in Brooklyn. The company also purchased quantity items and gold chains from independent suppliers in Taiwan and South Korea.

In addition to New York, Starrett stores were located in Boston, Chicago, Beverly Hills, San Francisco, Atlanta,

Dallas, Palm Beach, London, Paris, Zurich, Hong Kong, Honolulu, Cancun, Rome, and Brussels. Starrett did not have a mail order catalogue but sometimes sent favored customers drawings of new designs before they were made up and offered to the general public. Many of these were one-of-a-kind pieces: brooches, bracelets, rings, necklaces, tiaras.

Generally, all the Starrett stores, worldwide, offered the same merchandise, although the mix was often varied. The general manager of each shop ordered the items from New York that he thought would sell best in his area. In addition, every Starrett store had its own workshop and was encouraged to produce jewelry on special order for valued clients, usually personalized items designed to the customer's specifications.

During the last year, Clayton Starrett's second as president and chief executive officer, he had replaced the general managers of nine of the sixteen Starrett stores. Some of these men (and one woman) had been with the company for ten, fifteen, twenty years, and their termination had been the cause of the violent disagreement between Clayton and his father.

The late Lewis Starrett claimed they were all experienced, loyal employees who had proved their competence, and firing them was not only an act of ingratitude but, more important, would have an adverse effect on revenues and net profits.

But Clayton was adamant. The veterans would have to go because, he said, they knew little about modern merchandising, advertising, promotion, and public relations. They were content to cater to an aging clientele and made no effort to attract a new generation of Starrett customers.

The argument between father and son became so fierce that it began to affect the morale of personnel in the New York store. It was only resolved when Clayton, white-faced, threatened to resign and move out of his parents' apartment. Thereupon the old man backed down, and the son became the recognized and undisputed boss of Starrett Fine Jewelry, Inc.

The new general managers he hired for the subsidiary stores were mostly hard young men, smartly dressed, with an eye on the bottom line and a brusque manner with subordinates. A few were reputedly MBAs, and several were foreign-born. All seemed possessed of driving ambition and, shortly before his death, Lewis Starrett had to admit that revenues and net profits were increasing spectacularly.

When Lewis ran the company with iron fist and bellows of rage, he arrived for work each morning at 7:30 and frequently put in a twelve-hour day. Clayton's style of management was considerably more laid-back. He showed up around ten o'clock, took a lengthy lunch and, if he returned from that, was usually out of the office by five.

On this day he stepped from his chauffeured stretch limousine (a presidential perk) and entered the Starrett Fine Jewelry Building a few minutes before ten. He hardly glanced into the selling area, almost devoid of customers. He was not dismayed; Starrett's patrons were not early-morning shoppers; they preferred late afternoon.

A small, elaborately decorated elevator lifted him slowly to his private office on the top floor. His secretary, an English import hired more for her accent than her ability, took his homburg and chesterfield. A few minutes later she returned with a cup of black coffee and a toasted bagel.

This minibreakfast was served on bone china in an exclusive Starrett pattern called Belladonna.

As he gnawed his bagel, he reviewed the day's schedule. There was nothing that seemed to him of monumental importance, and he wondered if, about four or four-thirty that afternoon, he might call Helene Pierce and ask if she was willing to receive him.

He was paying $5,400 a month for her apartment, giving her $1,000 a week walking-around money, and occasionally bringing her small diamonds for her collection. But in spite of this largesse, he had to obey her rules: no unexpected visits, limited phone calls, no questions as to how she spent her time. He accepted these dictates cheerfully because, he admitted to himself, he was obsessed. Helene was half his age, had a body that never failed to arouse him, and was so practiced in the craft of love that he never ceased to wonder how one so young could be so knowing and experienced.

His first task of the morning was to review, on his desktop computer, the previous day's sales at the sixteen Starrett stores. It was then the height of the Christmas shopping season, a period that usually accounted for thirty percent of Starrett's annual revenues. He punched the keys and watched intently as numbers filled the screen.

The computer showed not only current sales but provided comparison with income of the same week during the previous five years. The numbers Clayton studied showed that Starrett's business was essentially flat; the increase was barely enough to cover the inflation rate. He was now more firmly convinced than ever that Starrett could not depend solely on retail sales for continued profits and growth.

He then switched to a software program for which only he possessed the access code. Now the numbers shown on the screen were much more encouraging. Exciting, in fact, and he blessed the day Helene and Turner Pierce had come into his life. Helene had brought joy, and sometimes rapture; Turner had provided financial salvation.

His first meeting was with an in-house designer to go over proposed designs for a new line of sterling silver key-rings in the shapes of mythological beasts. They had a surrealistic discussion as to whether or not the unicorn was a phallic symbol and if so, what effect it might have on sales. Clayton eventually initialed all the sketches except for the centaur, which he deemed too suggestive for public display and sale.

He accepted a phone call from Eleanor and spoke with her for almost fifteen minutes, marveling (not for the first time) how his adulterous affair had made him a better husband, more patient with his wife and amenable to her wishes. She had called to remind him that they were to attend a charity dinner and fashion show at the Metropolitan Museum.

Eleanor was not directly involved, but the Starretts had subscribed ($1,000 a couple) because one of Eleanor's close friends had organized the affair. These endless charity parties were, Clayton knew, a world of mutual back-scratching. He submitted because they kept his wife busy and happy, and because they were good public relations. Also, he enjoyed wearing a dinner jacket.

He then met with an interior decorator and went over plans to redecorate his office. The day after his father's funeral, Clayton had moved into his office, the largest in the executive suite. But it was crammed with dark oak furniture, the windows overlooking Park Avenue half hidden behind dusty velvet drapes, the walls covered with flocked paper. Clayton spent an hour describing exactly what he wanted: stainless steel, glass, Bauhaus-style chairs, bright Warhols on the walls, and perhaps a Biedermeier couch as a conversation piece.

He lunched at a Japanese restaurant, the guest of a Tokyo merchant who wanted Starrett to carry a choice selection of antique inro and netsuke. While they ate sashimi and drank hot sake, the exporter displayed a few samples of his exquisitely carved wares. Clayton was fascinated and agreed to accept a small shipment on consignment as a test of the sales potential.

He returned to his office, wondering if Starrett might emulate Gump's of San Francisco and offer imported curios, bibelots, and objets d'art. They could, he reckoned, be sold in the department now handling estate jewelry, and might very well find a market.

He dictated several letters to his secretary and, after she left, called Helene's apartment on his private line. But there was no answer, and he guessed she was out spending money. "Shopping," she had once told him, "is my second favorite pastime."

It was then almost 4:30, and Clayton decided to call his limousine, return home, and take a nap before he dressed for dinner. But then Solomon Guthrie phoned and asked if he could come up immediately. Guthrie was Starrett's chief financial officer, and Clayton knew what he wanted to talk about.

Sol was sixty-three, had worked for Starrett forty years, and called his bosses Mister Lewis and Mister Clayton. He had a horseshoe of frazzled white hair around a bald pate, and was possibly the last office worker in New York to wear celluloid cuff protectors. He had learned, with difficulty, to use computers, but still insisted in keeping a duplicate set of records in his spidery script in giant ledgers that covered half his desk.

He came stomping into Clayton's office carrying a thick roll of computer printout under his arm.

"Mister Clayton," he said aggrievedly, "I don't know what the hell's going on around here."

"I suppose you mean the bullion trades," Clayton said, sighing. "I explained it to you once, but I'll go over it again if you want me to."

"It's the paperwork," the CFO said angrily. "We're getting invoices, canceled checks, bills of lading, warehouse receipts, insurance premium notices—it's a snowfall! Look at this printout—one day's paper!"

"Just temporary," Clayton soothed him. "When our new systems integration goes on-line, the paperwork will be reduced to a minimum I assure you."

"But it never used to be like this," Sol complained. "I used to be able to keep up. All right, so I had to work late some nights—that comes with the territory. But with these bullion trades, I'm lost. I'm falling farther and farther behind."

"What are you telling me, Sol—that you need more people?"

"No, I don't need more people. By the time I tell them what to do, I could do it myself. What I want to know is the reason for all this. For years we were a jewelry store. Now suddenly we're gold dealers—a whole different business entirely."

"Not necessarily," Clayton said. "There's money to be made buying and selling bullion. Why should we let the dealers skim the cream? With our contacts we can buy in

35

bulk and sell to independent jewelers at a price they can't match anywhere else."

"But where are we buying the gold? I get the invoices, but I never heard of some of these suppliers."

"All legitimate," Clayton told him. "You get the warehouse receipts, don't you? That's proof they're delivering, and the gold is going in our vaults."

"And the customers—who are they?"

"First of all, I plan to make all our stores autonomous. They'll be more subsidiaries than branches. I want them to do more designing and manufacturing on their own. New York will sell them the raw materials: gold, silver, gemstones, and so forth. At a markup, of course. In turn, the subsidiaries can sell to small jewelers in their area."

Guthrie shook his head. "It sounds meshugenah to me. And right now we got too much invested in bullion. What if Russia or South Africa dumps, and the market price takes a nosedive. Then we're dead."

Clayton smiled. "We're hedged," he said. "There's no way we can be hurt. Sol, you see the bottom line. Are we losing money on our gold deals?"

"No," the CFO admitted.

"We're making money, aren't we? Lots of money."

Sol nodded. "I just don't understand it," he said fretfully. "I don't understand how you figure to unload so much gold. I think our inventory is much, much too heavy. And your father, God rest his soul, if he was alive today, believe me he'd be telling you the same thing."

Clayton took a cigar from a handsome mahogany humidor on his desk. It was a much better brand than his father had smoked. But he didn't light the cigar immediately. Just rolled it gently between his fingers.

"Sol," he said, "you're sixty-three—right?"

"Yes."

"Retirement in two years. I'll bet you're looking forward to it."

"I haven't thought about it."

"You should, Sol. It isn't too soon to start training someone to take your place."

"Who? These kids—what do they know. They come out of college and can't even balance a checkbook."

"How about the new man I hired—Dick Satterlee?"

"He's a noodle!" Sol cried.

"Teach him," Clayton urged. "Teach him, Sol. He comes very highly recommended."

"I don't like him," Sol said angrily. "Something creepy about that guy. Last week I caught him going through my ledgers."

"So?" Clayton said. "How else is he going to learn?"

"Listen, Mister Clayton," the older man said, "those ledgers are private business. Everyone in my office knows—*hands off!* I don't want anyone touching them; they're my responsibility."

Starrett slowly pierced and lighted his cigar. "Sol," he said, "when was your last raise?"

Guthrie was startled. "Two years ago," he said. "I thought you knew."

"I should have remembered," Clayton said, "but I've had a lot on my mind. Father's death and all . . ."

"Of course."

"Suppose you take a raise of fifty thousand a year until you retire. With your pension, that should give you a nice nest egg."

The CFO was shocked. "Thank you, Mister Clayton," he said finally.

"You deserve it. And Sol, stop worrying about the gold business. Trust me."

After Guthrie left his office, Clayton put his cigar carefully aside and called Turner Pierce. The phone was lifted after the sixth ring.

"Hello?"

"Turner? Clayton Starrett."

"How are you, Clay? I was just thinking about you. I saw Ramon last night, and there have been some interesting developments."

"Turner, I've got to see you as soon as possible."

"Oh? A problem?"

"It could be," Clayton said.

5

Dora Conti, listing to port under the weight of an over-stuffed shoulder bag, was admitted to the Starrett apartment at 2:30 P.M. The door was opened by a tall, bowed man she assumed was the butler, identified in newspaper clippings as Charles Hawkins.

He didn't look like a Fifth Avenue butler to her, or valet, footman, or even scullion. He seemed all elbows and knees, his gaunt cheeks were pitted, and a lock of dank, black hair flopped across his forehead. He was wearing a shiny gray alpaca jacket, black serge trousers just as shiny, and Space Shoes.

"Dora Conti," she said, "to see Mrs. Olivia Starrett. I have an appointment."

"Madam is waiting," he said in a sepulchral whisper, and held out his arms to her.

For one awful instant she thought he meant to embrace her, then realized he merely wanted to take her coat. She whipped off her scarf and struggled out of her heavy loden parka. He took them with the tips of his fingers, and she followed his flat-footed shuffle down a long corridor to the living room.

This high-ceilinged chamber seemed crowded with a plethora of chintz- and cretonne-covered chairs and couches, all in floral patterns: roses, poppies, lilies, iris, camellias. It was like entering a hothouse; only the scent was missing.

A man and a woman were sharing a love seat when Dora came into the room. The man stood immediately. He was wearing a double-breasted suit of dove-gray flannel, with a black silk dickey and a white clerical collar.

"Good afternoon," Dora said briskly. "I am Dora Conti, and as I explained on the phone, I am your insurance claims adjuster. Thank you for seeing me on such short notice."

"Of course," the man said with a smile of what Dora considered excessive warmth. "I hope you won't be offended if I ask to see your credentials."

She made no reply, but dug her ID out of the shoulder bag, handed him card and letter of authorization.

He examined them carefully, then returned them, his smile still in place. "Thank you," he said. "You must understand my caution; so many newspaper reporters have attempted to interview family members under a variety of pretexts that we've become somewhat distrustful. My name is Brian Callaway."

"*Father* Brian Callaway," the woman on the settee said, "and I am Olivia Starrett."

"Ma'am," Dora said, "first of all I'd like to express my condolences on the death of your husband."

"Oh, he didn't die," the woman said. "He passed into the divine harmony. My, what beautiful hair you have!"

"Thank you."

40

"And do construction workers whistle at you and shout, 'Hey, red!'?"

"No," Dora said. "They usually whistle and shout, 'Hey, fatso'!"

Olivia Starrett laughed, a warbling sound. "Men can be so cruel," she said. "You are certainly not fat. Plump perhaps—wouldn't you say, Father?"

"Pleasingly," he said.

"Now then," the widow said, patting the cushion beside her, "you come sit next to me, and we'll have a nice chat."

She was a heavy-bodied woman herself, with a motherly softness. Her complexion was a creamy velvet, and her eyes seemed widened in an expression of continual surprise. Silvery hair was drawn back in a chignon and tied with a girlish ribbon. Her hands were unexpectedly pudgy, and her diamond rings, Dora estimated, would have kept Mario supplied with prosciutto for two lifetimes.

"Mrs. Starrett," Dora began, "let me explain why I am here. If your husband had been ill and had, uh, passed away in a hospital, or even at home with a doctor in attendance, there probably would have been no need for our investigating the claim, despite its size. But because his, uh, passing was violent and unexpected, an investigation is necessary to establish the facts of the case."

Father Callaway seated himself in an armchair facing the two women. "Surely," he said, "an investigation of that horrible crime is a job for the police."

"Of course it is," Dora agreed. "But right now all they have is a theory as to how and why the homicide was committed. It may or may not be correct. But until the perpetrator is caught, there are unanswered questions we'd like to see cleared up. Mrs. Starrett, I hope I am not upsetting you by talking of your husband's, uh, death."

"Oh, not at all," she said, almost blithely. "I have made my peace."

"Olivia is a strong woman," Callaway said.

"As you said at the service, Father: Faith conquers all."

"Just a few questions," Dora said. "First of all, can you tell me the whereabouts of family members at the time your husband, uh, passed away?"

"Now let me see," Mrs. Starrett said, staring at the ceiling. "Earlier that evening the entire family was here, and we were having cocktails and little nibbles. Helene and Turner Pierce stopped by."

"I was also present, Olivia," Callaway interrupted.

"Of course you were! Well, we had a few drinks, and then Clayton and Eleanor left to attend a charity affair at the Waldorf. And Felicia had a dinner date, so she left. And then the Pierces."

"And I left at the same time they did," the Father reminded her. He looked directly at Dora. "I have a small tabernacle on East Twentieth Street—and I like to be present at the evening meal to offer what spiritual solace I can."

"Tabernacle?" Dora said. "Then you are not Roman Catholic?"

"No," he said shortly. "I am the founder and pastor of the Church of the Holy Oneness."

"I see," Dora said, and turned to the widow. "So only you and your husband were in the apartment at dinnertime?"

"And Charles, our houseman, and Clara, our cook."

"Charles' wife."

Olivia's eyes widened even more. "Now how did you know that?"

"It was in the newspapers," Dora lied smoothly. "You

had dinner, and then Mr. Starrett left to take his usual walk—is that correct?"

"Yes," Olivia said, nodding, "that's what happened. I remember it was threatening rain, and I wanted Lewis to take an umbrella and wear his rubbers, but he wouldn't." She sighed. "He was a very obstinate man."

Callaway corrected her gently. "Strong-minded, Olivia," he murmured.

"Yes," she said, "he was a very strong-minded man."

"Mrs. Starrett," Dora said, "do you know anyone who might wish to harm your husband? Did he have any enemies?"

The widow lifted her chin. "My husband could be difficult at times. At home and, I'm sure, at the office. I was aware that many people thought him offensive. He did have a temper, you know, and I'm sure he sometimes said things in anger that he later regretted. But no, I know of no one who wished to harm him."

"Was he ever threatened? In person or by letter?"

"Not to my knowledge."

"The police," Callaway observed, "believe he was killed by a stranger."

"Uh-huh," Dora said. "That's their theory. Mrs. Starrett, I don't want to take any more of your time. If I think of more questions, may I come back?"

Olivia put a warm hand on her arm. "Of course you may, my dear. As often as you like. Are you married?"

"Yes. We live in Hartford. My husband is a dispatcher for a trucking company."

"How nice! Does he love you?"

Dora was startled. "I believe he does. He says he does."

"And do you love him?"

"Yes."

Olivia nodded approvingly. "Love is the most important thing. Isn't it, Father?"

"The only thing," said Callaway, a broad-chested man who liked to show his teeth.

Dora stood up. The pastor rose at the same time and took a wallet from his inner jacket pocket. He extracted a card and handed it to her.

"The address of the Church of the Holy Oneness," he said. "Service every Friday evening at eight. But you'll be welcome anytime you wish to stop by."

"Thank you," she said, tucking the card in her shoulder bag. "I may just do that. Mrs. Starrett, it's been a pleasure meeting you, and I hope to see you again."

"And the insurance?" Callaway asked. "When may the beneficiaries expect to have the claim approved?"

Dora smiled sweetly. "As soon as possible," she said, and shook his hand.

Charles was waiting in the foyer, and she wondered how much of the conversation he had overheard. He helped her on with her parka.

"Thank you, Charles."

She thought he might have winked at her, but it was such an unbutlerlike act that she decided he had merely blinked. With one eye.

6

Clayton Starrett could see no physical resemblance between Helene and Turner Pierce, yet they both showed the same face to the world: cool, somewhat aloof, with tight smiles and brief laughs. And both dressed with careless elegance, held their liquor well, and had a frequently expressed distaste for the commonplace. "Vulgar!" was their strongest term of opprobrium.

Sitting with them in the living room of Helene's apartment, sharing a pitcher of gin martinis, Clayton noted for the first time how pale both were, how slender, how languid their gestures. In their presence he felt uncomfortably lumpish, as if his energy and robust good health were somehow vulgar.

"And what was Guthrie's reaction when you gave him the raise?" Turner asked.

"He was surprised," Clayton said. "Perhaps shocked is a better word. I know he never expected anything like that. I did it, of course, to give him a bigger stake in the company. You might call it a bribe—to keep his mouth shut about the gold deals."

"You think it'll work?"

"I don't know," Clayton said worriedly. "Sol is an honest man—maybe too honest. In spite of the raise he may keep digging. I got the feeling he wasn't completely satisfied with my explanation."

"Helene?" Turner said.

"Don't do anything at the moment," she advised. "The money may convince him it would be stupid to make waves. But you better tell Dick Satterlee to keep an eye on him, just in case."

"Yes, that would be wise," Turner said. "Since his New Orleans contact was eliminated, Ramon wants to increase his investments elsewhere. We'll be getting the lion's share, so the last thing we want right now is a snoopy accountant nosing around. I'll phone Satterlee at home and alert him." He glanced at his Piaget Polo, finished his martini, stood up. "I've got to run. Thanks for the drink, sis."

"I'll give you a call later," she said.

He swooped to kiss her cheek. "Much later," he said. "I won't be home until midnight."

"I hope you're behaving yourself," she said.

"Don't I always?" he said. "Clay, sometimes this sister of mine acts like she's my mother."

They all laughed. Turner gathered up his leather trench coat and trilby. "Clay," he said, "don't worry about Sol Guthrie. I'll take care of it."

"Good," Clayton said. "He's been with Starrett a long time and only has two years to go before he starts drawing a hefty pension. He'd be a fool to endanger that."

"Sometimes honest men do foolish things," Turner said. "You know the old saying: No good deed goes unpunished. I hope Mr. Guthrie knows it."

He waved a hand at them and left. Helene rose to bolt the door and put on the chain. "Another party tonight?" she asked Clayton.

He nodded. "The third this week. My wife is cohostess of this one. At the Pierre."

"For which charity?"

He shrugged. "Who the hell knows—or cares. For unwed mothers or to spay stray cats or *something.*"

"So you have to go home to dress?"

He smiled at her. "Not for an hour," he said.

"Time enough," she said. "We can go around the world in an hour."

If she seemed languid, almost enervated, when dressed and in the company of others, she displayed a totally different persona when naked and alone with him. Her strength was astonishing, her vigor daunting. Indifference vanished; now she was vital and determined. She gave Clayton credit for this transformation. "You make me a pagan," she told him.

He could scarcely believe his good fortune. This lovely, intense young woman seemed to have no wish but to give him pleasure. There was nothing he asked that she would not do, and their lovemaking became a new world for him. He was a sexual despot, and she his willing slave, eager to serve.

He thought he had never known an ecstasy to equal this, and only later did he begin to plot how he might change his life to insure that his happiness would endure forever.

7

Dora Conti had been trying for almost a week to pin down
a meeting with Felicia Starrett. Two appointments had
been made, but Felicia called at the last minute to cancel
both, offering excuses that seemed trivial to Dora: she had
to have her hands waxed, and Bloomies was having a panty
hose sale.

Finally she agreed, positively, to meet Dora for a drink
at the Bedlington cocktail lounge at 4:30 on Friday. She
was only twenty minutes late.

She came sailing into the bar wearing a mink Eisen-
hower jacket that Dora would have killed for. Under the
jacket she wore a white turtleneck sweater, and below was
a skirt of black calfskin, short and tight. Her only jewelry
was a solitaire, a marquise-cut diamond in a Tiffany setting.
Five carats at least, Dora guessed.

Felicia shook hands, took off her mink and tossed it onto
an empty chair. "Chivas neat," she yelled at the bartender.
"Perrier on the side." She sat down across the table from

Dora, looked around the cocktail lounge. "Ratty dump," she said.

"Isn't it," Dora said pleasantly. "Thank you for giving me a few minutes of your time, Miss Starrett. I appreciate it."

"I hope it's only a few minutes. I have an appointment for a trim and rinse at five-thirty, and if I'm late Adolph will probably scalp me. Who does your hair?"

"I do," Dora said. "Doesn't it look like it?"

"It's okay," Felicia said. "Like you don't give a damn how it looks. I like that. May I have one of your cigarettes?"

"Help yourself."

"I'm trying to stop smoking so I don't buy any. I'm still smoking but I'm saving a lot of money. Your name is Dora Conti?"

"That's right."

"Italian?"

"My husband is."

"How long have you been married?"

"Six years."

"Children?"

"No."

"That's smart," Felicia said. "Who the hell wants to bring kids into this rotten world. This is about the insurance?"

"Just a few questions," Dora said. "Your mother has already told me most of what I wanted to know. She said you were in the apartment having cocktails the evening your father was killed. But you left early."

"That's right. I had a dinner-date downtown. A new restaurant on Spring Street. It turned out to be a bummer. I told the cops all this. I'm sure they checked it out."

"I'm sure they did," Dora said. "Miss Starrett, do you know of any enemies your father had? Anyone who might have wanted to harm him?"

50

Felicia had been smoking with short, rapid puffs. Now tears came to her eyes, and she stubbed out the cigarette.

"Damn!" she said. "I thought I was finished with the weeping and wailing."

"I'm sorry I upset you."

"Not your fault. But every time I think of him lying there on the sidewalk, all alone, it gets to me. My father was a sonofabitch but I loved him. Can you understand that?"

"Yes."

"And no matter what a stinker he was, no one should die like that. It's just not right."

"No," Dora said, "it isn't."

"Sure, I guess he had enemies. You can't be a world-class bastard all your life without getting people sore at you. But no, I don't know of anyone who hated him enough to murder him."

"I met Father Callaway when I questioned your mother. He seems to agree with the police theory that your father was killed by a stranger."

"*Father* Callaway!" Felicia cried. "He's as much a Father as I am an astronaut. Don't pay any attention to what he says or thinks. The man's a phony."

"Oh?" Dora said. "How do you mean?"

"He's got this rinky-dink church in an empty store, and he cons money from a lot of innocent people like my mother who fall for his smarmy smile and bullshit about one world of love and harmony."

"Surely he does some good," Dora suggested. "He said his church runs a soup kitchen for the homeless."

"So he hands out a few cheese sandwiches while he's dining at the homes of his suckers on beef Wellington. My father had his number. Every time he saw Callaway in his preacher's outfit, he'd ask him, 'How's white-collar crime today?'"

Dora laughed. "But your father allowed him in your home."

"For mother's sake," Felicia said wearily. "She's a true believer in Callaway and his cockamamy church."

"Is anyone else in your family a true believer? Your sister-in-law, for instance."

"Eleanor? All she believes in are the society columns. If she doesn't see her name in print, she doesn't exist. I don't know why I'm telling you all this; it's got nothing to do with the insurance."

"You never know," Dora said, and watched the other woman light another cigarette with fingers that trembled slightly.

She figured Felicia had already endured the big four-oh. She was a tall, angular woman, tightly wound, with a Nefertiti profile and hands made for scratching.

"I'll tell you something about Eleanor," she said broodingly. "We used to be as close as this . . ." She displayed two crossed fingers. "Then she and Clay had a kid, a boy, a beautiful child. Lived eighteen months and died horribly of meningitis. It broke Eleanor; she became a different woman. She told everyone: 'No more kids.' That was all right; it was her decision to make. But—and this is my own idea—I think it also turned her off sex. After a while my brother started playing around. I know that for a fact. One-night stands, nothing serious. But who could blame him; he wasn't getting any at home. And then Eleanor got on the charity-party circuit, and that's been her whole life ever since. Sad, sad, sad. Life sucks—you know that?"

Dora didn't reply.

"Well, enough soap opera for one day," Felicia said, and rose abruptly. "I've got to dash. Thanks for the drink. If you need anything else, give me a buzz."

"Thank you, Miss Starrett."

She tugged on her mink jacket, stood a moment looking down at Dora.

"Six years, huh?" she said. "I've never been married. I'm an old maid."

"Don't say that," Dora said.

"Why not?" Felicia said, forcing a laugh. "It's true, isn't it? But don't feel sorry for me; I get my jollies—one way or another. Keep in touch, kiddo."

And with a wave of a hand she was gone. Dora sat alone, feeling she needed something stronger than beer. So she moved to the bar and ordered a straight Chivas, Perrier on the side. She had never before had such a drink, but Felicia Starrett had ordered it, and Dora wanted to honor her. Go figure it, she told herself.

She had the one drink, then went upstairs to the corporate suite and worked on notes that would be source material for her report to Mike Trevalyan. Then she took a nap that worked wonders because she awoke in a sportive mood. She showered and phoned Mario while she was still naked. It seemed more intimate that way. Mario said he missed her, and she said she missed him. She made kissing sounds on the phone.

"Disgusting!" he said, laughing, and hung up.

She dressed, pulled on her parka, and sallied forth. It was a nippy night, the smell of snow in the air, and when she asked the Bedlington doorman to get her a cab, he said, "Forget it!"

So she walked over to Fifth Avenue and then south,

pausing to admire holiday displays in store windows. She saw the glittering tree at Rockefeller Center and stopped awhile to listen to a group of carolers who were singing "Heilige Nacht" and taking up a collection for victims of AIDS.

She wandered on down Fifth Avenue, crisscrossing several times to inspect shop windows, searching for something unusual to give Mario for Christmas. The stone lions in front of the Library had wreaths around their necks, which she thought was a nice touch. A throng stood on line to view Lord & Taylor's animated windows, so she decided to see them another time.

She was at 34th Street before she knew it, and walked over to Herald Square to gawk at Macy's windows. It was then almost 7:30 and, having come this far, she suddenly decided to walk farther and visit Father Callaway's Church of the Holy Oneness.

It was colder now, a fine mist haloing the streetlights. She plodded on, hands deep in parka pockets, remembering what Detective Wenden had said about the stupidity of walking the city at night. She knew how to use a handgun but had never carried one, believing herself incapable of actually shooting someone. And if you couldn't do that, what was the point?

But she arrived at East 20th Street without incident, except for having to shoo away several panhandlers who accepted their rejection docilely enough. Stiffing them did not demonstrate the Christmas spirit, she admitted, but she had no desire to stop, open her shoulder bag, fumble for her wallet. Wenden didn't have to warn her about the danger of being fearless. She wasn't.

As Felicia Starrett had said, Callaway's church was

located in a former store. It apparently had been a fast-food luncheonette because the legend TAKE OUT ORDERS was still lettered in one corner of the plate glass window. A wide venetian blind, closed, concealed the interior from passersby, but a sign over the doorway read CHURCH OF THE HOLY ONENESS, ALL WELCOME in a cursive script.

Dora paused before entering and suddenly felt a hard object pressing into her back. "Your money or your life," a harsh voice grated. She whirled to see Detective John Wenden grinning and digging a knuckle into her ribs.

"You louse!" she gasped. "You really scared me."

"Serves you right," he said. "What the hell are you doing down here by yourself?"

"Curiosity," she said. "What are *you* doing here?"

"Oh, I had some time to kill," he said casually, "and figured I'd catch the preacher's act. Let's go in."

"Let's sit in the back," she suggested. "Mrs. Starrett may be here, and I'd just as soon she didn't see me."

"Suits me," he said. "I hope the place is heated."

It was overheated. About fifty folding chairs were set up in a long, narrow room, facing a low stage with a lectern and upright piano. The majority of the chairs were occupied, mostly by well-dressed matrons. But there were a few young couples, a scatter of single men and women, and a couple of derelicts who had obviously come in to warm up. They were sleeping.

A plump, baldish man was seated at the piano playing and singing "O Little Town of Bethlehem" in a surprisingly clarion tenor. The audience seemed to be listening attentively. Conti and Wenden took off their coats and slid into chairs in the back row. Dora craned and spotted Mrs. Olivia Starrett seated up front.

The hymn ended, the pianist rose and left the stage, exiting through a rear doorway. The audience stirred, then settled down and waited expectantly. A few moments later Father Brian Callaway entered, striding purposefully across the stage. He stood erect behind the lectern, smiling at his audience.

He was wearing a long cassock of white satin, the sleeves unusually wide and billowing. The front was edged with purple piping, cuffs and hem decorated with gold embroidery. A diamond ring sparkled on the forefinger of his right hand.

"Father Gotrocks," Wenden whispered to Dora.

"Shh," she said.

"Good evening, brothers and sisters," Callaway began in a warm, conversational tone. "Welcome to the Church of the Holy Oneness. After the service, coffee and cake will be served, and you will be asked to contribute voluntarily to the work of the Church which, as many of you know, includes daily distribution of food to those unfortunates who, often through no fault of their own, are without means to provide for themselves.

"Tonight I want to talk to you about the environment. Not acid rain, the pollution of our air and water, the destruction of our forests and coastline, but *personal* environment, the pollution of our souls and the need to seek what I call the Divine Harmony, in which we are one with nature, with each other, and with God."

He developed this theme in more detail during the following thirty minutes. He likened greed, envy, lust, and other sins to lethal chemicals that poisoned the soil and foods grown from it. He said that the earth could not endure such contamination indefinitely, and similarly the human soul could not withstand the corrosion of moral offenses that weakened, debilitated, and would eventually destroy the individual and inevitably all of society.

The solution, he stated in a calm, reasonable manner, was to recognize that just as the physical environment was one, interdependent, and sacred, so the moral environment was one, and it demanded care, sacrifice, and, above all, love if we were to find a Divine Harmony with nature, people, and with God: a Holy Oneness that encompassed all joys and all sorrows.

He was still speaking of the Holy Oneness when Wenden tugged at Dora's sleeve.

"Let's split," he said in a low voice.

She nodded, and they gathered up their coats and slipped away. Apparently neither the pastor nor anyone in that rapt audience noticed their departure. Outside, the mist had thickened to a freezing drizzle.

"I've got a car," the detective said, "but there's a pizza joint just around the corner on Third. We won't get too wet."

"Let's go," Dora said. She took his arm, and they scurried.

A few minutes later they were snugly settled in a booth, breathing garlicky air, sipping cold beers, and waiting for their Mammoth Supreme, half-anchovy, half-pepperoni.

"The guy surprised me," Wenden said. "I thought he'd be a religious windbag, one of those 'Come to Jesus!' shouters. But I have to admit he sounded sincere, like he really believes in that snake oil he's peddling."

"Maybe he does," Dora said. "I thought he was impressive. Very low-key, very persuasive. Tell me the truth: How come you found time to catch him in action?"

Wenden shrugged. "I really don't know. Maybe because he's so smooth and has too many teeth. How's that for scientific crime detection?"

They stared at each other for a thoughtful moment.

"Tell you what," Dora said finally, "I'll ask my boss to run Callaway through our computer. But our data base only includes people who have been involved in insurance scams."

"Do it," the detective urged. "Just for the fun of it."

Their giant pizza was served, and they dug in, plucking paper napkins from the dispenser.

"How you coming with the Starrett family?" Wenden asked her.

"All right, I guess. So far everyone's been very cooperative. The net result is zilch. Why do I have a feeling I'm not asking the right questions?"

"Like what?" he said. "Like 'Did you kill your husband?' or 'Did you murder your father?'"

"Nothing as gross as that," she said. "But I'm convinced that family has secrets."

"All families have secrets."

"But the Starretts' secrets may have something to do with the homicide. I tell you, John—"

"John?" he interrupted. "Oh my, I thought you told me you were happily married."

"Oh, shut up," she said, laughing. "If we're going to pig out on a pizza together, it might as well be John and Dora. What I was going to say is that I mean no disrespect to the NYPD, but I think the official theory of a stranger as the murderer is bunk. And I think you think it's bunk."

He carefully lifted a pepperoni wedge, folded it lengthwise, began to eat holding a paper napkin over his shirtfront.

58

He had a craggy face, more interesting than handsome: nose and chin too long, cheekbones high and prominent, eyes dark and deeply set. Dora liked his mouth, when it wasn't smeared with pizza topping, and his hair was black as a gypsy's. The best thing about him, she decided, was his voice: a rich, resonant baritone, musical as a sax.

He wiped his lips and took a gulp of beer. "Maybe it is bunk," he said. "But I've got nothing better. Have you?"

She shook her head. "Some very weak threads to follow. Father Callaway is one. Clayton Starrett is another."

"What's with him?"

"Apparently he's cheating on his wife."

"That's a crime?" Wenden said. "The world hasn't got enough jails to hold all the married men who play around. What else?"

"You got anything on Charles Hawkins, the butler?"

He smiled. "You mean the butler did it? Only in books. You ever know a homicide where the butler was actually the perp?"

"No," she admitted, "but I worked a case where the gardener did the dirty work. I think I'll take another look at Mr. Hawkins. You going to drive me back to my hotel?"

"Sure," he said. "You going to ask me up for a nightcap?"

"Nope," she said. "A shared pizza is enough intimacy for one night. Let me get the bill; the Company can afford it."

"Okay," he said cheerfully. "My alimony payment is due next week and I'm running short."

"Need a few bucks till payday?" she asked.

He stared at her. "You're a sweetheart, you are," he said. "Thanks, but no thanks. I'll get by."

She paid the check and they dashed through a cold rain to his car, an old Pontiac she figured should be put out to stud. But the heater worked, and so did the radio. They rode uptown listening to a medley of Gershwin tunes and singing along with some of them. Wenden's voice might have been a rich, resonant baritone, but he had a tin ear.

He pulled up outside the Bedlington and turned to her. "Thanks for the pizza," he said.

"Thanks for the company, John," she said. "I'm glad I bumped into you."

She started to get out of the car, but he put a hand on her arm.

"If you change your mind," he said, "I hope I'll be the first to know."

"Change my mind? About what?"

"You and me. A little of that divine harmony."

"Good night, Detective Wenden," she said.

8

Clayton Starrett, flushed with too much rich food and good wine, stood patiently, waiting for his wife to finish cheek-kissing and air-kissing with all her cohostesses in the hotel ballroom. Finally she came over to him, smile still in place. Eleanor was a plain woman, rather bony, and her strapless evening gown did nothing to conceal prominent clavicles and washboard chest. But parties always gave her a glow; excitement energized her, made her seem warm and vital.

"I thought it went splendidly," she said. "Didn't you?"

"Good party," he said, nodding.

"And the speeches weren't too long, were they, Clay?"

"Just right," he said, although he had dozed through most of them. "Can we go now?"

Most of the limousines had already departed, so theirs was called up almost immediately. On the ride home she chattered animatedly about the food, the wine, the table decorations, who wore what, who drank too much, who made a scene over a waiter's clumsiness.

"And did you see that twit Bob Farber with his new wife?" she asked her husband.

"I saw them."

"She must be half his age—or less. What a fool the man is."

"Uh-huh," Clayton said, remembering the new Mrs. Farber as a luscious creature. No other word for her—luscious!

Charles, clad in a shabby bathrobe, met them at the door. He told them that both Mrs. Olivia and Miss Felicia had retired to their bedrooms. At Eleanor's request, he brought two small brandies to their suite, closed the door, and presumably went about his nightly chores: locking up and turning off the lights.

Clayton loosened his tie, cummerbund, and opened the top button of his trousers. He sprawled in a worn velvet armchair (originally mauve) and watched his wife remove her jewelry. He remembered when he had given her the three-strand pearl choker, the black jade and gold bracelet, the mabe pearl earrings, the dragon brooch with rubies and diamonds set in platinum. Well, why not? She was a jeweler's wife. He reckoned a woman who married a butcher got all the sirloins she could eat.

Eleanor came over to his chair and turned her back. Obediently he reached up and pulled down the long zipper. He saw her pale, bony back.

"Losing too much weight, aren't you, hon?" he said.

"I don't think so," she said lightly. "You know the saying: You can never be too rich or too thin."

She went into the bedroom to undress. He sipped his brandy and thought of Bob Farber's new wife. Luscious!

Eleanor returned pulling on a crimson silk bathrobe.

Before she knotted the sash, he saw how thin she really was. There was a time, before their son died, before Eleanor changed, when to watch her dress and undress in his presence was a joy. He had cherished those moments of warm domesticity. But now all the fervor had disappeared from their intimacy. His joy had dried up, just as Eleanor's body had become juiceless and her passions spent on table settings for charity benefits.

She took one sip of her brandy, then handed him the glass. "You finish it," she said. "I'm going to bed."

She swooped to kiss his cheek, then went back into the bedroom. He knew she would don a sleep mask and insert ear stopples. He suspected the mask and plugs were intended as armor, to protect herself from unwanted physical overtures. That didn't offend him, though it saddened him; he had no intention of forcing himself upon her. His last attempt, almost two years ago, had been a disaster that ended with tears and hysterical recriminations.

He finished his brandy, put the glass aside, and drank from Eleanor's. He saw the bedroom light go out, and wondered how much longer he could endure this marriage that was all form and no content.

Since meeting Helene Pierce, he had become concerned about age and the passing of time. It seemed to be accelerating. My God, here it was Christmas again! A year almost over, so quickly, gone in a flash. He felt the weight of his years: His mind was sharp as ever, he was convinced, but the body inexorably slowing, gravity claiming paunch and ass, vigor dulled and, worst of all, his capacity for fun dwindling—except when he was with Helene. She restored him: the best medicine a man could want.

Bob Farber had done it, and so had a dozen other friends

and acquaintances. It was easy to make crude jokes about old goats and young women, but there was more to it than a toss in the hay and proving your manhood. There was rejuvenation, a rebirth of energy and resolve.

It would be difficult, he acknowledged. He would have to move slowly and carefully. If he could not win his mother's approval, at least he would need her neutrality. As things stood now, she was, in effect, the owner of Starrett Fine Jewelry, and he could not risk her displeasure.

As for Helene, he could not see her rejecting him even if he was old enough to be her father. In addition to her physical attractions, she had a sharp mind, a real bottom-line mentality. He knew of no other lovers she had, and while he was no Adonis, he offered enough in the way of financial security to convince her to disregard his age. And, of course, Turner Pierce was dependent on Starrett Jewelry for a large hunk of his income. He could count on Turner's endorsement.

Eleanor would be saddened. Naturally. But there were many women in Manhattan, in their circle, who had endured the same experience. There was nothing like a generous cash settlement to cushion the shock.

Clayton finished the brandy, rose and stretched. The matter would demand heavy deliberation and prudent judgment. But he thought it was doable and needed only a clever game plan to make it a reality.

He went to bed, thought more of his decision and how it might be implemented. And never once, in all his speculation, did he put a name to what he planned. Just as, not too long ago, people spoke of cancer as the Big C, because naming the tragedy was too shocking. So Clayton Starrett never said, even to himself, "Divorce." Or even the Big D.

9

The Company's Hartford office opened officially at 9:00 A.M., but Dora knew Mike Trevalyan arrived every morning at eight to get his day's work organized. She called him early on his private line and grinned to hear his surly growl.

"Tough night, Mike?" she asked.

"No tougher than usual. I had to go to a testimonial dinner for a cop who's retiring. A very wet party. What's up?"

She told him what she wanted: Run Brian Callaway through the computer and see if there was anything on him. And get her some inside poop on Starrett Fine Jewelry: who owned it, their assets, revenues, profits, and so forth.

"Callaway will be easy," Trevalyan said. "I should have an answer for you later today. Starrett will take some time. It's a privately held company, so there won't be much public disclosure. But I have some contacts in the jewelry trade, and I'll see what I can dig up."

"Thanks, Mike," Dora said. One of the things she liked about her boss was that he never asked unnecessary questions, like, "What do you need this stuff for?" She couldn't have answered that.

She had an appointment at noon with Helene and Turner Pierce. It gave her enough time to have a leisurely New York breakfast (lox and cream cheese on bagel) and then wander about the selling floors of Starrett's store on Park Avenue. Miniature Christmas trees were everywhere, decorated with gold tinsel, and muted carols were coming from concealed speakers. There were few customers, but not a single clerk came forward to ask, "May I help you?"

Dora spent almost an hour inspecting jewelry in showcases and silver, crystal, and china on open display. All price tags were turned facedown or tucked discreetly beneath the items. But Dora knew she could never afford the things she liked—except, perhaps, a sterling silver barrette in the shape of a dolphin.

She arrived at Helene Pierce's apartment house a little before noon. It was a shiny new high-rise on Second Avenue, all glass and rosy brick with a gourmet food shop and a designer's boutique on the street level. The doorman wore a plumed shako and military cape of crimson wool. Inside, the concierge behind a marble counter wore a swallowtail of white silk. Dora was impressed and wondered what kind of rent Helene Pierce was paying. Even if the apartments were co-ops or condos, she figured the maintenance would be stiff; plumed shakos and silk swallowtails cost. And so do elevators lined with ebony panels and antiqued mirrors.

The woman who opened the door of the 16th-floor apartment looked to be ten years younger than Dora, six inches taller, and thirty pounds lighter. She had the masklike features of a high-fashion model, her smile distant. She was wearing a cognac-colored jumpsuit belted with what seemed to be a silver bicycle chain. Her long feet were bare.

"Dora Conti?" she asked, voice flat and drawly.

"Yes, Miss Pierce. Thank you for seeing me. I promise not to take too much of your time."

"Come on in. My brother should be along any minute."

The apartment was not as lavish as Dora expected. The rugs and furnishings were attractive, but hardly luxurious. The living room had a curiously unlived-in look, as if it might be a model room in a department store. Dora got the feeling of impermanence, the occupant a transient just passing through.

They sat at opposite ends of a couch covered with beige linen and both half-turned to face each other.

"What a lovely building," Dora said. "The lobby is quite unusual."

Helene's smile was mocking. "A little garish," she said. "I would have preferred something a bit more subdued, a bit more elegant. But apparently people like it; all the apartments have been sold."

"It's a co-op?"

"That's correct."

"How long have you lived here, Miss Pierce?"

"Oh . . . let me see . . . It's been a little over a year now."

"I hope you don't mind my saying, but you don't talk like a New Yorker. The Midwest, I'd guess."

Helene stared at her, then reached for a pack of cigarettes on the end table. "Would you like one?" she asked.

"No, thank you."

"Do you mind if I smoke?"

"Not at all."

Dora watched her light up slowly, wondering if this lovely, self-possessed young woman was stalling.

"Yes, you're quite right," Helene said with a short laugh. "The Midwest it is."

"Oh?" Dora said, trying to keep her prying light and casual. "Where?"

"Kansas City."

"Which one? Missouri or Kansas?"

"Missouri. Does it show?"

"Only in your voice," Dora said. "Believe me, your looks are pure Manhattan."

"I hope that's a compliment."

"It is. Have you ever modeled, Miss Pierce?"

"No. I've been asked to, but—" There was a knock at the hallway door. "That must be my brother. Excuse me a moment."

The man who followed Helene back into the living room was wearing a mink-collared cashmere topcoat slung carelessly over his shoulders like a cape. There was a hint of swagger in his walk, and when he leaned down to shake Dora's hand, she caught a whiff of something else. Cigar smoke, she guessed. Or perhaps brandy.

"Miss Conti," he said, smiling. "A pleasure. What's this? My sister didn't offer you a drink?"

"Sorry about that," Helene said. "Would you like something—hard or soft?"

"Nothing, thank you," Dora said. "I'll just ask a few questions and then be on my way."

The Pierces agreed they had attended a small cocktail

party at the Starrett apartment the night Lewis had been killed. And no, neither knew of any enemies who might have wished the older Starrett dead. It was true he was sometimes a difficult man to get along with, but his occasional nastiness was hardly a reason for murder.

"How long have you known the Starretts?" Dora asked, addressing Turner.

"Oh . . . perhaps two years," he replied. "Maybe a little longer. It began as a business relationship when I landed Starrett Jewelry as a client. Then Helene and I met the entire family, and we became friends."

"What kind of business are you in, Mr. Pierce?"

"I'm a management consultant. It's really a one-man operation. I specialize in computer systems, analyzing a client's needs and devising the most efficient setup to meet those needs. Or sometimes I recommend changing or upgrading a client's existing hardware."

"And that's the kind of work you did for Starrett?"

"Yes. Their new state-of-the-art systems integration is just coming on-line now. I think it will make a big difference in back-room efficiency and give Starrett executives the tools to improve their management skills."

That sounded like a sales pitch to Dora, but she said politely, "Fascinating."

"I haven't the slightest idea what my brother is talking about," Helene said. "Computers are as mysterious to me as the engine in my car. Do you use computers in your work, Miss Conti?"

"Oh yes. The insurance business would be lost without them. I'd like to ask both of you an additional question, but first I want to assure you that your replies will be held in strictest confidence. Has either of you, or both, ever noticed any signs of discord between members of the Starrett family? Any arguments, for instance, or other evidence of hostility?"

The Pierces looked at each other a brief moment.

"I can't recall anything like that," Turner said slowly. "Can you, sis?"

She shook her head. "They seem a very happy family. No arguments that I can remember. Sometimes Lewis Starrett would get angry with Father Brian Callaway, but of course the Father is not a member of the family."

"And even then Lewis was just letting off steam," Turner put in swiftly. "I'm sure he didn't mean anything by it. It was just his way."

"What was he angry about?" Dora said.

Turner rose from his armchair. "May I have one of your cigarettes, sis?" he asked.

Dora watched him light up, thinking these two used the same shtick to give themselves time to frame their replies.

Turner Pierce was a tall man, slender and graceful as a fencer. His complexion was dark, almost olive, and he sported a wide black mustache, so sleek it might have been painted. He had the same negligent manner as Helene, but behind his casual attention, Dora imagined, was something else: a streak of uncaring cruelty, as if the opinions or even the suffering of others were a bore, and only his own gratification mattered.

"I believe," he said carefully, "it concerned the contributions Olivia was making to Father Callaway's church. It was nonsense, of course. The Starretts have all the money in the world, and the Father's church does many worthwhile things for the poor and homeless."

Dora nodded. "And I understand Mrs. Eleanor is quite

70

active in charity benefits. It seems to me the Starrett women are very generous to the less fortunate."

"Yes," he said shortly, "they are."

"Felicia Starrett as well?" she asked suddenly.

"Oh, Felicia has her private charities," Helene said in her flat drawl. "She does a lot of good, doesn't she, Turner?"

"Oh yes," he said, "a lot."

They didn't smile, but Dora was conscious of an inside joke there, a private joke, and she didn't like it.

"Thank you both very much," she said rising. "I appreciate your kind cooperation."

Turner stood up, helped her on with her bulky anorak. "It's been a pleasure meeting you, ma'am," he said. "If there's anything more you need, my sister and I will be delighted to help."

She shook hands with both: identical handclasps, cool and limp. She walked down the marble-tiled corridor to the elevator, thinking those two were taking her lightly; scorn was in their voices. And why not? They were elegant animals, handsome and aloof. And she? She was a *plumpmobile,* not quite frumpy but no *Elle* cover girl either.

It was in the elevator that she decided to start a new diet immediately.

She spent the afternoon Christmas shopping. She selected a nice pipe for her father who, since her mother's death, was living alone in Kennebunkport and refused to leave town, even for a visit. And she bought scarves, mittens, brass trivets, soup tureens, books of cartoons, music boxes, hairbrushes, and lots of other keen stuff. She paid with credit cards, had everything gift-wrapped and mailed out to her and her husband's aunts, uncles, nieces, nephews, cousins, and friends. She still didn't find anything ex- actly right for Mario.

She had dinner in a restaurant in the plaza of Rockefeller Center: the best broiled trout she had ever eaten. She had one glass of Chablis, but when the dessert cart was rolled up, her new resolve vanished and she pigged out on a big chocolate-banana mousse. And then punished herself by walking back to her hotel, convinced the calories were melting away during her hike.

The desk clerk at the Bedlington had a message for her: Call Mike Trevalyan. She went up to her suite, kicked off her shoes, and phoned. Mike sounded much friskier than he was that morning, and Dora figured he had had one of his three-martini lunches.

"This Brian Callaway you asked about," he said. "Is he a big, beefy guy, heavy through the shoulders and chest, reddish complexion, lots of charm and a hundred-watt smile?"

"That's the man," Dora said. "You found him?"

"Finally. In the alias file. His real name, as far as we know, is Sidney Loftus, but he's used a half-dozen fake monikers."

"Is he a preacher?"

"A *preacher?*" Trevalyan said, laughing. "Yeah, I guess he could be a preacher. He's already been a used-car sales- man, a psychotherapist, an investment advisor, and—get this—an insurance consultant."

"Oh-oh," Dora said. "A wrongo?"

"So twisted you could screw him into the ground. Ac- cording to the computer, he's never done hard time for any of his scams. He's always worked a deal, made restitu- tion, and got off with a suspended sentence or probation:

Then he blows town, changes his name, and starts another swindle. About five years ago he put together a stolen car ring. If you couldn't keep up the payments on your jalopy, or needed some ready cash, you'd go to him and he'd arrange to have your car swiped. He never did it himself; he had a crew of dopers working for him. The car would be taken to a chop shop, and by the time the insurers got around to looking for it, the parts were down in Uruguay. The cops infiltrated the ring and were twenty-four hours away from busting Sidney Loftus when he must have been tipped off because he skipped town and hasn't been heard of since, until you asked about him. You know where he is, Dora?"

She ignored the question. "Mike," she said, "this stolen car ring—where was it operating?"

"Kansas City."

"Which one? Missouri or Kansas?"

"Missouri."

"Thank you very much," said Dora.

10

Despite working for Starrett Fine Jewelry for forty years, CFO Solomon Guthrie knew little about the techniques of jewelry making. All he knew were numbers. "Numbers don't lie," he was fond of remarking. This honest man never fully realized how numbers can be cooked, and how a Park Avenue corporation based on fiddled data might have no more financial stature than an Orchard Street pushcart.

But despite his naiveté, Guthrie could not rid himself of the suspicion that something was wrong with the way Mister Clayton was running the business. All those new branch managers. That new computer systems integration that Sol didn't understand. And the tremendous purchases and sales of gold bullion. He couldn't believe any jewelry store, or chain of stores, could use that much pure gold. And yet, at the end of each month, Starrett showed a nice profit on its bullion deals. Guthrie was bewildered.

Finally he phoned Arthur Rushkin, who had been Starrett's attorney almost as long as Sol had slaved over Starrett's ledgers.

"Baker and Rushkin," the receptionist said.

"This is Solomon Guthrie of Starrett Jewelry. Can I talk to Mr. Rushkin, please."

"Sol!" Rushkin said heartily. "When are we going to tear a herring together?"

"Listen, Art," Guthrie said, "I've got to see you right away. Can you give me an hour this afternoon?"

"A problem?"

"I think it is."

"No problem is worth more than a half-hour. See you here at three o'clock. Okay?"

"I'll be there."

He stuffed a roll of computer printout into his battered briefcase and added a copy of Starrett's most recent monthly statement. Then he told his secretary, Claire Heffernan, that he was going over to Arthur Rushkin's office and would probably return by four o'clock.

He had no sooner departed than Claire strolled into the office of Dick Satterlee.

"He's gone to see the lawyer," she reported.

"Thanks, doll," Satterlee said.

"Party tonight?" she asked.

"Why not," he said, grinning.

The moment she was gone, he phoned Turner Pierce. Turner wasn't in, but Satterlee left a message on his answering machine, asking him to call back as soon as possible; it was important.

Solomon Guthrie knew he'd never get a cab, so he walked over to the offices of Baker & Rushkin on Fifth Avenue near 45th Street. It was an overcast day, the sky heavy with dirty clouds, a nippy wind blowing from the northwest. Christmas shoppers were scurrying, and the Salvation Army Santas on the corners were stamping their feet to keep warm.

Rushkin came out of his inner office to greet him in the reception room. The two men embraced, shook hands, patted shoulders.

"Happy holidays, Sol," Rushkin said.

"Yeah," Guthrie said. "Same to you."

The attorney was the CFO's age, but a different breed of cat entirely. A lot of good beef and bourbon had gone into that florid face, and his impressive stomach was only partly concealed by Italian tailoring and, if the truth be told, an elastic, girdlelike undergarment that kept his abdomen compressed.

He settled Guthrie in an armchair alongside his antique partners' desk, then sat back into his deep swivel chair and laced fingers across his tattersall waistcoat. "All right, Sol," he said, "what's bothering you?"

Guthrie poured it all out, speaking so rapidly he was almost spluttering. He told Rushkin about the new branch managers; Clayton's plan to make every Starrett store autonomous; the new computer system that Sol couldn't understand. And finally he described all the dealing in gold bullion. Long before he ended his recital, Rushkin was toying with a letter opener on his desktop and staring at the other man with something close to pity.

"Sol, Sol," he said gently, "what you're complaining about are business decisions. Clayton is president and CEO; he has every right to make those decisions. Is Starrett losing money?"

"No."

"Making money?"

"Yes."

"Then Clayton seems to be doing a good job."

"Look," Sol said desperately, "I know I've got no proof, but something's going on that just isn't kosher. Like those gold deals."

"All right," the attorney said patiently, "tell me exactly how those deals are made. Where does Starrett get the gold?"

"We buy it from overseas dealers in precious metals."

"How do you pay?"

"Our bank transfers money from our account to the dealers' banks overseas. It's all done electronically. By computer," he added disgustedly.

"Then the overseas dealer ships the gold to the U.S.?"

"No, the dealers have subsidiaries over here. The gold is warehoused by the subsidiaries. When we buy, the gold is delivered to our vault in Brooklyn."

"How is it delivered?"

"Usually by armored truck."

"Good security?"

"The best. Our Brooklyn warehouse is an armed camp. It costs us plenty, but it's worth it."

"All right," Rushkin said. "Starrett signs a contract to buy X ounces of gold. You get copies of the contract?"

"Naturally."

"The subsidiary of the overseas dealer then delivers the gold to Starrett's vault. The amount delivered is checked carefully against the contract?"

"Of course."

"Have you ever been short-weighed?"

"No."

"So now Starrett has the bullion in its vault. Who do you sell it to?"

"To our branches around the country. Then they sell it to small jewelry stores in their area."

"Correct me if I'm wrong, but I presume because of its size, resources, and reputation, plus the volume of its purchases, Starrett buys gold at a good price from those overseas dealers."

"That's correct."

"And tacks on a markup when it sells to its branches?"

"Yes."

"Which, in turn, make a profit when they sell to independents in their area?"

"Yes."

Arthur Rushkin tossed up his hands. "Sol," he said, laughing, "what you've just described is a very normal, conventional way of doing business. Buy low, sell high. You get complete documentation of every step in the procedure, don't you? Contracts, bills of lading, shipping invoices, and so forth?"

"Yes. On the computer."

"And the final customers—the small, independent jewelry stores—have they ever stiffed you?"

"No," Guthrie admitted, then burst out, "but I tell you something stinks! There's too much gold coming in, going out, floating all over the place. And some of those small shops that buy our gold—why, they weren't even in business a couple of years ago. I know; I checked."

"Small retail stores come and go, Sol; you know that. I really can't understand why you're so upset. You haven't told me anything that even hints of illegal business practices—if that's what you're implying."

"Something's going on," Guthrie insisted. "I know it is. We're buying too much bullion, and too many independent stores are buying it from us. Listen, what do they need it for? Everyone knows pure gold is very rarely used in jewelry. It's too soft; it bends or scratches. Maybe twenty-four-karat or twenty-two-karat will be used as a thin plating on some other metal, but gold jewelry is usually an eighteen- or fourteen-karat alloy. So why do these rinky-dink stores need so much pure stuff?"

Arthur sighed. "I don't know, but if their checks don't bounce, what the hell do you care what they do with it? Sol, what is it exactly you want me to do? Talk to Clayton? About what? That he's making money for Starrett by dealing in gold bullion?"

Guthrie opened his briefcase, piled the statement and computer printout on the attorney's desk. "Just take a look at this stuff, will you, Art?" he asked. "Study it. Maybe you'll spot something I can't see." He paused a moment, then almost shouted, "You know what Clayton did the other day?"

"What?"

"Gave me a fifty-thousand-dollar-a-year raise."

"Mazeltov!" Rushkin cried.

Sol shook his head. "Too much," he said. "It doesn't make business sense to give me so much. And he gave it to me right after I complained about what's going on at Starrett Fine Jewelry. You don't suppose he did it so I'll keep my mouth shut, do you?"

The attorney stared at him. "Sol," he said, "I've got to tell you that sounds paranoid to me. In all honesty, I think you're making something out of nothing."

"Just look over this printout, Art—will you do that for me?"

"Of course."

"And please don't tell Clayton I came to see you. Well, you can tell him if he asks; my secretary knows I came here. But don't tell Clayton what we talked about."

"Whatever you say, Sol."

The CFO stood up, tucked the empty briefcase under his arm. "I'm going to keep digging," he vowed. "I'll find out what's going on."

Rushkin nodded, walked out to the reception room with Guthrie, helped him on with his coat. "Keep in touch, Sol," he said lightly.

When the outside door closed, the lawyer turned to the receptionist and stared at her a moment.

"Too bad," he said.

"What's too bad, Mr. Rushkin?"

"Growing old is too bad, for some people. They can't keep up with new developments, like computers. They resent younger people coming into their business and doing a good job. They want things to remain the way they were. Change confuses them. They get the feeling the world is passing them by, and they start thinking there's a conspiracy against them. Don't ever grow old, Sally."

"Do I have a choice?" she asked.

He laughed. "I have to meet Mr. Yamoto at the Four Seasons bar," he said. "That means I won't be back this afternoon. There's a pile of computer printout on my desk. Will you put it away in a filing cabinet, please."

"Which filing cabinet?"

"I couldn't care less," Arthur Rushkin said.

11

Mrs. Eleanor Starrett sat at a white enameled table in Georgio's Salon on East 56th Street, having a set of false fingernails attached. Next to her, Dora Conti was perched uncomfortably on a small stool on rollers. Across the table from Mrs. Starrett, the attendant, a buxom lady from Martinique, bent intently over her gluing job, saying nothing but not missing a word of the conversation.

"So sorry I couldn't meet you at home," Eleanor said, "but I'm due at Tiffany's in a half-hour to select door prizes for a benefit. With the holidays coming on, it's just rush, rush, rush."

"That's all right," Dora said, wondering how this woman could pull on gloves with rocks like that on her fingers. "I just have a few questions to ask."

"I really don't understand why the insurance company is investigating my father-in-law's death. I should think that would be a job for the police."

"Of course it is," Dora said. "But the policy is so large

and the circumstances of Mr. Starrett's death so puzzling, we want to be absolutely certain the claim is, ah, unencumbered before it is paid."

"Well, the poor man could hardly have stabbed himself in the back, could he?" Eleanor said tartly. "Which means, I suppose, that you think one of the beneficiaries may have done him in."

"Mrs. Starrett," Dora said, sighing, "no one is accusing anyone of anything. We would just like to see the murder solved and the case closed, that's all. Now, do you know of any enemies Lewis Starrett had? Any person or persons who might wish to harm him?"

"No."

"How did *you* get along with him?"

Eleanor turned her head to look directly at her questioner. "Dad—that's what I always called him: Dad—could be a dreadful man at times. I'm sure you've heard that from others as well. But for some reason he took a liking to me, and I got along with him very well. Olivia and Clayton and Felicia suffered more from his temper tantrums than I did. And the servants were targets, too, of course. But he never raised his voice to me. Perhaps he knew that if he had, I'd have marched out of that house and never returned."

"I understand Father Brian Callaway was sometimes the cause of his anger."

"My, my," Mrs. Starrett said mockingly, "you have been busy, haven't you? Well, you're right; Dad couldn't stand the man. The fact that Olivia was giving the preacher money infuriated him. He finally forbade her to give Father Callaway's so-called church another red cent."

"And what was his argument with the servants?"

"Oh, that was a long-running civil war. Stupid things like

84

Charles' fingernails were too long, the Sunday *Times* had a section missing, Clara was using the good wine to cook with—picky things like that."

"Did they ever threaten to quit?"

"Of course not. They're being very well paid indeed, and though I wouldn't call them incompetent, they're far from being super. Just adequate, I'd say. If they quit, who'd pay them what dad was giving them—plus their own little suite of rooms as well."

"I understand you're very active in charity benefits, Mrs. Starrett."

"I do what I can," she said in a tone of such humility that Dora wanted to kick her shins.

"Does your sister-in-law ever join in these activities?"

"I'm afraid Felicia's favorite charity is Felicia. We get along. Period."

"But not close?"

"No," Eleanor said with a short bark of laughter. "Not close at all."

"Could you tell me something about Helene and Turner Pierce. How long have you known them?"

"Oh, perhaps a couple of years."

"How did they become friends of the Starrett family?"

"Let me think . . ." Eleanor considered a moment. "I do believe Father Callaway brought them around. He knew them from somewhere, or maybe they were members of his church—I really don't recall."

"And how do you get along with them?"

"Excellently. I admire them. They are two attractive young people, very *chic*, very *with* it. And it's a pleasure to see a brother and sister so affectionate toward each other."

"More affectionate than Clayton and Felicia?"

Eleanor stared at her. "No comment," she said.

Dora rose from the low stool with some difficulty. "Thank you for your time, Mrs. Starrett," she said. "You've been very helpful."

"I have?" the other woman said. "I don't know how."

Dora left the beauty salon, went next door to a small hotel, and used the public phone in the lobby.

"The Starrett residence," Charles answered.

"This is Dora Conti. Is any member of the family home? I'd like to speak to them."

"Just a moment, please."

It took longer than a moment, but finally Felicia came on the line, breathless.

"Hiya, kiddo," she said. "Listen, I can't talk right now. Gotta run. Heavy lunch date."

"Wait, wait," Dora said hastily. "I just want to know if it's okay if I come over and talk to Charles and Clara for a few minutes."

"Of course," Felicia said. "I'll tell them to let you in and answer your questions. 'Bye!"

Dora walked over to Madison Avenue and boarded an uptown bus. It had turned cold, almost freezing, and everyone was bundled up; the bus smelled of mothballs. Traffic was clogged, and it took almost forty-five minutes before she arrived at the Starrett apartment. Charles opened the door and led the way into the kitchen where a short, stout woman was standing at the sink, scraping carrots.

Clara Hawkins looked as dour as her husband. Her iron-gray hair was pulled up in a bun, and her lips seemed eternally pursed in a grimace of disapproval. She was wearing a soiled apron over a dress of rusty bombazine, and her fat feet were shoved into heelless slippers. What was most remarkable, Dora decided, was that Clara had a discernible mustache.

No one offered her a chair so she remained standing, leaning against the enormous refrigerator. She looked around at the well-appointed kitchen: copper-bottomed pots and pans hanging from an overhead frame; a Cuisinart on the counter; a hardwood rack holding knives and a butchers' round; a double-sink of stainless steel; gleaming white appliances; and glass-doored cupboards holding enough tableware to feed a regiment.

"I just have a few questions," Dora said, addressing Charles. "I understand that on the evening Mr. Starrett was killed, there was a cocktail party for family and friends."

He nodded.

"Where was it held—in the living room?"

"Mostly," he said. "That's where I served drinks and canapes. But people wandered around."

"You mean they all weren't in the living room constantly during the party?"

"They wandered," he repeated. "Only Mrs. Olivia remained seated. The others stood and mingled, went to their bedrooms to fetch something or make a phone call."

Clara turned from the sink. "Sometimes they came in here," she said. "For more ice, or maybe for another drink while Charles was busy passing the tray of hors d'oeuvres."

"Were there any arguments during the party? Did anyone make a scene?"

Wife and husband looked at each other, then shook their heads.

"How long have you been with the Starretts?" Dora

asked, bedeviled by the fear that she wasn't asking the right questions.

"Seven years, come March," Charles replied. "I started with them first. Then, about a year later, the cook they had left and Clara took over."

"Both of you get along well with the family?"

Charles shrugged. "No complaints," he said.

"I understand the late Mr. Starrett had a short temper."

Again the shrug. "He liked everything just so."

"And when it wasn't, he let you know?"

"He let everyone know," Clara said, turning again from her task at the sink. "He was a mean, mean man."

"Clara!" her husband warned.

"Well, he was," she insisted. "The way he treated people—it just wasn't right."

"Speak only good of the dead," her husband admonished.

"Bullshit," Clara said unexpectedly.

Hopeless, Dora decided, realizing she was getting nowhere. These people weren't going to reveal any skeletons in the Starretts' closet, and she couldn't blame them; they had cushy jobs and wanted to hang on to them.

She took a final look around the kitchen. Her gaze fell on that hardwood knife rack attached to the wall. It had eight slots. Two were empty. She stepped to the rack, withdrew a long bread knife with a serrated edge, and examined it.

"Nice," she said.

"Imported," Charles said. "Carbon steel. The best."

Dora replaced the bread knife. "Two are missing," she said casually. "What are they?"

Clara, at the sink, held up a paring knife she was using to scrape carrots. "This is one," she said.

"And the other?" Dora persisted.

Charles and Clara exchanged a quick glance. "It was an eight-inch chef's knife," he said. "I'm sure it's around here somewhere, but we can't find it."

"It'll probably turn up," Dora said, knowing it wouldn't.

12

Mike Trevalyan had frequently urged Dora to use a tape recorder during interviews. Most of the investigators on his staff used them, but she refused.

"It makes witnesses freeze up," she argued. "They see that little black box and they're afraid I'm going to use their words in court, or they might say something they'll want to deny later."

So she worked without a recorder, and didn't even take notes during interviews. But as soon as possible she wrote an account of her conversations in a thick spiral notebook: questions asked, answers received. She also made notes on the physical appearance of the witnesses, their clothing, speech patterns, any unusual gestures or mannerisms.

She returned to the Bedlington after her session with Clara and Charles Hawkins and got to work writing out the details of her meeting with the servants and with Mrs. Eleanor Starrett. That completed, she slowly read over everything in the notebook, all the conversations and her personal reactions to the people involved. Then she phoned Detective John Wenden.

He wasn't in, but she left a message asking him to call her at the Bedlington. She went into the little pantry and poured herself a glass of white wine. She brought it back into the sitting room and curled up in a deep armchair. She sipped her wine, stared at her notebook, and wondered what Mario was doing. Finally she put the empty glass aside and read through her notebook again, searching for inspiration. Zilch.

She went downstairs for an early dinner in the hotel, and had a miserable meal of meat loaf, mashed potatoes, and peas. At that moment, she mournfully imagined, Mario was dining on veal scaloppine sautéed with marsala and lemon juice. Life was unfair; everyone knew that.

She returned to her suite and, fearing Wenden might have called during her absence, phoned him again. But he had not yet returned to his office or called in for messages. So she settled down with her notebook again, convinced those scribbled pages held the key to what actually happened to Lewis Starrett—and why.

When her phone rang, she rushed to pick it up, crossing her fingers for luck.

"Hiya," Wenden said hoarsely. "Quite a surprise hearing from you."

"How so?" she asked, genuinely puzzled.

"The way I came on to you the other night; I thought you'd be miffed."

"Nah," she said. "It's good for a girl's ego. When the passes stop, it's time to start worrying. My God, John, you sound terrible."

"Ah, shit," he said, "I think I got the flu. I have it all: sneezing, runny nose, headache, cough."

"Are you dosing yourself?"

"Yeah. Aspirin mostly. I get these things every year. Nothing to do but wait for them to go away."

"Why didn't you call in sick, stay home, and doctor yourself?"

"Because three other guys beat me to it, and the boss got down on his knees and cried. You feeling okay?"

"Oh sure. I'm healthy as a horse. John, I was hoping to see you tonight, but I guess you want to get home."

"Not especially. I feel so lousy I don't even want to think about driving to Queens."

"That's where you live?"

"If you can call it that. What's up?"

"A couple of interesting things. Listen, if you can make it over here, I'll fix you a cup of hot tea with a slug of brandy. It won't cure the flu but might help you forget it."

"On my way," he said. "Shouldn't take more than twenty minutes or so."

She put a kettle on to boil, set out a cup and saucer for him, and then went into the bathroom to brush her hair and add a little lip gloss, wondering what the hell she was doing.

When Wenden arrived, carrying an open box of Kleenex, he looked like death warmed over: bleary eyes, unshaven jaw, his nose red and swollen. And, as usual, his clothes could have been a scarecrow's castoffs.

She got him seated on the couch, poured him a steaming cup of tea, and added a shot of brandy to it. He held the cup with both hands, took a noisy sip, closed his eyes and sighed.

"Plasma," he said. "Thank you, Florence Nightingale."

"You should be in bed," she said.

"Best offer I've had today," he said, then sneezed and grabbed for a tissue.

"Now I know you're not terminal," she said, smiling. "Anything new on the Starrett case?"

"Nothing from our snitches. We've checked the whole neighborhood for three blocks around. No one saw anything or heard anything. We searched every sewer basin and trash can. No knife. We've got fliers out in every taxi garage in the city. The official line is still homicide by a stranger, maybe after an argument, maybe by some nut who objected to Starrett's cigar smoke—who the hell knows."

"Uh-huh. John, did you see the medical examiner's report?"

"Sure, I saw it. I love reading those things. They really make you want to resign from the human race. The things people do to people . . ."

"Did the report describe the wound that killed Starrett?"

"Of course."

"How deep did it go—do you remember?"

He thought a moment. "About seven and a half inches. Around there. They can never be precise. Tissue fills in. The outside puncture was a slit about two inches long."

Dora nodded. "I think you need another brandy," she said.

"I'll take it gladly," he said, sneezing again, "but why do I need it?"

"I went up to see the Starretts' servants today. We talked in the kitchen. There's a knife rack on the wall. Nice cutlery. Imported carbon steel. One of the knives is missing. An eight-inch chef's knife. We have one at home. It's a triangular blade. Close to the handle it's about two inches wide."

Wenden set his cup back on the saucer. It rattled. "How long has it been missing?" he asked, staring at her.

"I didn't ask them," Dora said. "But when I noticed it, Clara and Charles glanced at each other. I think it probably disappeared at that cocktail party the night Starrett was killed, but the servants didn't want to come right out and say so."

"Why didn't you lean on them?"

"How the hell could I?" she said angrily. "You're a cop; you can lean. I'm just a short, fat, housewife-type from the insurance company. I've got no clout."

"All right, all right," he said. "So *I'll* lean on them. If the knife disappeared on the night of the murder, that opens up a whole new can of worms."

"It also clears three in this cast of characters," she said. "Olivia and the two servants stayed in the apartment for dinner and presumably were still there when Lewis went for his walk. Did you check the whereabouts of the others at the time of the killing?"

The detective looked at her indignantly. "You think we're mutts? Of course we checked. They all have alibis. None of them are rock solid, but alibis rarely are. Felicia was at a new restaurant down on Spring Street. Confirmed by her date—a twit who wears one earring. Helene and Turner Pierce were at a theatre on West Forty-sixth Street. They have their ticket stubs to prove it. Father Callaway was down at his church, passing out ham sandwiches to the homeless. He was seen there. Eleanor and Clayton Starrett were at a charity bash at the Hilton. Sounds good, but there's not one of them who couldn't have ducked out and

95

cabbed back to East Eighty-third Street in time to chill Lewis. They all knew his nightly routine. Hey, what do I call you?"

"Call me? My name is Dora."

"I know that, but it's too domestic. Will you be sore if I call you Red?"

She sighed. "Delighted," she said.

"Could I have another brandy, Red?"

"You're not going to pass out on me, are you?"

"Hell, no. I'm just getting my head together."

She brought the brandy bottle and set it on the cocktail table in front of the couch.

"Help yourself," she said.

"Some for you?"

"No, thanks," she said. "I'm not driving to Queens."

He laughed and poured more brandy into his teacup. "I could make that trip even if I was comatose, I've driven it so many times. Okay, let's assume someone at the cocktail party lifted the knife. Eliminate Olivia and the servants; that leaves us with six possibles."

"Here's my second goody of the evening," Dora said. "Remember I told you I was going to ask my boss to run Father Brian Callaway through our computer."

"Sure, I remember. Come up with anything?"

"His real name is Sidney Loftus. He's a con man with a sheet as long as your arm."

"Oh-oh. Anything violent?"

"I don't know. I told you our data base includes only insurance fraud. You better run Callaway, or Loftus, through your records."

"Yeah, I better."

"And while you're at it, do a trace on Helene and Turner

Pierce. I asked my boss, but we have nothing on them in our file."

"Why should I check out the Pierces?"

"Callaway's most recent scam was a stolen car game in Kansas City, Missouri. That's where Helene Pierce comes from."

"How do you know?"

"She told me."

Wenden studied her a moment, then shook his head in wonderment. "You're something, you are. Red, how do you get people to talk?"

"Sometimes you tell things to strangers you wouldn't tell your best friend. Also, I come across as a dumpy homebody. I don't represent much of a threat, they think, so they talk."

"A dumpy homebody," he repeated. "I'm beginning to believe you're more barracuda." He sneezed again, wiped his swollen nose with a tissue. "All right, I'll ask for a rundown on Callaway and the Pierces. I warn you it's going to take time; Records is undermanned and overworked, like the rest of the Department."

"I can wait," Dora said. "That insurance claim isn't going to get paid until I say so."

He took a deep breath, put his head back, stared at the ceiling. "I guess I shouldn't be surprised that a member of his family or a close friend might have iced the old man; it happens all the time. But I thought those people were class. What do you figure the motive was?"

"Money," Dora said.

"Yeah," Wenden said, "probably. When money comes in the door, class goes out the window. Every time."

She laughed. "I didn't know you were a philosopher."

97

"How can you be a cop and not be a philosopher?" He lowered his head, stared at her with bleary eyes. "I lied to you, Red."

"How so?"

"I told you I wasn't going to pass out. Now I'm not so sure."

"Whatever," she said, "you're in no condition to drive. I have an extra bedroom; you can sack out in there."

"Thanks," he said.

"What time do you want to get up?"

"Never," he said. "Give me a hand, will you."

She helped him to his feet and half-supported him into the bedroom. He sat down heavily on the edge of the bed.

"Can you undress?" she asked him.

"I can get my shoes off," he said in a mumble. "That's enough. I've slept in my clothes before."

"I never would have guessed," she said. "Want more aspirin?"

"Nope. I've had enough."

"I'd say so. I'm not going to wake you up in the morning. Sleep as long as you can. It'll do you the world of good."

"Thanks again, Red. And listen . . ." He tried a grin. "You don't have to lock your bedroom door."

"I know that," she said.

But she did.

13

Solomon Guthrie lived alone in a six-room apartment on Riverside Drive near 86th Street. The prewar building had gone co-op in 1974, and Guthrie had bought his apartment for $59,500. His wife had told him it was a lot of money—and it was, at the time. And why, she had asked, did they need so much space since their two grown sons had moved away: Jacob, an ophthalmologist, to Minneapolis, and Alan, an aerospace designer, to Los Angeles.

But Solomon didn't want to give up an apartment he loved and in which he and his wife had lived most of their married life. Besides, he said, it would be a good investment, and it turned out to be exactly that, with similar apartments in the building now selling for $750,000 to a million.

Then Hilda died in 1978, of cancer, and Solomon was alone in the six rooms. His sons, their wives and children visited at least once a year, and that was a treat. But generally he lived a solitary life. After all these years it was still a wrench to come home to an empty house, especially on dark winter nights.

Every weekday morning Guthrie left his apartment at 7:30, picked up his *Times* from a marble table in the lobby, and walked over to West End Avenue to get a taxi heading south. An hour later and it would be almost impossible to find an empty cab, but Solomon usually had good luck before eight o'clock.

This particular morning was cold, bleak, with a damp wind blowing off the river. He was glad he had worn his heavy overcoat. He was also wearing fur-lined gloves and lugging his old briefcase stuffed with work he had taken home the night before. One of the things he had labored over was a schedule of Christmas bonuses for Starrett employees.

Solomon arrived at the southwest corner of West End and 86th Street, stepped off the curb, looked uptown. There was a cab parked across 86th, but the off-duty light was on, and the driver appeared to be reading a newspaper. He moved farther into the street to see if any other cabs were approaching. He raised an arm when he saw one a block away, coming down West End.

But then the cab parked across 86th went into action. The off-duty light flicked off, the driver tossed his newspaper aside, and the cab came gunning across the street and pulled up in front of Solomon. He opened the back door and crawled in with some difficulty, first hoisting his briefcase and newspaper onto the seat, then twisting himself into the cramped space and turning to slam the door.

"Good morning," he said.

"Where to?" the driver said without turning around.

"The Starrett Building, please. Park Avenue between Fifty-sixth and Fifty-seventh."

He settled back and unbuttoned his overcoat. He put on his reading glasses and began to scan the front page of the *Times.* Then he became conscious of the cab slowing, and he looked up. Traffic lights were green as far as he could see, but his taxi was stopping between 78th and 77th streets, pulling alongside cars parked at the curb.

"Why are you stopping here?" he asked the driver.

"Another guy going south," the driver said. "You don't mind sharing, do you?"

"Yes, I mind," Guthrie said angrily. "I'm paying you full fare to take me where I want to go, and I have no desire to stop along the way to pick up—"

He was still talking when the cab stopped. A man wearing a black fur hat and short leather coat came quickly from between parked cars and jerked open the passenger door.

"Hey!" Guthrie cried. "What the hell do you think—"

But then the stranger was inside, crouching over him, the door was slammed, and the cab took off with a chirp of tires.

"What—" Guthrie started again, and then felt a sear in his abdomen, a flash of fire he couldn't understand until he looked down, saw the man stab him again. He tried to writhe away from that flaming blade, but he was pressed back into a corner, his homburg and glasses falling off as the man stabbed again and again, sliding the steel in smoothly, withdrawing, inserting it. Then he stopped.

"Make sure," the driver said, not turning.

"I'm sure," the assailant said, and pushed Guthrie's body onto the floor. Then he sat down, wiped his blade clean on Solomon's overcoat, and returned the knife to a handsome leather sheath strapped to his right shin.

The cab stopped for the light at 72nd Street. When it

101

turned green, it went south to 71st, made a right into the dead-end street, drove slowly between parked cars to a turnaround at the western end.

The cab stopped on the curve and the two men looked about casually. There was a woman walking a Doberman farther east, but no one else was on the street.

"Let's go," the driver said.

Both men got out of the cab and closed the doors. They paused a moment to light cigarettes, then walked toward West End Avenue, not too fast, not too slow.

14

"How do you feel?" she asked.

"Still got the sniffles," John Wenden said, "but I'll live to play the violin again. Actually, I feel a helluva lot better. It was the tea and brandy that did it."

"It was a good night's sleep that did it," Dora insisted. "You were whacked-out. Want to take a hot shower?"

"You bet."

"Help yourself. There are plenty of towels. If you want to shave, you can borrow my razor. I'll even throw in a fresh blade."

"Thanks, but I'll skip. I keep an electric shaver in my office; the beard can wait till I get there. Sorry I crashed last night, Red."

"You're entitled. While you're showering I'll make us a cup of coffee. But it'll be instant and black. Okay?"

"My favorite brew," he said.

She was preparing coffee when she suddenly thought of what to buy her husband for Christmas. An espresso machine! One of those neat, shiny gadgets that make both espresso and cappuccino. Mario, a coffee maven, would be delighted.

They stood at the sink and sipped their black instant. Wenden looked at her reflectively.

"You think Father Callaway was the perp, don't you?" he said.

Dora shrugged. "I think he's the front-runner. You're going to check him out, aren't you? And the Pierces."

"Oh sure. I'll start the ball rolling as soon as I get back to my desk. What're you doing today?"

"I've got a ten o'clock appointment with Clayton at the Starrett Building. It was the only time he could fit me in."

"What do you expect to get from him?"

"I'm getting confusing signals on how the Pierces became such good friends with the Starrett family. Whether it was before or after Turner Pierce landed Starrett Fine Jewelry as a client and designed their new computer system. I'd also like to know if Father Callaway made the introduction."

He looked at her admiringly. "You're a real sherlock. You enjoy your job?"

"Oh hell, yes."

"What does your husband think of your being a gumshoe?"

She flipped a hand back and forth. "He doesn't mind what I do. What he doesn't like is my being away from home so much. It means he has to cook for only one— which isn't much fun. Mario is a super chef. Do you prepare your own meals?"

"Not exactly," Wenden said. "I have a cook—Mrs. Paul.

Listen, Red, I've got to run. Thanks again for the brandy. And the shower. And the coffee. I owe you."

"Just remember you said that," Dora told him. "I may call in my chits."

"Anytime," the detective assured her.

She let him kiss her cheek before he left.

She spent a few minutes straightening up the suite, not accustomed to maid service. Then she went out into a raw morning. It was too cold to hike all the way, so she took a Fifth Avenue bus south and then walked east to Park Avenue, stopping frequently to look in the shop windows on 57th Street.

She was on time for her appointment but had to wait awhile in a cramped reception room. Most of the magazines on the cocktail table were jewelry trade journals, but there was one copy of *Town & Country.* Leafing through it, Dora spotted a full-page Starrett ad. It showed a magnificent necklace of alternating white and yellow diamonds draped across a woman's bare breasts (the nipples hidden). The only print on the page, in a small, discreet script, read: *Starrett Fine Jewelry. Simply Superior.*

A secretary with an English accent ushered her into Clayton Starrett's office at about 10:15. He bounced up from behind his desk, beaming and apparently chockablock with early-morning energy.

"Good morning!" he caroled, shaking her hand enthusiastically. "Sorry to keep you waiting. The Christmas season, you know—our busiest time. Here, let me take your coat. Now you sit right here. Dreadful office, isn't it? So dark and gloomy. I'm having the whole place done over. Bright colors. Much livelier. Well, I hope you've brought me good news about the insurance."

"Not quite yet, Mr. Starrett," Dora said with a set smile, "but we're getting there. We'd like the mystery of your father's death cleared up before the claim is approved. As I'm sure you would."

"Of course, of course," he cried. "Anything I can do to help. Anything at all."

He seemed in an antic mood, and she decided to take advantage of it. "Just a few little questions. Really extraneous to my investigation, but I like to dot the *i*'s and cross the *t*'s. Could you tell me how you and your family met Helene and Turner Pierce?"

He was startled by the question, then sat back, tapped fingertips together. "How did we meet the Pierces? Now let me see . . . I think it was a few years ago. Yes, at least two. Father Callaway was over for dinner and I happened to mention something about the inadequacy of our computers. The Father said he had just the man for me, a management consultant who specialized in designing and upgrading computer systems. So I said to send him around. He was Turner Pierce, and he's done a marvelous job for us. And through Turner I met his sister Helene. A charming couple. They came over for dinner several times, and we all became good friends."

"I see," Dora said. "And did you investigate Turner's credentials before you—"

But then the phone on Starrett's desk jangled, and he looked at it, frowning.

"Damn it," he said. "I told my secretary to hold all my calls. Excuse me a moment, please."

He leaned forward, elbows on the desk, and picked up the phone. "Yes? Who? All right, put him on." He looked up at Dora, puzzled. "A police officer," he said. Then:

"Hello? Yes, this is Clayton Starrett. That's correct. What? What? Oh my God! When did this happen? Oh God, how awful! Yes, of course. I understand. I'll be there as soon as possible."

He hung up. He stared blankly at Dora, and she rose to her feet, fearing he might collapse. He was stricken, face broken and sagging, eyes wide and staring, lips trembling.

"The police," he said, voice cracking. "They say Solomon Guthrie has been killed. Murdered."

"Who?"

"Sol Guthrie, our chief financial officer. He's been with Starrett forty years. A good friend of my father."

He began to blink rapidly, but it didn't work; tears overflowed. He wiped them away angrily with the back of his hand.

"How was he killed?" Dora asked.

"Stabbed to death. Like father. Oh, this lousy, rotten city! I hate it, just hate it!"

"It's not only New York, Mr. Starrett. It's happening everywhere."

He nodded, stood up, took a deep breath. "I've got to go. The police asked me to come to, uh, where Sol was found. They want me to, uh, identify the body. West End Avenue and Seventy-first Street. Yes, that's what he said."

Dora moved behind the desk to put a hand on his arm. "Mr. Starrett, would you like me to go with you? Perhaps it would be a little easier if you weren't alone."

He looked at her, face twisted. "Would you do that? Thank you. Yes, please come with me. I'd really appreciate it. Listen, there's a bottle of Scotch in that sideboard over there, and glasses. Would you pour us a drink while I call down and have my driver bring the car around."

107

She poured him a stiff shot of whiskey, but none for herself. He finished on the phone and downed his drink in two gulps. Then he coughed, and his eyes began to water again.

"Let's go," he said hoarsely.

On the drive uptown he kept his head turned away from her, staring out the limousine's tinted windows at the mean streets of his city.

"How old a man was he, Mr. Starrett?"

"Sol was sixty-three."

"Married?"

"A widower. He has two grown sons, but they don't live in New York. They'll have to be notified as soon as possible. I hope we have their addresses in our personnel file."

"The police will find them," Dora assured him. "Did they say if the killer had been caught?"

"They didn't say."

"What do you suppose he was doing there—where his body was found?"

"Probably on his way to work. He lived on Eighty-sixth and Riverside Drive."

They found West 71st Street blocked by two uniformed police officers. Clayton Starrett identified himself and the limo was allowed to move slowly down to the far end of the block. There were squad cars, an ambulance, a van from the police lab, all parked in a jagged semicircle around a yellow cab with opened doors. Crime scene tape, tied to trees and iron fences, held back a small throng of gawkers.

A burly man wearing a plaid mackinaw, ID clipped to his lapel, came over to them.

"Mr. Starrett?"

Clayton nodded.

"I'm Detective Stanley Morris. I spoke to you on the phone. Thanks for helping us out. We need positive identification. This way, please."

He took Clayton firmly by the arm and started to lead him toward the cab.

"Can I come?" Dora asked.

The detective stopped, looked back at her. "Who are you?"

"Dora Conti. I'm a friend of Mr. Starrett."

"Did you know the victim?"

"No," she said.

"Then you stay here."

Left alone, she looked about and saw John Wenden leaning against the door of a squad car, talking to a uniformed officer. She moved around to his line of sight and waved her arm wildly. He spotted her and came over, face expressionless.

"What the hell are you doing here, Red?" he asked her.

"I was in Clayton's office when he got the call. I thought he should have someone with him."

"How did he take the news?"

"Total shock. And he wasn't faking. This Solomon Guthrie—he was stabbed?"

Wenden nodded.

"Like Lewis Starrett?"

"No. From the front. And more than one wound. Several, in fact."

"Same kind of knife? An eight-inch triangular blade?"

"I doubt it. It looks more like a kind of stiletto, but we won't know for sure until the autopsy."

"Any leads?"

"Nothing worth a shit."

"What about the cab?"

"It was stolen early this morning from Broadway and Seventy-ninth. The driver parked for a minute to run into a deli to pick up a coffee and bagel. He left his motor running—the schmuck! When he came out, the cab was gone. It ended up here."

"Robbery?"

"Doesn't look like it. Guthrie's wallet and credit cards are all there. And a gold Starrett pocket watch. Nothing was touched. He was carrying a briefcase full of Starrett business papers. That's how come Clayton was called."

Dora shook her head. "I don't get it. Clayton says he was probably on his way to work. Then the driver turns in here, goes to the dead end, stops, gets out of the cab, opens the back door, stabs his passenger to death, and walks away. Do you believe it?"

"No," John said, "it doesn't fit. The victim would have plenty of time to scream or get out the other side of the cab or put up a fight. But there's no sign of a struggle. I'm betting on two perps: the driver and another guy in back with Guthrie."

"A planned homicide?"

"I'd guess so. Probably professionals. A contract killing most likely. They knew exactly what they were doing. The lab crew is vacuuming the cab now. They'll be able to tell us more. What does this do to your theory that Father Callaway offed Lewis Starrett?"

"Knocks it into left field," Dora admitted. "The chairman and principal stockholder of Starrett Fine Jewelry gets stabbed to death on East Eighty-third Street. Then the chief financial officer of Starrett gets knifed on West Seventy-first. You don't believe in coincidences, do you?"

"Hell, no. Not in this business."

"So where does that leave your official theory that Lewis Starrett's death was a random killing by a stranger?"

"Right next to yours," he said, "out in left field. It seems obvious the two homicides are connected, and Starrett Jewelry is probably the key. So now we start searching through their files for fired employees or someone who might have a grudge against the company and decided to knock off its executives to get even."

"You going to put a guard on Clayton?"

"We can't baby-sit him twenty-four hours a day. Haven't got the manpower. But we'll warn him and suggest he beef up security at his stores and hire personal bodyguards for himself, his family and top executives. He can afford it. Oh-oh, here he comes now."

Clayton Starrett, supported by Detective Stanley Morris, returned to the limousine. He was almost tottering; his face was ashen.

"I'll ride back to his office with him," Dora said, "or to his home, if that's where he wants to go. Listen, John, will you call me tonight if anything new breaks on this case?"

"I'll call you tonight even if nothing breaks," Wenden said. "Okay, Red?"

"Sure," Dora said. "I'm glad you shaved. Keep up the good work."

15

"I'm ready," Felicia Starrett said.

"You're always ready," Turner Pierce said, and she giggled.

The bedroom of Turner's sublet in Murray Hill was like the rest of the apartment: dark with heavy oak furniture, worn oriental rugs, and drapes of tarnished brocade. On every flat surface was artfully arranged the owner's collection of porcelain figurines: shepherds, ballerinas, courtiers, elves and fairies—all in pinks and lavenders.

Few of Turner's possessions were in view: mostly scattered newspapers, magazines, and computer trade journals. A closed Compaq laptop was on the marble sideboard and, in the bedroom, a bottle of Tanqueray vodka was in an aluminum bucket of ice cubes alongside the bed. Also thrust into the bucket was a clump of baby Vidalia onions.

Felicia rose naked from the crumpled sheets, stood shakily. She put hands on her hips and drew a deep breath before heading into the bathroom.

Turner stretched to pour himself a wineglass of chilled vodka. He selected one of the onions and began to gnaw on the white bulb. Felicia came from the bathroom, tugging snarls from her hair with a wide-toothed comb. She paused to pull on Turner's shirt, then sat on the edge of the bed and watched him drink and chew his onion. He offered her the glass of vodka, but she shook her head.

"Not my shtick," she said, "as you well know. Where did you learn to make love like that?"

"My mother taught me," he said.

She laughed. "Not your sister?"

"No, she taught dad."

Felicia laughed again. "You bastard," she said, "you always top me. Listen, I'm going to make you an offer you can't refuse."

"Oh?" he said, dropping an ice cube into his vodka.

"When the insurance money comes in, I'm going to have a cool million. I own ten percent of Starrett Fine Jewelry, and that pays me about fifty grand a year in dividends. And when mother shuffles off, I'll be a very, very wealthy lady."

"So?"

"I want to buy you," she said. "I'm proposing, you stinker. Marry me, and you'll be set for life. I'll sign any kind of a prenuptial agreement your shyster comes up with."

He showed no sign of surprise or shock; just began to nibble on the green onion top.

"Why would you want to do that?" he asked.

"Because I'm tired of alley-catting around. I'm tired of one-night stands. I'm tired of burned-out men who are scared of making a commitment. I'm tired of living in my father's house, now my mother's. I want my own home and my own man. I'm about ten years older than you—correct?"

"More like fifteen," he said casually.

"Swine!" she said. "But what the hell difference does age make? I'm as young as you in bed. Right or wrong?"

"Right," he said.

"You betcha. There's nothing you've asked me to do that I haven't done. I can keep up with you. The body's not so bad, is it?"

"The body's good," he acknowledged.

"It should be—the money I spend on it. I may not be a centerfold, but I'm not a dried-out husk either. And you'll be getting financial security for the rest of your life. What do you say?"

He poured more vodka, and this time she lifted the drink from his fingers and took a gulp. She grimaced and handed back the glass.

"What would your family say?" he asked. "Your mother? Clayton?"

"Screw my family," she said wrathfully. "I've got my own life to live. I can't keep living it the way they want me to. I'll bet you don't let Helene run your life."

"Your mother could disown you," he pointed out.

"Not without a helluva court fight," Felicia said. "If she dies and I don't get half the estate, some lawyer is going to earn mucho dinero representing me. But that's all in the future. Right now I've got enough loot so that you and I could live the lush life. Well?"

"Interesting proposition," Turner said. "I'll have to think about it."

"Sure," she said. "Run it through your little computer and see if it doesn't make sense. Now let me prove that

115

marrying me would be the smartest deal you ever made."

He finished his vodka, set the empty glass on the floor. "I have something for you," he said. "Want it now?"

"I thought you'd never ask," she said. "Where is it?"

"Top bureau drawer."

"How much?"

"A gram."

"You darling!" she cried.

16

Two days before Christmas, Dora Conti went home to Hartford, lugging an espresso machine in a bulky carton. She had spent more than she intended, but it was a marvelous gadget. Not only did it make espresso and cappuccino, but it also ground coffee beans. And it had enough shiny spigots, valves, dials, and switches to keep Mario happily busy for days while he learned to brew a perfect cup of coffee.

Before she left New York, Dora called John Wenden. He reported there was nothing new on either the Lewis Starrett or Solomon Guthrie homicides. The Department was checking out all discharged employees of Starrett Fine Jewelry, but it was going to be an arduous task.

"We got their employment records," Wenden said, "but there's been a big turnover in the last two years. This is going to take a long, long time."

"Did you get anything from Records about Callaway or the Pierces?"

"Not yet. They say they're working on it, and if I push them, they're liable to get pissed off and stall just to teach me a lesson. That's the way the world works."

"Tell me about it," Dora said. "I have the same problem in my shop."

Then she told him she would return to Manhattan on January 2nd and would call him when she got back. She wished him a Merry Christmas and a Happy New Year.

"Likewise," John said.

So she went home, feeling guilty about leaving him alone for the holidays, and thinking what an irrational emotion that was. But he seemed such a weary, lost man that she worried about him and wished she had bought him a Christmas gift. A maroon cashmere muffler would have been nice. But then she wondered if NYPD detectives wore mufflers.

Mario was at work when Dora arrived home, so she was able to conceal his gift in the back of her closet. In the living room he had erected a bushy six-foot Douglas fir and alongside it, brought up from the basement, were boxes of ornaments, tinsel, garlands, and strings of lights. There was a big bottle of Frascati in the fridge, and in the wine rack on the countertop were bottles of Lacrima Cristi, Soave, Valpolicella, and—Dora's favorite—Asti Spumante.

They had a splendid holiday, all the better because they spent it alone. On Christmas Eve they made love under the glittering tree because it seemed a holy thing to do. Mario gave her a marvelous tennis bracelet, and even if the diamonds were pebbles compared to the rocks that Starrett women wore, Dora thought it the most beautiful gift she had ever received, and her happiness was doubled by Mario's joy with his new espresso machine.

During the remainder of the week, Dora went to the office every day and wrote a progress report on the word processor, consulting her spiral notebook to make certain she could justify her surmises and conclusions. She left the nineteen-page report on Mike Trevalyan's desk late one evening, and the next morning she was summoned to his office, a dank chamber cluttered with files and bundles of computer printout tied with twine. The air was fetid with cigar smoke; during crises or explosions of temper, Trevalyan was known to keep two cigars going at once.

He was a porcine man with small eyes, a pouty mouth, and all the sweet reasonableness of a Marine drill instructor. But the Company didn't pay him an enormous salary for affability. They *wanted* him to be irascible, suspicious, and to scan every insurance claim as if the money was coming out of his own pocket. He had worked as a claims adjuster all his life, expected chicanery and, it was said, was furiously disappointed when he couldn't find it.

"This case," he said, pointing his cigar at Dora's report, "it reeketh in the nostrils of the righteous. There's frigging in the rigging going on here, kiddo, and I'm not paying a cent until we know more."

"I agree," Dora said. "Too many unanswered questions."

"The cops think it was a disgruntled ex-employee taking out his grudge on Starrett executives?"

"That's what they think," she said.

"You know what's wrong with that theory?" Trevalyan demanded.

"Of course I know," Dora said. "It doesn't account for the knife disappearing from the Starretts' apartment, maybe on the night Lewis was killed. That's the first thing I want to check out when I get back to New York."

119

"This Detective Wenden you mention—he should have seen that. Is the guy a bubblehead?"

"No, he's just overworked, running a half-dozen homicide cases at the same time. He happens to be a very experienced and conscientious professional."

Trevalyan stared at her. "You wouldn't have the hots for this guy, would you?"

"Oh Mike, don't be such an asshole. No, I haven't got the hots for him. Yes, we are friends. You want me to make an enemy of the detective handling the case?"

"Just don't get too close," he warned. "It's your brains I'm buying, not your glands. If he's as overworked as you say, he might try to sweep the whole thing under the rug."

"No," Dora said firmly, "John would never do that."

"Oh-ho," Trevalyan said, mashing out his cigar butt in an overflowing ashtray, "it's *John,* is it? Watch yourself, sister. This big-city slicker may be warm for your form, and is feeding you just enough inside poop to keep you coming back to him. And meanwhile he's working an angle you haven't even thought of."

"You're crazy!" she said angrily. "It's me that gave him the scoop on the missing knife and Callaway's record. I'm way ahead of him."

"Keep it that way," Trevalyan advised, lighting a fresh cigar. "If he's not playing you, like you claim, then you play him. Don't tell him everything; just enough to make him want to cooperate. What else are you planning when you get back to Sodom on the Hudson?"

"A couple of things," Dora said. "Mostly I want to dig deeper on how Father Callaway fits into the picture. Like where was he and what was he doing the morning Solomon Guthrie was stabbed to death."

"You think Callaway did it?"

"I'm not sure about Guthrie, but I think there's a good possibility he killed Lewis Starrett."

Trevalyan inspected the glowing end of his cigar. "What was his motive?"

"I haven't figured that out yet. I guess Starrett said some nasty things to him, but nothing dirty enough to trigger a murder."

Mike looked up at her and laughed. "Dora, you better read your own report again. Callaway's motive is in there."

"What?"

"You heard me. Your report includes a very logical reason why Callaway might have iced Lewis Starrett."

"Mike, what *is* it?"

He shook his head. "You find it; it's your case. And keep an eye on that New York cop. I still think he's trying to get in your drawers."

"Where the hell were you when God was handing out couth?" she said indignantly.

"Waiting for seconds in the cynics' line," he said. "Now let's go drink some lunch. Your treat."

He was exaggerating, of course; they actually had food for lunch: thick corned beef sandwiches with french fries and a schooner of beer each at an Irish bar near the Company's headquarters. And while they lunched, Mike told her what he had been able to pick up about Starrett Fine Jewelry, Inc.

Little was known because it was a privately held corporation, and public disclosure of its structuring and current financial condition was not required. But through rumors and hearsay, Trevalyan had learned that Olivia, Clayton, and Felicia each owned ten percent of the stock. Lewis had owned seventy percent which, presumably, would go to his widow.

"So as of now," Dora said, "Olivia really controls the whole shebang."

Mike nodded. "From what I hear, back in the 1950s and '60s, Starrett Fine Jewelry was a cash cow. That's when they opened all their branch stores. Then, beginning about ten years ago, their sales and profits went down, down, down. The problem was a-g-e. Their clientele was getting older, putting money in annuities and Treasury bonds instead of diamonds. And the baby-boomers were doing their jewelry shopping at trendier places. They thought Starrett was old-fashioned and stuffy. So about two years ago Lewis went into semiretirement and turned over the reins to Clayton.

"Well, Clayton's first year at the helm was a disaster. He brought in a bunch of kooky designers and started pushing a line of what was really horribly overpriced costume jewelry. Not only did it not attract the yuppies, but it turned off what few old customers were left. Starrett was drowning in red ink, and there was talk in the trade that they might end up in Chapter Eleven. Then, about a year ago, Clayton turned the whole thing around. He got rid of all the designers with ponytails and went back to Starrett's classic fine jewelry. He fired most of his branch managers and brought in young hotshots who knew something about modern merchandising. And he started trading bullion, buying gold overseas at a good price and selling it to small independent jewelers in this country at a nice markup. From what I heard, Starrett is back in the bucks again, and everyone is happy."

"Except Lewis," Dora said. "And Solomon Guthrie."

"Yeah," Trevalyan said, "except them. Have you talked to Starrett's attorney yet?"

"Not yet, but he's on my list."

"He probably won't tell you a thing, but it's worth a try. Ask him if Lewis kept a bimbo on the side."

Dora stared at him. "Why should I ask him that?"

"Just for the fun of it. You never know."

She sighed. "All right, Mike, I'll ask him. Now I'm going to pay for our lunch. But I warn you, I'm putting it on my expense account."

"Suits me," Trevalyan said.

On New Year's Eve, Dora and Mario walked to their church for a noon service. Afterwards, they went looking for Father Piesecki and found him in the church basement where he and a fat altar boy were gilding a plaster saint. They told him about the open house they were having that night and urged him to stop by.

"I'll try," he said, "but I have four other parties to visit."

"Homemade kielbasa," Mario said.

"I'll be there when the doors open," Father Piesecki promised.

It was a wild and wonderful evening, with friends and family members coming and going. Most of the guests brought a covered dish or a bottle, so there was plenty to eat and drink. Neighbors had been invited to forestall complaints about the noise. Father Piesecki showed up with his accordion and never did get to those four other parties.

No one got too drunk or too obstreperous, and if the Christmas tree was knocked over during a violent polka, it was soon set aright. Even Mike Trevalyan and Mario's trucker friends were reasonably well-behaved, and the

123

worst thing that happened was when Dora's elderly uncle dropped his dentures into the punch bowl.

Mario started serving espresso from his new machine at 1:00 A.M., but it was almost three o'clock in the morning before the last guests went tottering off. It was an hour after that before the remaining food was put away, empty glasses and scraped dishes stacked in the sink, ashtrays wiped clean, and Dora and Mario could have a final Asti Spumante, toast each other, and fall thankfully into bed. They didn't make love until they awoke at eleven o'clock on January 1.

She returned to New York the following day. Manhattan was still digging out from a five-inch snowfall, but that was pleasant; garbage on the sidewalks was covered over, and the snow was not yet despoiled by dog droppings. Streets had been cleared, buses were running, and the blue sky looked as if it had been washed out and hung up to dry.

She called John Wenden from her suite at the Bedlington, but it was late in the afternoon before he got back to her.

"Hey, Red," he said, "how was the holiday?"

"Super," she said. "How was yours?"

"No complaints. I drank too much, but so did everyone else. How's your D.O.H.?"

"My *what?*"

"Your D.O.H. Dear Old Hubby."

"My husband is fine, thank you," she said stiffly, and Wenden laughed.

"Listen, Red," he said, "I finally heard from Records. What they dug up on Father Brian Callaway is pretty much what you told me: real name Sidney Loftus, small-time scams and swindles but no violent crimes. He's never

124

done a day in the clink—can you believe it? Nothing on either Turner or Helene Pierce. That doesn't mean they're squeaky clean, just that they've never been caught. Let's see, what else . . . Oh yeah, I had a nose-to-nose talk with the Starrett servants. They finally admitted the eight-inch chef's knife disappeared the evening Lewis Starrett was killed."

"John," she said, "I thought you were convinced Lewis and Solomon Guthrie were murdered by an ex-employee."

"Convinced? Hell no, I wasn't convinced. But when two guys from the same company get iced, it's S.O.P. to check out former employees who might be looking for revenge. It's something that has to be done, but there's no guarantee it's the right way to go."

"I'm glad to hear you say that. So you still think it might have been someone at that cocktail party?"

"It could have been Jack the Ripper for all I know," the detective said. "What's your next move?"

She thought a moment, remembering Trevalyan's warning not to reveal too much. "I don't know," she said. "Just poke around some more, I guess."

"Bullshit," Wenden said. "Unless I miss my guess, you're going to investigate where Callaway was at the time Solomon Guthrie took his final ride in a yellow cab."

"I might do that," she admitted.

"Don't hold out on me, Red," he said, "or I'll bring this beautiful friendship to a screeching halt. Forget about Callaway; I've already checked him out. He was in a hospital the morning Guthrie was offed."

"A hospital? What for?"

"Minor surgery. I'd tell you what it was, but I don't want to make you blush. Let's just say he's now sitting on a big

125

rubber doughnut. Anyway, there's no possibility he could have aced Guthrie. Disappointed?"

"Yes," Dora said, "I am."

"Welcome to the club," John said. "How about lunch tomorrow?"

"Sure," Dora said. "Think you can stand hotel food again?"

"I can stand anything," he said, "as long as it's free. Can you make it early? Noon?"

"Fine."

"It'll be good seeing you again," he said. "I've missed you, Red."

"And I've missed you," she replied, shocked at what she was saying. Then: "John, what's the name of Starrett's attorney?"

"Oh-ho," he said, "the wheels keep turning, do they? His name is Arthur Rushkin. Baker and Rushkin, on Fifth Avenue. That's another one you owe me."

"I'll remember," she promised.

"See that you do," he said, and hung up.

She called Baker & Rushkin on Fifth Avenue, explained who she was and what she wanted. She was put on hold for almost five minutes while "Mack the Knife" played softly in the background. Finally Arthur Rushkin came on the phone. Again she identified herself and asked if he could spare her a few minutes of his time.

"I have to be in court tomorrow," he said, "but I should be back in the office by four o'clock. How does that sound?"

"I'll be there, Mr. Rushkin."

Then she dug out a copy of the progress report she had submitted to Trevalyan. She reread it for the umpteenth time, searching for what Mike had said was a logical motive for Callaway killing Lewis Starrett. She still hadn't found it, and thought maybe Trevalyan was putting her on; he was capable of a stupid trick like that.

But this time she saw it and smacked her forehead with her palm, wondering how she could have been so dense.

17

Turner had warned Helene of Clayton's reaction to Solomon Guthrie's death and had suggested the spin she put on it.

"You'll have no trouble," he predicted. "Most people believe what they *must* believe, to shield themselves from reality."

"But not you," Helene said.

"Oh no," Turner said airily. "I take reality raw à la sauce diable. Delicious, but it might make you sweat a bit."

Still, it was no easy task to convince Clayton that Guthrie's murder had been a simple mugging gone awry. He admitted that such senseless killings occurred every day on the hard streets of New York, but Helene could see that guilt gnawed; he could not rid himself of the notion that somehow he had contributed to Sol's death, that he was in fact an accessory. That was the word he used: accessory.

Finally she ignored Turner's instructions on how to handle this crybaby and resorted to a more elemental and effective method: She took him to bed. Within minutes sorrow was banished, guilt forgotten, and he was exhibiting the frantic physical ardor of a man who had been brooding too much on mortality.

She understood his passion was death-driven, but no less enjoyable for that. Afterwards, though, she had to listen to his banal maunderings on how fleeting life was; how important it is to "Gather ye rosebuds while ye may"; how no man on his deathbed had ever said, "I should have paid more attention to business"—all hoary clichés Helene had heard dozens of times before, usually from older men.

But this time the peroration was different.

Lying flat on his back, legs together, arms at his sides, staring at the ceiling for all the world like a stripped corpse being fitted for a shroud, Clayton declared:

"I've decided to change my life. Change it completely."

It was said in a challenging tone, as if he expected opposition and was prepared to overcome it.

"Change it how, Clay?" she asked.

"I'm going to leave Eleanor. People are supposed to grow closer together in a marriage; we've grown farther apart. We're strangers. I don't know her anymore, and she doesn't know me. It's not the way I want to spend the rest of my life."

"Have you said anything to her?"

"No, not yet. Before I do, I want to get mother's reaction. And yours."

"Mine?" Helene said, fearing what was coming. "I have nothing to do with it."

He turned his head on the pillow to stare at her. "You do. Because if mother approves—or at least is neutral—and I leave Eleanor, I want to marry you."

She was nothing if not an accomplished actress, and her

face and voice displayed all the proper reactions: shock, pleasure, dubiety. "Clay," she started, "I'm not—"

But he held up a palm to stop her. "Wait a minute; let me make my case. First of all, my marriage has become unendurable. That's a given. And I see no possibility of the situation improving. Absolutely not. So no matter what you decide, my life with Eleanor is finished. You mustn't think you're responsible for the breakup. It would have happened even if I had never met you."

"Shall I get us a drink?" she asked.

"No, not yet; I don't need it. Helene, I know I'm twice your age, but surely there are other things more important. We think alike, laugh at the same things, get along beautifully, and we're building up a lot of shared memories, aren't we?"

"Yes."

"I may not be the world's greatest stud, but I'm not a complete dud, am I?"

"It's all I can do to keep up with you," she assured him, and he smiled with pleasure.

"The most important thing is your future," he said earnestly. "Your financial future. And that I can guarantee. I know that if I wasn't helping you out, you'd be depending on your brother's generosity. But how long do you want to do that? And what if he suffers financial reverses—it's always possible—then where are you? What I'm offering you is security, now and for the future. You must think about your future."

"Yes," she said, "I must."

"Marry me, and we can draw up some kind of agreement so that even if I die suddenly or our marriage doesn't work out, you'll be well taken care of. I know how much you enjoy the good life. This is your chance to make certain you can keep enjoying it."

"You're quite a salesman," she said with a tinny laugh. "I think I better have a drink now. May I bring you one?"

"Yes," he said. "All right."

Naked in the kitchen, leaning stiff-armed on the countertop, she wondered how she might finesse this complication. She wished Turner was there to advise her, but then she knew what he'd say: stall, stall, stall. Until they could figure out the permutations and decide where their best interest lay.

She poured vodka over ice, added lime wedges, and carried the two glasses back to the bedroom: a proud, erect young woman with a dancer's body and appetites without end.

She handed Clayton his drink, then sat cross-legged at the foot of the bed.

"I won't say anything about your leaving your wife," she said. "I've never suggested it, have I? Never even hinted at it. It's really your decision and none of my business. But I don't understand why you feel you must marry me. Why can't we continue just the way we have been? I'm perfectly content."

He shook his head. "First of all, I happen to be a very conventional man. Tradition and all that. If I'm to have a long-term relationship with a woman, it should be legal; that's the way I was brought up. Second, for purely selfish reasons I want you for my wife. I want to be seen with you in public, take you to the theatre and parties, hear you introduced as Mrs. Clayton Starrett. I don't want people smirking and whispering, 'There's Clay with his floozy.' That wouldn't reflect well on Starrett Fine Jewelry. Bad public relations."

"I can see you've given this a lot of serious thought."

"Yes, I have," he said, missing the irony completely, "and I think you should, too. I don't expect an answer this minute, but if you think it over carefully, I know you'll see the advantages, especially security-wise."

"You don't mind if I tell my brother about this, do you?"

"Of course not," he said with a rapscallion grin. "I was counting on it. I know how close you two are, and I'm betting he'll be all for it. He'll tell you it's the smart thing to do: look out for Numero Uno."

She didn't reply.

He finished his drink and climbed out of bed. "Listen, I've got to get back to the office. Things are in a mess since Sol passed. Dick Satterlee has taken over and is doing what he can. But Sol carried a lot in his head, and it's going to take a while to get things straightened out."

After he was dressed, he tugged a small suede pouch from his side pocket and tossed it onto the bed. "Two carats. Pear-shaped. There's a tiny inclusion in the base but you'll never notice it."

"Thank you," she said faintly.

"I hope the next stone I give you will be in a solitaire," he said. "And I promise it'll be larger than two carats."

"Clay," she said, "do you love me?"

He waved a hand. "That goes without saying," he said, and bent down to kiss her.

After he was gone, the door locked, bolted, and chained behind him, she added the new diamond to her hoard and sat staring at the glittering heap. She didn't want to call Turner immediately. She needed time to think, to plan, to figure the best way to look out for Numero Uno.

18

The snow had melted, but the gutters were awash with garbage and some street corners were small lakes. But having gained almost five pounds during the holiday at home, Dora decided the walk downtown would do her good. This was after lunch with John Wenden during which she virtuously nibbled on a small tuna sandwich and drank nothing but tea.

"Are you sick?" John asked.

"Diet," she explained. "My New Year's resolution."

"I made one, too," he said, swilling his beer. "To cut out the beer."

Strangely, they spoke little of the Starrett case at lunch. Mostly they exchanged memories of Christmases past when they were children and the world was bright with hope and their dreams without limit.

"That didn't last long," Wenden said. "By the time I was ten I knew I would never be president, of anything."

"Even as a kid I was chubby," Dora said. "All the beautiful, popular girls chose me for a friend because they didn't want any competition."

"No one chose me for a friend," he said. "I've always been a loner. Maybe that's why my marriage flopped."

"Do you ever see your ex?"

"No," he said shortly. "I hear she's been dating a barber from Yonkers. Serves her right."

Dora laughed. "I think you should get married again, John."

He brightened. "My first proposal this year!"

"Not me, dummy," she said. "I'm taken."

"Not even for a week?" he asked, looking at her.

"Not even for a night. You just don't give up, do you?"

"You've never cheated on your husband?"

"Never."

"He wouldn't know. It would be an act of charity."

"It would be an act of stupidity," she said.

Plodding downtown, trying to leap over puddles and avoid a splashing from passing cabs, Dora thought of that luncheon conversation and smiled at John's persistence. It was a compliment, she supposed, to have a man come on so strongly. But it was worrisome, too, and she wondered how the hell Mike Trevalyan had guessed immediately what Wenden's motives were, without even meeting the guy. Maybe, she thought shrewdly, because Trevalyan had similar desires.

Men, she decided, were born to perpetual hankering. Except Mario, of course. Right? Right?

She was early for her appointment with Arthur Rushkin and walked over to the Starrett store on Park Avenue. There were few shoppers, and most seemed to be browsing, wandering about to examine the showcases of diamond rings, gold watches, brooches set with precious gems and, in particular, one fantastic three-strand choker of emeralds and rubies that, Dora guessed, probably cost more than the Contis' bungalow in Hartford.

On the way out she picked up a small, slick-paper leaflet: an application for a charge account. It also included a short history of Starrett Fine Jewelry and listed the addresses of all the branch stores. Dora slipped it into her shoulder bag, to be added to the Starrett file, and then headed for the attorney's office on Fifth Avenue.

She waited only five minutes in the reception room before Arthur Rushkin came out, introduced himself, shook her hand, and asked if she'd care for coffee. She declined, but was pleased with his hearty friendliness. If he was putting on an act, it was a good one.

He got her seated alongside the antique desk in his private office, then relaxed into his big swivel chair. He laced fingers across his bulging paisley waistcoat and regarded her with a benign smile.

"It's *Mrs.* Conti, isn't it?" he asked.

She nodded.

"I hope you won't be offended, Mrs. Conti, but after you called I made inquiries about you. I like to know something about the people I meet with. Perhaps you'll be happy to learn that you are very highly regarded. The people I spoke to praised you as a very intelligent, professional, and dedicated investigator."

"Yes," she said, "I am happy to hear it."

"I suppose," he said, still smiling, "your job is to make certain, before the claim is approved, that none of the beneficiaries was involved in the death of Lewis Starrett."

"That's part of it," she said cautiously.

"And what have you discovered?"

"Nothing definite," she said. "There are still many unanswered questions. Mr. Rushkin, do you know of any enemies Lewis Starrett had who might have wished him harm?"

He shook his head. "Lew could be a very difficult man at times, but I know of no one who disliked him enough to plunge a knife in his back."

Dora sighed. "That's what everyone says. And the whole situation has been further complicated by the murder of Solomon Guthrie."

Rushkin stopped smiling. "Yes," he said in a low voice, "I can understand that." Then he was silent for such a long time that she wondered if he was waiting for her to speak. Finally he rose, walked over to the windows facing Fifth Avenue. He stood there, staring out, his back turned to her, hands thrust into his trouser pockets.

"A hypothetical question, Mrs. Conti," he said, his deep voice a rumble. "If I was to reveal to you material that might possibly—and I repeat the word *possibly*—aid in your investigation, and should that material result in your uncovering *possible* evidence of wrongdoing and illegality, would you feel impelled to present that evidence to the authorities?"

"Of course," she said instantly.

He whirled to face her. "I would never, of course," he said sternly, "ask you *not* to. After all, I am, in a manner of speaking, an officer of the court. But what would your reaction be if I were to ask that if you did indeed uncover what you considered incriminating evidence, you would be willing to reveal that evidence to me before you took it to the police?"

She pondered that a moment. Then, lifting her chin, she said decisively, "I think not, Mr. Rushkin. This is no reflection on your trustworthiness or on your ethics, but I must consider the possibility that the evidence I find might implicate someone close to you, someone to whom you feel great personal attachment. In which case, revealing the evidence to you before it's turned over to the police might possibly—and I repeat the word possibly—result in the quick disappearance of the suspect."

Rushkin smiled wryly. "The praise of your intelligence was justified," he said, and came back to sit down again in his swivel chair. He fiddled with a pen on his desk, and she noted the sag of the heavy folds in his face and neck. He was a man she would ordinarily label "fat-faced," but sorrow gave his fleshy features a kind of nobility.

"I have had a problem these past few weeks," he confessed, not looking at her. "A problem you may feel is ridiculous, but which has cost me more than one night's sleep. The question is this: To whom do I owe my loyalty? In this whole sad affair, who is my client? Was it Lewis Starrett? Is it the Starrett family or any member thereof? And what of the Starrett employees, including Sol Guthrie? Whom do I represent? I have come to a conclusion you may find odd, but I have decided that my client is the one that pays my bills. In this case, it's Starrett Fine Jewelry, Incorporated. My client is a corporation, not the several owners or employees of that corporation, but the corporation itself, and it is to that legal entity that my responsibility is due."

"I don't think that's odd at all," Dora said. "He who pays the piper calls the tune."

"Yes," Rushkin said, "something like that. My wrestling

with the problem was made more difficult because of my personal relationship with Lewis Starrett and Solomon Guthrie. They were both old and dear friends, and I don't have many of those anymore. I would not care, by my actions, to impugn their reputation or distress their families. I believe they were both men of integrity. I would like to keep on believing it."

"Mr. Rushkin," Dora said softly, "there is obviously something you know about this case that is bothering you mightily. I suggest you tell me now what it is. I cannot promise complete and everlasting confidentiality because I may, someday, be called to testify about it in a court of law. All I can tell you is that I'll make every effort I can to treat whatever you tell me as a private communication, not to be repeated to anyone without your permission."

He nodded. "Very well," he said, "I accept that."

He then told her that a few days before his murder, Solomon Guthrie came to that very office, "sat in that very chair where you're now seated, Mrs. Conti," and voiced his suspicions that something illegal was going on at Starrett Fine Jewelry, Inc. He had no hard evidence to back up his accusation, but he was convinced skulduggery was going on, and he felt it probably involved Starrett's trading in gold bullion.

"He described to me exactly how the trading is done," Arthur Rushkin told Dora, "and I could see nothing wrong with it. It seemed like a conventional business practice: buying low and selling high."

"Did Mr. Guthrie name any person or persons he suspected of being involved in the illegalities?"

"He didn't actually accuse anyone," the attorney said, "but he certainly implied that Clayton Starrett was aware of what was going on."

Rushkin then related how Solomon Guthrie had left a large bundle of computer printout and pleaded with the lawyer to review it and perhaps discover evidence of thievery, fraud, embezzlement—whatever crime was being perpetrated.

"I filed it away and forgot about it," Rushkin confessed. "Then Sol was killed, and you can imagine the guilt I felt. I dragged it out and spent hours going over it, item by item. I found nothing but ordinary business transactions: the purchase and sale of gold bullion by Starrett Fine Jewelry during the last three months. I was somewhat surprised by the weight of gold being traded, but there is ample documentation to back up every deal."

Rushkin said he had then called in a computer expert, a man he trusted completely, and asked him to go over the printout to see if he could spot any gross discrepancies or anything even slightly suspicious. The expert could find nothing amiss.

But, the attorney went on, he could not rid himself of the notion that the printout was, in effect, Solomon Guthrie's last will and testament and he, Rushkin, would be failing his client, Starrett Fine Jewelry, by not investigating the matter further.

"Yes," Dora said, "I think it should be done. Tell me something, Mr. Rushkin: Did anyone at Starrett know that Solomon Guthrie had come to your office?"

The lawyer thought a moment. "He asked me not to tell Clayton Starrett of his visit, but then he said his secretary—Sol's secretary—knew he was coming over here."

"And other than what he thought might be on the computer printout, he had no additional evidence to prove his suspicions?"

"Well, he did say that Clayton had raised his salary by

141

fifty thousand a year. I congratulated him on his good fortune, but Sol was convinced it was a bribe to keep his mouth shut and not rock the boat. He was in a very excitable state, and I more or less laughed off what I considered wild and unfounded mistrust of his employer. I think now I was wrong and should have treated the matter more seriously."

"You couldn't have known he'd be killed. And there's always the possibility that his suspicions had nothing to do with his murder."

"Do you believe that?" Rushkin demanded.

"No," Dora said. "Do you?"

The lawyer shook his head. "I told you I feel guilt for ignoring what Guthrie told me. I also feel a deep and abiding anger at those who killed that sweet man."

"Clayton Starrett?" she suggested.

Rushkin glared at her. "Absolutely not! I'm that boy's godfather, and I assure you he's totally incapable of violence of any kind."

"If you say so," Dora said.

The attorney took a deep breath, leaned toward her across his desk. "Mrs. Conti, I want to hand over the printout to you. Perhaps you can find something in it that both the computer expert and I missed. Will you take a look?"

"Of course," Dora said. "A long, careful look. I was hoping you'd let me see it, Mr. Rushkin. But tell me: How do you think possible illegality in the gold trades relates to the death of Lewis Starrett?"

He shrugged. "I have no idea. Unless Lew found out something and had to be silenced."

"And then Solomon Guthrie found out that same something and also had to be silenced?"

He stared at her. "It's possible, isn't it?"

"Yes," Dora said. "Very possible."

Sighing, Rushkin opened the deep bottom drawer of his desk and dragged out the thick bundle of computer print-out. He weighed it in his hands a moment. "You know," he said, "I don't know whether I hope you find something or hope you don't. If you find nothing, then my guilt at treating Sol so shabbily will be less. If you find something, then I fear that people I know and love may be badly hurt."

"It comes with the territory," Dora said grimly, took the bundle from his hands, and jammed it into her shoulder bag. "Thank you much for your help, Mr. Rushkin. I'll keep in touch. If you want to reach me, I'm at the Hotel Bedlington on Madison Avenue."

He made a note of it on his desk pad and she started toward the door. Then she stopped and turned back.

"You knew Lewis Starrett a long time?" she asked.

Rushkin's smile returned. "Since before you were born. He was one of my first clients."

"My boss told me to ask you this: Did he have a mistress?"

The smile faded; the attorney stared at her stonily. "Not to my knowledge," he said.

Dora nodded and had the door open when Rushkin called, "Mrs. Conti." She turned back again. "Many years ago," the lawyer said.

She waited a long time for the down elevator and then descended alone to the street, aware of how a lonely elevator inspired introspection. In this case, her thoughts dwelt on how fortunate she was to give the impression of a dumpy hausfrau. If she had the physique and manner of a femme fatale–private eye, she doubted if Arthur Rushkin,

143

attorney-at-law, would have revealed that his beamy smiles masked an inner grief.

She hustled back to the Bedlington, clutching her shoulder bag as if it contained the Holy Grail. Double-locked into her corporate suite, she kicked off her shoes, put on reading glasses, and started poring over the computer printout, convinced she would crack its code where two others before her (men!) had failed.

She scanned it quickly at first, trying to get an overview of what it included. It appeared to be a straightforward record of gold purchases abroad; shipments of gold by the sellers' subsidiaries in the U.S. to Starrett's Brooklyn vault; sales of bullion by Starrett to its branch stores; sales by the branches to small, independent jewelers in their areas.

Then she went over it slowly, studying it carefully. The documentation was all there in meticulous detail: numbers and dates of sales contracts, shipping invoices, warehouse receipts, checks, and records of electronic transmission of Starrett's funds overseas. Dora reviewed every trade, even double-checking addition, subtraction, and percentages with her pocket calculator. Everything was correct to the penny.

Suddenly, at about 9:30 P.M., she realized she was famished; nothing to eat all day but that measly tuna sandwich at lunch. She called downstairs hastily and caught the kitchen just as it was about to close for the night. She persuaded an annoyed chef to make her two chicken sandwiches on wheat toast—hold the mayo. While she awaited the arrival of room service, she brewed a pot of tea, using three bags.

And that was her dinner: sandwiches that tasted like wet cardboard and tea strong enough to strip varnish from a tabletop. As she ate, she started again on the computer printout, going slowly and methodically over every trade, looking for any evidence, however slight, of something awry. She found nothing.

By midnight her eyesight was bleary and she gave up. She took a hot shower, thinking that perhaps Solomon Guthrie had been imagining wrongdoing. And if there was something amiss, as Mike Trevalyan had suggested, she couldn't find it in Starrett's gold trades.

But she could not sleep; her brain was churning. She tried to approach the problem from a new angle. If Arthur Rushkin, his computer expert, and she had been unable to find anything wrong in the *details* of the printout, perhaps the corruption was implicit in the whole concept of bullion trading. Maybe there was a gross flaw, so obvious that they were all missing it, just as Mario sometimes said, "Where's the dried oregano?" when the jar was in plain view on the countertop. Then Dora would say, "If it had teeth, it'd bite you."

At 2:00 A.M. she got out of bed, turned on the lights, donned her reading glasses again. This time she flipped through the printout swiftly, trying to absorb the "big picture." She saw something. Not earthshaking. And perhaps it was innocent and could easily be explained. But it was an anomaly, and frail though it might be, it was her only hope.

She searched frantically through her shoulder bag for that folder she had picked up at Starrett Fine Jewelry the previous morning: the charge account application that also listed the addresses of Starrett's branch stores. She checked the location of the stores against the computer printout.

Then, smiling, she went back to bed and fell asleep almost instantly.

19

"This kir is too sweet," Helene Pierce complained.

"You were born a woman," Turner said, "and so you're doomed to eternal dissatisfaction. Also, it's a kir royale. Now eat a grape."

He had frozen a bunch of white seedless grapes. They were hard as marbles, but softened on the tongue and crunched delightfully when bitten.

The Pierces were slumped languidly in overstuffed armchairs in Turner's frowsy apartment, having returned from lunch at Vito's where they had pasta primavera, a watercress salad, and shared a bottle of Pinot Grigio. Now they were sodden with food and wine, toying with the kirs and frozen grapes, both smiling at the memory of their rice-and-beans days.

"I have something to tell you," Helene said.

"And I have something to tell *you*," he said. "But go ahead; ladies first."

"Since when?" she said. "Anyway, Clayton asked me to marry him."

Turner's aplomb shattered. He drained his glass.

"When did this happen?" he asked hoarsely.

"A few days ago."

"Why didn't you tell me immediately?"

"No rush," she said. "He has to ask mommy's permission first."

"Sure," Turner said, "she owns the company now. He's really going to divorce Eleanor?"

"That's what he says."

"Shit!"

"My sentiments exactly," Helene said. "How are we going to handle it?"

"Before we compute that, I better tell you *my* news; it'll give you a hoot. Felicia wants to marry me."

They stared at each other. They wanted to laugh but couldn't.

"This family's doing splendidly," Turner said with a twisted smile. "What did Clayton offer?"

"Financial security. A prenuptial agreement on my terms."

"Pretty much what Felicia offered me. There's a lot of loot there, kiddo."

"I know."

"Damn it!" he exploded. "Things were going so great, and now this. How long can you stall Clayton?"

She shrugged, "As long as it takes him to get a divorce. If Eleanor hires a good lawyer, it could be a year. Stop biting your nails."

He took a deep breath. "It means we'll have to revise our timetable. Another year on the gravy train and that's it."

"What about Felicia?"

"I'll think of something."

"You want to cut and run right now?" she asked curiously.

He shook his head. "It took a lot of time and hard work to set up this deal. It's just beginning to pay off; I'm not walking away from it. And besides, if I split, Ramon would be a mite peeved."

"The understatement of the year," she said.

He nodded gloomily. "I'll figure out how to handle Felicia; it's Clayton I'm worried about."

"You worry too much," she told him. "Leave it to me."

"If you say so," he said doubtfully, and went into the kitchen to mix more kir royales.

Helene straightened up in her armchair, lighted a cigarette slowly. She heard him moving about, the gurgle of wine, clink of glasses. She looked toward the kitchen door, frowning.

She had caught something in his voice that disturbed her. Not panic—not yet—but there was an uncertainty she had never heard before. He was the one who had taught her self-assurance.

"Just don't give a dam'," he had instructed her. "About *anything*. That gives you an edge on everyone who believes in something."

And that's the way they had played their lives; amorality was their religion, and they had flourished. And as they thrived, their confidence grew. They thumbed their noses at the world and danced away laughing. But now, it seemed to her, his surety was crumbling. She imagined all the scenarios that could result from his weakness and how they would impact on her life.

He brought fresh drinks from the kitchen, and she smiled at him, thinking that if push came to shove, she might have to make a hard choice.

20

Dora awoke the next morning convinced that her brainstorm of the previous night had been exactly that: a storm of the brain. Now, in the sunny calm of a new day, it seemed highly unlikely that the peculiarity she had spotted in the computer printout had any significance whatsoever. There were a dozen innocent explanations for it. It was a minor curiosity. It would lead her nowhere.

But still, she reflected glumly, it was all she had, and it deserved, at least, a couple of phone calls. So she dialed Arthur Rushkin. He wasn't in his office yet, and Dora continued calling at fifteen-minute intervals until, at about 10:30, she was put through to him.

"Did you find anything?" he asked eagerly.

"Not really," she said, wondering if dissembling was part of her job or part of her nature. "I just have a technical question, and I was hoping you'd be willing to give me the name of that computer expert you consulted."

"I don't see why not," Rushkin said slowly. "His name is

Gregor Pinchik, and he's in the Manhattan directory. He has his own business: computer consultant for banks, brokerages, credit card companies, and corporations."

"Sounds like just the man I need."

"There are two things you should know about him," the attorney went on. "One, he charges a hundred dollars an hour. And two, he's an ex-felon."

"Oh-oh," Dora said. "For what?"

"Computer fraud," Rushkin said, laughing. "But since he's been out, he's discovered there's more money to be made by telling clients how to avoid getting taken by computer sharpies like him. Shall I give Pinchik a call and tell him he'll be hearing from you? That way you won't have to go through the identification rigmarole."

"It would be a big help. Thank you, Mr. Rushkin."

Then she phoned Mike Trevalyan in Hartford.

"Are you on to anything?" he asked.

"Not really," Dora said again, "but something came up that needs a little digging. Mike, remember when you were telling me about Starrett Fine Jewelry? You said that about a year ago Clayton Starrett fired most of his branch managers and put in new people. And about the same time he started trading in gold bullion."

"So?"

"Starrett has fifteen branches in addition to their flagship store in New York. What I need to know is this: Which of the branch stores got new managers a year ago."

"I'm not sure I can get that," Trevalyan said, "but if it's important, I'll try."

"It's important," Dora assured him.

"How come I always end up doing your job for you?"

"Not all of it. The other thing I wanted to tell you is that I'm going to hire a computer consultant."

"What the hell for?"

"Because I need him," she said patiently. "Technical questions that only an expert can answer."

"How much does he charge?"

"A hundred dollars an hour."

"What!" Trevalyan bellowed. "Are you crazy? A hundred an hour? That means the Company will be paying twenty-five bucks every time this guy takes a crap!"

"Mike," Dora said, sighing, "*must* you be so vulgar and disgusting? Look, if you needed brain surgery—which sometimes I think you do—would you shop around for the cheapest surgeon you could find? You have to pay for expertise; you know that."

"Are you sure this guy's an expert?"

"The best in the business," she said, not mentioning that he had done time for computer fraud.

"Well . . . all right," Trevalyan said grudgingly. "But try to use him only for an hour."

"I'll try," she promised, keeping her fingers carefully crossed.

Her third call of the morning was to Gregor Pinchik, whose address in the directory was on West 23rd Street.

Dora gave her name and asked if Mr. Arthur Rushkin had informed Pinchik that she'd be phoning.

"Yeah, he called," the computer consultant acknowledged in a gravelly voice. "He tell you what my fees are?"

"A hundred an hour?"

"That's right. And believe me, lady, I'm worth it. What's this about?"

"I'd rather not talk about it on the phone. Could we meet somewhere?"

"Why not. How's about you coming down here to my loft."

153

"Sure," Dora said, "I could do that. What time?"

"Noon. How does that sound?"

"I'll be there," she said.

"It's just west of Ninth Avenue. Don't let the building scare you. It's being demolished, and right now I'm the only tenant left. But the intercom still works. You ring from downstairs—three short rings and one long one—and I'll buzz you in. Okay?"

"Okay," Dora said. "I'm on my way."

The decrepit building on West 23rd Street had scaffolding in place, and workmen were prying at crumbling ornamental stonework and brick facing, allowing the debris to tumble down within plywood walls protecting the sidewalk.

Dora nervously ducked into the littered vestibule and pressed the only button in sight: three shorts and a long. The electric lock buzzed; she pushed her way in and cautiously climbed five flights of rickety wood stairs, thinking that at a hundred dollars an hour Gregor Pinchik could afford a business address more impressive than this.

The man who greeted her at the door of the top-floor loft was short, blocky, with a head of Einstein hair and a full Smith Brothers beard, hopelessly snarled. But the eyes were alive, the smile bright.

"Nice place, huh?" he said grinning. "I'm moving to SoHo next week, as soon as they bring in power cables for my hardware. Watch where you step and what you touch; everything is muck and mire."

He led her into one enormous room, jammed with sealed wooden crates and cardboard cartons. His desk was a card table, the phone covered with a plastic cozy. He used his pocket handkerchief to wipe clean a steel folding chair so

Dora could sit down. She rummaged through her shoulder bag, found a business card, handed it over.

Pinchik inspected it and laughed. "I know the Company," he said. "Their computer system has more holes than a cribbage board. I got into it once—just for the fun of it, you understand—and looked around, but there was nothing interesting. Tell your boss his computer security is a joke."

"I'll tell him," Dora said. "You're a hacker?"

"I'm a superhacker," he said. "I protect my clients against electronic snoops like me. Which means I have to stay one step ahead of the Nosy Parkers, and it ain't easy. By the way, your first hour of consultation started when you rang the doorbell."

Dora nodded. "Mr. Rushkin tells me you reviewed the computer printout from Starrett Jewelry and found nothing wrong."

Pinchik made a dismissive gesture. "That wasn't real computer stuff," he said. "It was just data processing. You could have done the same thing with an adding machine or pocket calculator, if you wanted to spend the time."

"But it was accurate?" she persisted.

"Accurate?" Pinchik said, and coughed a laugh. "As accurate as what was put into it. You know the expression GIGO? It means Garbage In, Garbage Out. If you feed a computer false data, what you get out is false data. A lot of people find it hard to realize that a computer has no conscience. It doesn't know right or wrong, good or evil. You program it to give you the best way to blow up the world, and it'll chug along for a few seconds and tell you; it doesn't care. Did Rushkin say I've done time?"

She nodded.

"Let me tell you how that happened," he said, "if you don't mind wasting part of your hundred-dollar hour."

"I don't mind," Dora said.

"I've got an eighth-grade education," Pinchik said, "but I'm a computer whiz. Most hackers have the passion. With me, it's an obsession. I was a salesman in a computer store on West Forty-sixth Street. I could buy new equipment at an employee's discount, and I was living up here paying bupkes for rent. I worked eight hours a day at the store and spent eight hours hacking. I mean I was writing programs and corresponding electronically with people all over the world as nutty as I was. I can't begin to tell you the systems I got into: government, universities, research labs, military, banks—the whole schmear.

"Now you gotta know I'm a divorced man. My wife claimed she was a computer widow, and she was right. She's living in Hawaii now, and I understand she's bedding some young stud who wears earrings, beats a drum, and roasts pigs for tourists. But that's her problem. Mine was that I had to send her an alimony check every month. Getting bored?"

"No, no," Dora said, thinking of Detective John Wenden and his alimony problems. "It's interesting."

"Well, those monthly alimony checks were killing me," Pinchik went on. "I could have afforded them if it hadn't been for my obsession; all my loose bucks were going for new hardware, modems, programs, and so forth. So one night I'm up here noodling around, and I break into the computer system of an upstate New York bank. Just for the fun of it, you understand."

"How did you get in?" Dora asked curiously.

Pinchik gave her his bright smile. "If you want to know

the truth, lady, most bankers are morons. This was the case of a brand-new integrated computer system installed in an old bank that had more than twenty local branches. There were seven top bank executives who were given private access code words to the entire system. All right, you have seven guys who can tap into the system and move it any way they want anytime they want. Now you guess what passwords those seven guys selected."

"Days of the week?" Dora suggested.

"Try again."

"The Seven Deadly Sins?"

"Try again."

Dora thought a moment. "The Seven Dwarfs?" she said. "From 'Snow White'?"

"Now you've got it," Pinchik said approvingly. "They thought they were being so cute. It's easy for hackers to break into so-called secure systems. It took me about ten minutes to get into this bank's records, using the password 'Dopey.' I was just looking around, reading all their confidential stuff, and I got this absolutely brilliant idea."

"And that's what put you in jail," Dora said.

"Yeah, lady," the expert said ruefully, "but it wasn't the idea; that was a winner. I just screwed it up, that's all. Here's how it worked. . . . The bank I invaded, like most banks everywhere, carried a lot of what they call dormant accounts. These are old savings and checking accounts that haven't had any action—deposits or withdrawals—for years and years. Maybe the depositor forgot he had money in that bank. Maybe he died and his heirs didn't know he had the account. Maybe he's in jail and doesn't want to touch it until he gets out. Maybe he's hiding the money from his wife or girlfriend. Or maybe he *stole* the money and parked it in a bank until the statute of limitations runs out. For whatever reason, these are inactive accounts that keep getting bigger and bigger as the interest piles up."

"But don't the banks have to advertise the accounts?"

"Sure they do, after a period of years. Then some of the depositors come forward. In most states, if the money isn't claimed after a period of X years, it goes into the state's general funds. So I saw all these dormant accounts on the records of that bank I invaded in upstate New York, and I thought 'Why not?' So every month I'd have Dopey transfer my alimony payment electronically to my ex-wife's account in a Hilo bank, making withdrawals from a large dormant account. The depositor didn't scream; no one knew where the hell he was. Maybe he was dead. And my ex didn't object; all she saw were those monthly payments coming in. The bank's books showed legitimate withdrawals with no evidence that they were being made by Dopey, who was me."

"You were right," Dora said, "it's a brilliant idea. What went wrong?"

"I did," Pinchik said. "Every month I would get into the computer as Dopey and instruct the New York bank to transfer the alimony payment electronically to the Hawaiian bank. What I should have done was feed instructions into the New York bank's computer telling it to make those payments *automatically* every month. It would have been an easy job, but I had other things on my mind and never got around to it. So one month I forgot to tell the New York bank to transfer the alimony money."

"Oh-oh," Dora said.

"Yeah, oh-oh," Pinchik said disgustedly. "It was my own stupid fault. My ex-wife didn't see her payment show up on her statement that month and asked her Hilo bank to check up on it. They contacted the New York bank and asked where the alimony money was. New York said, 'What alimony money?' Naturally my ex gave them my name—she wasn't ratting on me; she really thought it was my dough she was getting—and the New York bank discovered I didn't have an account there. One thing led to another, and I ended up behind bars. But it was a sweet deal while it lasted."

"You don't seem bitter about it."

The superhacker shrugged. "Don't do the crime if you can't do the time."

"Is there a lot of computer crime going on?"

Pinchik rolled his eyes. "More than you and everyone else realizes. Want a rough estimate? I'd guess a minimum of two or three *billion* dollars a year is being siphoned off by computer thievery, fraud, and swindles. And most of it you never hear about."

"Why not?"

"Because the victims—mostly banks—are too embarrassed by their idiotic carelessness to make public their losses. In most cases, even when the crook is caught, they refuse to prosecute; they don't want the publicity. They let their insurance companies cover the shortfall."

"Thanks a lot," Dora said. "That makes me feel great. Tell me something else: Is there a national list somewhere of all the computer thieves and swindlers who have been caught, even if they've never been prosecuted?"

"No, lady, I don't know of any data base that lists only computer felons. But I imagine the FBI's computerized files are programmed so they could spit out a list like that."

Dora shook her head. "The people I'm interested in aren't in the FBI files."

"Ah-ha," Pinchik said, trying to comb his tangled beard

with his fingers, "now we get down to the nitty-gritty. You got people you suspect of being computer crooks?"

"It's a possibility. The NYPD has done a trace on them, and they have no priors. The Company's data base of insurance swindlers also shows nothing. I thought maybe, with your contacts, you could do a search and see if these people have ever been involved in computer hanky-panky."

"Sure, I could do that," the expert said, and then gestured around the littered loft. "But you caught me at a bad time. All that stuff in crates and boxes is my hardware, disks, files, and programs, packed up and ready to go. It'll be at least a week, maybe two, before I'm really back in business."

"I can wait," Dora said.

"Good. Meanwhile, if you give me names and descriptions, I can get started calling hackers I know on the phone. When I'm set up and functioning in my new place in SoHo, I'll be able to make it a more thorough worldwide search. How does that sound?"

"Sounds fine," Dora said. "Please keep a very accurate record of the time you spend on it and your expenses. I've got a tightwad boss."

"I meet them all the time," Pinchik said. "Now let me turn on my handy-dandy tape recorder, and you dictate everything you know about these people. Be as detailed as you can, lady; don't leave anything out."

So Dora spoke into his notebook-sized tape recorder, stating and spelling the names of Turner and Helene Pierce, mentioning their roots in Kansas City, MO, describing their physical appearance, and what little she knew of their ages, habits, Turner's occupation as computer consultant, their style of living, their accents, their connection with Starrett Fine Jewelry, their home addresses and phone numbers.

"And that's all I have," she finished.

"Enough to get me started," Gregor Pinchik said, switching off the recorder. "The names mean nothing to me, but maybe one of my contacts will make them."

"I'm staying at the Hotel Bedlington on Madison Avenue," Dora said. "Can you give me weekly reports?"

"Nope," Pinchik said. "A waste of time. If I come up with something, I'll let you know immediately. But there's no point in sending you a weekly report of failure."

"How long do you think the search will take, Mr. Pinchik?"

He considered a moment. "Give me three weeks to a month," he said. "If I haven't nailed them by then, they're clean—guaranteed. Trust me."

"I do," Dora said, rising. "Send your bills to me at the Bedlington—all right?"

"Oh sure," he said. "Those you'll get weekly. Depend on it. Nice meeting you, lady."

21

The decorator stepped back to the office door, turned and examined her work through narrowed eyes. "Well, Mr. Starrett," she said, "how do you like it?"

Clayton, standing alongside his new stainless steel desk, looked around the refurbished office. "That painting over the couch," he said, "shouldn't it be a bit higher?"

"No," the decorator said decisively. "You're a tall man; the painting seems low to you. But it's actually at the eye level of the average person. The proportions of the wall composition are just right, and a Warhol over a Biedermeier lends a certain je ne sais quoi to the room."

"Yeah," he said, grinning happily, "that's exactly that I wanted—a certain je ne sais quoi. I think you did a beautiful job."

"Thank you," she said, and discreetly placed her bill, tucked into a mauve envelope, on a corner of his desk. She took a final look around. "I just adore the ambience," she breathed, and then she was gone.

Clayton thrust his hands into his pockets and strutted about the office a moment, admiring the black leather directors' chairs set at a cocktail table with a top of smoky glass. The entire office, he decided, now reflected the importance and prosperity of the occupant. As the decorator had said, the ambience was right: a wealthy ambience; good-taste ambience; up-to-date ambience.

He opened the mauve envelope, glanced at the statement, blanched, then smiled. His father, he knew, would have had apoplexy at a bill like that for redecorating an office. But times change, as Clayton well knew, and if you didn't change along with them you were left hopelessly behind.

And he had changed, was changing; he could feel it. He had lived in the shadow of his father so many years. He had been a follower, a lackey, really nothing more than a gofer. But now he was living his own life, he was *doing.* In the midst of his glittery office, he felt a surge that made him take a deep breath, suck in his gut, stand tall. Now he was *creating*—there was no other word for it.

He used his new phone, a marvelous instrument that had been coded with frequently called numbers so he had to touch only one button to call home.

"Charles?" he said. "This is Clayton Starrett. May I speak to my mother, please."

While he waited for her to come on the line, he slid into his "orthopedically correct" swivel chair that cushioned him like a womb. It was a sensual experience just to relax in that chair, enjoy its soft but firm comfort, close his eyes and drift, savoring the rewards of his creativity.

"Mother?" he said. "Clayton. Are you going to be in for a while? Good. Has Eleanor gone out? Also good. There's something important I'd like to talk to you about. I'll be home in twenty minutes or so. See you . . ."

He hung up briefly, then lifted the handset again and touched the button labeled H.P.

"Helene?" he said. "Clayton. Will you be in this afternoon? Oh, in about two hours. Good. I'd like to stop by for a few minutes. I won't be able to stay long; my advertising people are coming in later. Fine. See you . . ."

When he arrived home, Mrs. Olivia Starrett was in her flowery bedroom, seated at a spindly desk, working on correspondence. Clayton leaned down to kiss her downy cheek.

"I'll never get caught up," she said, sighing. "All the letters of condolence after father passed. And then Christmas and New Year's cards and letters. It's just too much."

"You'll answer them all," he assured her, pulling up a cushioned armchair too small for him. "You always do. Did Eleanor say when she'll be back?"

"I don't recall," his mother said vaguely. "Something about planning a dinner-dance on a cruise ship. Does that sound right, Clay?"

"Probably," he said. "I want to talk to you about Eleanor, mother. Eleanor and me."

Olivia removed her half-glasses and turned to him. "Oh dear," she said, "I do hope it's not a quarrel. You know how I dislike quarrels."

"I'm afraid it's more serious than that," Clayton said, and plunged right in. "Mother, you know that things haven't been right between Eleanor and me for several years now. Since little Ernie died, she's been a changed woman. Not the woman I married. You're intelligent and sensitive,

165

mother; you must have realized that things weren't going well between us."

Mrs. Starrett made a fluttery gesture. "God's will be done," she said. "We must learn to accept pain and sorrow as part of the holy oneness."

"Yes, yes," Clayton said impatiently, "but I can't go on living like this. It's—it's hypocritical. My marriage is a sham. There's just nothing to it. It's putting up a front at charity benefits and everything else is empty. I can't live that way anymore. It's tearing me apart."

She stared at him, her big eyes luminous. "Have you spoken to Eleanor about the way you feel?"

"Eleanor and I don't speak about *anything*. At least nothing important. We've become strangers to each other. Mother, I'm going to ask for a—for a *divorce.*" The word caught in his throat.

He was returning her stare but had to turn away when he saw her eyes fill with tears. She reached out to put a soft hand on his arm.

"Please, Clayton," she said. *"Please."*

He stood abruptly and stalked about the room, unable to face her. "It's got to be done," he said roughly. *"Got* to be. Our marriage is a great big zero. Eleanor has her charity parties, I have the business to take care of, and we have nothing in common. We just don't *share.* I want a chance at happiness. At least a *chance.* Don't you think I deserve that? Everyone deserves that."

"Have you considered a marriage counselor?" she said timidly. "Or perhaps you could talk to Father Callaway; he's very understanding."

He shook his head. "This isn't a temporary squabble. It goes deeper. We've just become incompatible, that's all. I know this is a shock to you, mother, but I wanted to tell you what I plan to do before I spoke to Eleanor about it. I wanted to get your reaction."

"My reaction?" she cried. "Another death in the family—that's my reaction."

"Come on!" he said heartily. "It's not that bad. People get divorced all the time and survive. Sometimes it's the healthiest thing to do. A loveless marriage is like a wasting disease."

She lowered her head, looked down at her hands, twisted her wedding band around and around. "What will you do then?" she asked. "Marry again?"

He had not intended to tell her. He had planned to take it a step at a time: inform her about the divorce at an initial meeting; then, after giving her time to adjust, he would tell her about Helene in another intimate conversation.

But now, because she did not seem unduly disturbed, he suddenly decided to go all the way, get it all out, thinking that she might be mollified if she knew that he wanted to remarry and would not be alone.

He sat down alongside her again and clasped her hands in his. "Mother, the first thing I want to do is end an impossible situation and divorce Eleanor. Believe me, she'll be well taken care of; she won't have a thing to worry about for the rest of her life. I'm talking about money worries. You know I'll make certain she's financially secure."

She nodded. "Yes, you *must* do that."

"Of course. And when the divorce becomes final"—he took a deep breath—"I want to marry Helene Pierce—if she'll have me."

Olivia raised her eyes to his, and he saw something that surprised him: a kind of peasant shrewdness. "How long has this been going on?" she asked.

He concealed his guilt by feigning bewilderment. "How

long has *what* been going on? You've known Helene as long as I have. She and her brother have become good friends to all of us. I think Helene is a lovely, sweet, sensitive person—don't you?"

"She's awfully young, Clayton—for you."

He shook his head. "I don't think so. Perhaps *she* does. Naturally I haven't even hinted to her about the way I feel. Maybe she'll turn me down."

"She won't," Mrs. Starrett said, the peasant again. "She's not that foolish."

He shrugged. "But that's all in the future. I just want you to know that I hope to remarry. I have no intention of living the rest of my life as a bachelor. When I remember how happy you and father were for so many years, I know that marriage—the *right* marriage—is what I want."

"Yes," his mother said.

He leaned toward her, serious and intent. "I know this must come as a shock to you, and a disappointment. I'd do anything in the world to keep from hurting you. I love you, and I know you love me."

"I do, but I love Eleanor, too. What you're doing to her seems so—so unkind."

He gave her a sad smile. "You know what they say: Sometimes you have to be cruel to be kind. Eleanor will be happier without me."

"You don't know that."

"Mother! She'll still have her life: her friends, her charities, her benefits. And perhaps she'll remarry, too. That's possible, isn't it?"

"I don't think so," Mrs. Starrett said.

He straightened up, trying to keep anger out of his voice. "If you don't want me to divorce Eleanor, I'll continue that miserable marriage the rest of my life. Is that what you want? Doesn't my happiness mean anything to you?"

Then she did weep and bent forward to embrace him. "Yes," she said, sobbing, "oh yes, I want you to be happy. I'd give my life to make you happy."

"I know you would, mother," he said in almost a croon, soothing her, stroking her wet cheek. "What's most important to me is that this doesn't come between us. I don't want to risk losing your love, and if you tell me not to do it, I won't."

"No," his mother said, "I can't tell you that. It's your life; I can't control it. Clayton, please let's not talk about it anymore. Not now. I'm so shaken I can't think straight. I think I'll take an aspirin and lie down for a while."

"You do that. And try not to worry about it. I know it's hard for you to accept, but things will work out—you'll see."

He said again that he loved her and then he left. On the way down in the elevator he thought of additional arguments he might have used, but generally he was satisfied with the way things had gone. On the way to Helene's, he had his chauffeur stop at a florist's shop where he ordered a dozen roses to be delivered immediately to his mother with a signed card that read: "I love you most of all."

He was still energized when Helene opened the door of her apartment. He embraced her, laughing, and really didn't calm down until she persuaded him to take off his hat and coat and sit in a living room armchair while she poured him a vodka. He gulped it greedily as he told her of the conversation with his mother.

"She'll go along," he predicted confidently. "Maybe it knocked her for a loop at first, but she'll get used to the

169

idea. I'll hit her again in a day or so, and gradually she'll accept it."

"Then she's not going to fire you?"

"No," he said, grinning, "I don't think so."

"I hope you're right, Clay," Helene said. "I'd hate to be the cause of a breakup between you and Olivia."

"You won't be. She thinks you're too young for me, but I told her that's your decision to make."

"And what did she say?"

"She said you won't turn me down; you're not that fool-ish."

Helene's smile was chilly. "Sometimes you and your family treat Olivia like she was a bubblehead. She happens to be a very wise lady."

"If you say so. Are you ready to become Mrs. Helene Starrett the day after my divorce is granted?"

"Oh Clay, that's months and months away. It seems to me you're rushing things."

"Look, if you're going to do something, then *do* it. You still haven't answered my question."

"You really want to marry me?"

"Absolutely!"

She came up close, pressed her softness against his arm, caressed the back of his neck. "Then why don't we go practice," she said throatily. "Right now."

"You're on," he said at once and stood up. He put his drink aside and began to take off his jacket.

"What about your advertising people, darling?" she said, unbuttoning his shirt.

"Let them wait," he said. "I own them; they don't own me."

22

The phone rang a little before eight o'clock, and Dora roused from a deep sleep. "H'lo," she said groggily.

"Did I wake you up, kiddo?" Mike Trevalyan said. "Good. That makes my day."

"Yeah, it would," she said, swinging her legs out of bed. "Is that why you called—just to wake me up?"

"Listen, you asked me to check on which managers got canned from which Starrett branch stores a year ago."

"You got it?"

"Nope, I struck out on that one. My contacts in the jewelry business were no help. I even had a researcher go through jewelry trade journals for the past few years, but she came up with zilch. Sometimes those magazines publish personnel changes in the business, but only when the company involved sends them press releases. I guess Starrett didn't want to publicize the firings."

"Thanks anyway, Mike. I appreciate your trying."

"How you coming on the Starrett claim?" he asked.

"Slowly," Dora said. "It gets curiouser and curiouser the deeper I dig. By the way, I found that statement in my report that gives a good motive for Father Brian Callaway killing Lewis Starrett."

Trevalyan laughed. "You should read your own reports more often. You think Callaway aka Sidney Loftus did the dirty deed?"

"I don't know," she said doubtfully. "He's got a perfect alibi for the Solomon Guthrie murder."

"Maybe the two killings aren't connected."

"Come on, Mike. The two victims were old friends and worked for the same company. There's got to be a connection."

"Then find it," her boss said. "Now go back to sleep."

"Fat chance," Dora said, but he had already hung up.

She sat on the edge of the bed yawning and knuckling her scalp. She reflected, not for the first time, that she really should do morning exercises. Maybe a few deep knee-bends, a few push-ups. The thought depressed her, and she went into the bathroom to take a hot shower.

She was standing in the kitchen, drinking her first decaf of the day and thinking of what Mike had said, when she realized where she might be able to get the information she wanted. She phoned Detective John Wenden and was surprised to find him at his desk.

"What are you doing at work so early?" she asked.

"I didn't get home last night," Wenden said. "We had a mini-riot down in the East Village, and all available troops were called in."

"What was the riot about?"

"About who can use a public park. How does that grab you? This city is nutsville—right? What's up, Red?"

"John, you told me the Department was going through employment records from Starrett Fine Jewelry to find someone who was fired and was sore enough to snuff Lewis Starrett and Solomon Guthrie."

"Yeah, we're working on it. Nothing so far."

"Well, about a year ago Starrett terminated a bunch of managers at their branch stores. Could you check the records and find out how many managers were canned and at which stores?"

"I could probably dig that out," he said slowly, "but why should I?"

"As a favor for me?" Dora said hopefully.

"Red, this isn't a one-way street, you know. It can't be caviar for you and beans for me. If you want that information, you better tell me what's percolating in that devious mind of yours."

She hesitated a moment. "All right," she said finally, "I can understand that. If you get me what I want, I'll tell you why I need it."

"You're all heart," Wenden said, sighing. "Okay, Red, I'll get the skinny for you. But only on condition that I deliver it in person. I want to see you again."

"And I want to see you."

"Just so you can pick my brain?"

She didn't answer.

"Well?" he said. "I'm waiting."

"No," Dora said faintly, "I just want to see you."

"That's a plus," he said. "A small plus. I'll let you know when I've got the info."

She hung up the phone, wondering why her hand was shaking. It wasn't much of a tremor, but it was there. To stop that nonsense, she immediately called Mario. There

173

was no answer. He was probably at work, and he didn't like to be phoned there. So Dora had another cup of coffee and resolutely banished John Wenden from her thoughts. For at least five minutes.

She spent the day doing research at the public library on Fifth Avenue. She started with the basics: The atomic number of gold was 79, its symbol was Au, it melted at 1064°C and boiled at 2875°. It had been discovered in prehistoric times and used in jewelry and coinage almost as long.

She then started reading about the mining and smelting of gold, and its casting into ingots, bars, and sheets, including gold leaf so thin (four millionths of an inch) you could tear it with a sneeze.

She took a break at 12:30, packed up all her notes, and went out into a drizzly day to look for lunch. There was a vendor on 42nd Street selling croissant sandwiches from an umbrella stand, and Dora had one ham and one cheese, washed down with a can of Diet Dr Pepper. By the time she returned to the library, she figured she was two pounds heavier, but half of that was in her sodden parka.

In the afternoon she concentrated on jewelry: how it was designed and fabricated, the metals and alloys used. By four o'clock, eyes aching, her shoulder bag crammed with photocopies and notes, she left the library, slogged over to Madison Avenue, and bused uptown to the Bedlington.

She peeled off her cold, wet clothes, took a hot shower, and popped a couple of aspirin, just in case. Then she made a pot of tea, put on her reading glasses, and settled down in her bathrobe to try to find some answers in her research. She found no answers, but she did find a new puzzle and was mulling over that when John Wenden called around 7:30.

"Miserable day and miserable night," he said. "You eat yet, Red?"

"No, not yet."

"Neither have I, but I wouldn't ask you to come out on a lousy night like this. You like Chinese food?"

"Right now I'd like anything edible."

"Suppose I stop by a take-out place and pick up some stuff. I'll get it to the hotel while it's still warm."

"Sounds good to me," Dora said. "I have a thing for shrimp in lobster sauce. Could you get some of that?"

"Sure, with wonton soup, fried rice, tea, and fortune cookies."

"You can skip the tea," she said. "I can provide that. But load up on the hot mustard."

"All right," he said. "See you in an hour."

She put all her research away in a closet and dressed hurriedly in a tweed skirt and black turtleneck pullover floppy enough to hide her thickening waist.

Monday starts the diet, kiddo, she told herself sternly. I really mean that.

She had a fresh pot of tea ready by the time John arrived. His coat and hat were pimpled with rain, and his ungloved hands were reddened and icy. Dora poured him a pony of brandy to chase the chill while she opened the Chinese food he had brought. All the cartons were arranged on the cocktail table in front of the couch, and Dora set out plates, cutlery, and mugs for their tea.

He hadn't forgotten the shrimp in lobster sauce, and there was also a big container of sweet and sour pork cooked with chunks of pineapple and green and red pep-

175

pers. Also egg rolls, barbecued ribs, and ginger ice cream.

"A feast!" Dora exulted. "I'm going to stuff myself."

"Be my guest," Wenden said. "You're looking good, Red. Losing weight?"

Dora laughed. "You sweet liar," she said. "No, I haven't lost any weight, and I'm not about to if you keep feeding me like this. I'll be a real Fatty, Fatty, two-by-four."

"More of you to love," he said, and when she didn't reply, he busied himself with a barbecued rib.

"Let's talk business," Dora said, smearing an eggroll with hot mustard. "Were you able to get the information about which Starrett branch managers were fired a year ago?"

"Yeah, I got it. And you said you'd tell me why you want it."

"All right," she said. "Did you know that Starrett has been dealing in gold bullion for about a year now?"

"Sure, I knew that," Wenden said, filling his plate with fried rice and sweet and sour pork.

Dora was startled. "How did you know?" she asked.

He looked up at her and grinned. "Surprised that we're not total stupes? When Solomon Guthrie was knocked off, he was carrying a briefcase stuffed with company business papers. We went through it. Most of it was about Christmas bonuses for Starrett employees. But there was also a file on recent purchases and sales of gold bullion."

"Oh," she said, somewhat discomfited. "Did you do anything about it?"

"Wow!" he said, wiping his forehead with a paper napkin. "That mustard is *rough.* Sure, I did something about it; I asked Clayton Starrett what gives. He said the company buys the gold overseas at a good price and sells it to small jewelry stores around the country at a nice markup. He showed me his records. Everything looks to be on the up-and-up. Isn't it?"

"Maybe," Dora said. "I got hold of a computer printout showing all of Starrett's gold business for the last three months, and it—"

"Whoa!" the detective said, holding up a palm. "Wait a minute. Where did you get the printout?"

"Let's just say it was from a reliable source. Will you accept that?"

He ate a moment without answering. Then: "For the time being."

"Well, I went over the printout many, many times and finally found something interesting. In addition to its flagship store on Park Avenue, Starrett has fifteen branches all over the world. Seven of them are overseas, and eight are in the U.S., including Honolulu. All the gold bullion Starrett was selling went to the domestic branches, none to the foreign stores."

Wenden showed no reaction. He helped himself to more fried rice. "So?" he said. "What's that supposed to mean?"

"I don't know what it means," Dora said crossly, "but it's unusual, don't you think?"

He sat back, swabbed his lips with a paper napkin, took a swig of tea. "There could be a dozen explanations. Maybe the overseas stores buy their gold from local sources. Maybe there are hefty import duties on gold shipped to those countries. Maybe the foreign branches don't *need* any gold because they get all their finished jewelry from New York."

"I guess you're right," Dora said forlornly. "I'm just grabbing at straws."

"On the other hand," John said, leaning forward again to start on his ice cream, "you may be on to something. About a year ago nine branch managers, including the guy in Manhattan, were fired and replaced with new people. All the firings and replacements were in Starrett's U.S. branches, none in the foreign stores."

They stared at each other a moment. Then Dora took a deep breath. "You got any ideas?" she asked.

"Nope," Wenden said. "You?"

"Not a one. There could be an innocent reason for it."

"Do you believe that?"

"No."

"I don't either," he said. "Something fishy is going on. Do you know anything you're not telling me, Red?"

"I've told you all I know," she said, emphasizing the *know* and figuring that made it only a half-lie.

"Well, keep digging, and if you come up with any ideas, give me a shout. Someone is jerking us around, and I don't like it."

She nodded, stood up, and began clearing the mess on the cocktail table. "John, there's leftovers. Do you want to take it home with you?"

"Nah," he said. "I'm going back to the office tonight for a few hours, and I won't be able to heat it up. You keep it. You can have it for breakfast tomorrow."

"With the hot mustard?" she said, smiling. "That'll start me off bright-eyed and bushy-tailed. Thank you for the banquet. You were a lifesaver."

"Is the way to a woman's heart through her stomach?" he asked.

"That's one way," she said.

Working together, they cleaned up the place, put uneaten food in the refrigerator, washed plates, cutlery

178

and mugs. Then they returned to the living room and Dora poured them tots of brandy.

"John, you look tired," Dora said. "Well, you usually look tired, but tonight you look *beat*. Are you getting enough sleep?"

He shrugged. "Not as much as I'd like. Did you know that in one eight-hour period over New Year's Eve there were thirteen homicides in New York. Ten by gunshot."

"That's terrible."

"We can't keep up with it. That's why I don't give the Starrett thing the time I should be giving it. I'm depending on you to help me out."

"I'll try," she said faintly, feeling guilty because of the things she hadn't told him. "Don't you get days off? A chance to recharge your batteries?"

"Yeah, I get days off occasionally. But they don't really help. I keep thinking about the cases I'm handling, wondering if I'm missing anything, figuring new ways to tackle them."

"You've got to relax."

"I know. I need a good, long vacation. About a year. Either that or a good woman."

She nodded. "That might help."

"You?" he said.

She tried a smile. "I told you; I'm taken."

"One of these days you'll be leaving New York—right? Whether the Starrett thing is cleared up or not. Whether the insurance claim is approved or not. You'll be going home to Hartford. Correct?"

"That's right."

"So we could have a scene while you're here, knowing it's not going to last forever. Who'd be hurt?"

She shook her head. "That's not me."

"Oh Red," he said, "life is too short to be faithful. You think your husband is faithful?"

She lifted her chin. "I think he is. But it's really his decision, isn't it? If he's going to cheat on me because he's a man or because he's Mario—that's his choice. No way can I affect it."

"Would it kill you to learn he's been cheating?"

She pondered a moment. "I don't know how I'd feel. It wouldn't *kill* me, but I'd probably take it hard."

"But you'd forgive him?"

"I probably would," she said.

"And if things were reversed, he'd probably forgive you."

"Probably," Dora said, "but I don't want to find out. Look, John, you said life is too short to be faithful. But I think the shortness of life is all the more reason to try to make it something decent. I see an awful lot of human corruption on my job—not as much *violent* corruption as you see, thank God—so I want to try as hard as I can to be a Girl Scout. Maybe it's because I want to prove I'm superior to the creeps I deal with. Maybe it's because if I make the one little slip voluntarily, it'll be a weakening and the first small step down a steep flight of stairs. Whatever, I want to live as straight as I can—which can be a mighty tough assignment at times."

"Is this one of them?" he asked. "You and me?"

She nodded dumbly.

He finished his drink, rose, and pulled on his damp coat. He looked at her so sadly that she embraced him and tried to kiss his cheek. But he turned to meet her lips and, despite her resolve, she melted. They clung tightly together.

"You better go," she said huskily, pulling away. "Give me a break."

"All right," he said. "For now."

After he was gone, she locked the door and paced up and down, hugging her elbows. She thought of what he had said and what she had said—and what she *might* have said, and what the result of that would have been.

She knew she should dig her library research out of the closet and get back to trying to solve the puzzle it contained. But she could not turn her thoughts away from her personal puzzle: what to do about this weary, attractive man who for all his flip talk was serious. Yes, yes, he was a *serious* man and fully aware that he was on his way to burnout.

"And who appointed *you* his nurse?" she asked herself aloud.

23

Mrs. Olivia Starrett and Father Brian Callaway sat at the long dining room table and waited silently, with folded hands, while Charles served tea. He was using bone china from Starrett Fine Jewelry in their exclusive Mimosa pattern.

He offered a tray of assorted pastries from Ferrara, then left the platter on the table and retired, closing the door softly behind him.

"Very distressing news indeed, Olivia," Father Brian said, adding cream and sugar to his tea. "You must have been devastated."

"I was," Mrs. Starrett said, "and I am. We have *never* had a divorce in our family, on either side."

"Has he spoken to Eleanor yet?"

"Not to my knowledge. He said he wanted to tell me first. Clayton is a good son."

"Yes," Callaway said. "Dutiful. Was he asking for your approval?"

"Not exactly. He did say that if I forbade it, he would remain married to Eleanor. But I cannot order him to continue what he calls a loveless marriage. The poor boy is obviously suffering. Do have an éclair."

"I think I shall; they look delicious. And how do you feel about his marrying Helene Pierce if the divorce goes through?"

"And I think I shall have an anise macaroon. Why, I believe Helene is a lovely, personable young lady, but much too young for Clayton. However, he feels the age difference is of little importance. And I must confess I have a selfish motive for wanting Clayton remarried, to Helene or any other woman of his choice. Before I pass over, I would like to hold a grandchild in my arms. Is it wicked of me to think of my own happiness?"

He reached across the table to pat one of her pudgy hands. "Olivia, you are incapable of being wicked. And your desire for a grandchild is completely natural, normal, and understandable. Eleanor cannot have another child?"

"Cannot or will not," Mrs. Starrett said sorrowfully. "She has never fully recovered from the passing of little Ernie. Do help yourself to more tea, Father."

"What a tragedy," he said, filling their cups. "But pain, sadness, and passing are all parts of the holy oneness. We must accept them and indeed welcome them as a test of our faith. For from the valley of despair the soul emerges renewed and triumphant. Do try a napoleon; they're exquisite."

"But so fattening!" she protested.

"No matter," he said, smiling at her. "You are a very regal woman, Olivia."

"Thank you," she said, glowing with pleasure. "Father, may I ask a favor?"

"Of course," he said heartily. "Anything you wish."

"I suggested to Clayton that he might consult a marriage counselor or speak to you before his decision becomes final. If there is any way at all the marriage can be saved, I must try it. Would you be willing to talk to Clayton and give him the benefit of your experience and spirituality?"

"I would be willing," Callaway said cautiously, "but would he?"

"Oh, I'm sure he would," Olivia said warmly. "Especially if you told him it was my express wish that the two of you get together and try to find a solution to this problem."

Callaway nibbled thoughtfully on a slice of panettone. "I gather that the solution you prefer is that the marriage be preserved?"

"That is my preference, yes. But if, in your opinion, the happiness of both Clayton and Eleanor would be better served by a divorce, then I'll accept that. I trust your judgment, Father, and will agree to whatever you think is best."

"It is an awesome responsibility, Olivia, but I shall do what I can. May I tell Clayton that you have told me all the details of your conversation with him?"

"Of course."

"Then I'll see what can be done. I agree with you, dear lady, that marriage is a sacred trust and those vows may only be broken for the most compelling reasons. We were put on this earth to nurture one another, to *share,* and every effort must be made to keep intact that holy oneness."

"I knew I could count on your understanding, Father," Mrs. Starrett said. "You're such a comfort. Now do have more tea and perhaps a slice of the torte. I believe it's made with Grand Marnier."

When Brian Callaway departed from the Starrett apartment, he paused a moment in the outside corridor to loosen his belt a notch. He then descended to the lobby and used a public phone to call Clayton at Starrett Fine Jewelry. It was almost 4:30 and Callaway guessed the man would be ready to leave his office.

Clayton was cordial enough, and when the Father asked for a meeting as soon as possible, to discuss a personal matter of "utmost importance," he agreed to meet Callaway at the bar of the Four Seasons at five o'clock or a little later.

"What's this all about?" he asked curiously.

"I prefer not to discuss it on the phone," the Father replied in magisterial tones.

He was the first to arrive and quickly downed a double vodka. He then ordered a plain tonic water and was sipping that when Clayton Starrett appeared, smiling broadly. The two men shook hands. Clayton ordered a gin martini.

"I'm afraid I'll have to make this short," Clayton said. "We have another charity benefit tonight, and I have to go home to dress."

The Father nodded. "I'll be brief," he promised. "I've just come from having tea with your mother. She asked me to meet with you. She informed me of your intention to divorce Eleanor and hopes I may persuade you to change your mind."

Clayton stared at him for a startled moment, then drained his martini. "Mother told you everything I said to her?" he asked hoarsely.

Callaway nodded. "She did. And gave me permission to tell you that she had. Clay, this is very embarrassing for me.

I really have no desire to intrude on your personal affairs, but I could hardly reject your mother's request."

"Did she also tell you I want to marry Helene Pierce?"

"She told me. Clay, what's the problem between you and Eleanor?"

The younger man took a gulp of his fresh drink. "A lot of problems, Father. I guess the big one is sex—or the lack thereof. Does that shock you?"

"Hardly," Callaway said. "I guessed that might be it. Eleanor is not an unattractive woman, but compared to Helene . . ." His voice trailed off.

"Exactly," Clayton said. "I want a little joy in my life."

"That's understandable. But what if you ask Eleanor for a divorce and then Helene turns you down? Your mother said you told her you haven't even hinted to Helene about the way you feel."

Starrett turned his glass around and around, looking down at it. "That wasn't precisely true. I have told Helene about the way I feel about her and what I plan to do."

"And what was her reaction?"

"I don't know why I'm telling you all this. I hope I can depend on your discretion."

"I assure you this conversation has all the confidentiality of a confessional booth."

"Some booth," Clayton said, looking around at the crowded, noisy bar. "Well, if you must know, Helene will marry me the moment the divorce is a done deal."

"She told you that?"

"Not in so many words, but I'm positive that's the way she feels. Even if the divorce takes a year, Helene is willing to wait. After all, it means status and financial security for her."

"It does indeed," Callaway said. "I think I'll have another drink if you don't mind. Perhaps a straight vodka on ice this time."

"Of course," Clayton said, and summoned the bartender. "Father, I appreciate your efforts—I know you mean well—but there's no way you can change my mind."

"I didn't expect to."

"How did mother sound when she told you about it. Is she still upset?"

"She is, and somewhat confused. She wants you to be happy, and she hopes to have grandchildren someday, but the very idea of a divorce in the family disturbs her. And, of course, she's aware of the distress Eleanor will suffer."

"So mother really hasn't made up her mind?"

"Not really. As a matter of fact, she said she would be willing to accept whatever recommendation I make."

Clayton's laugh was tinny. "In other words," he said, "my fate is in your hands."

"Yes," the Father said, and took a swallow of his vodka, "you might say that. My main aim in this affair is not to cause your mother any unnecessary pain. She is a splendid woman and has made very generous contributions to the Church of the Holy Oneness."

As he said this, Callaway turned to look directly into Clayton's eyes. "Very generous contributions," he repeated.

The two men, their stare locked, were silent a moment.

"I see," Clayton said finally. "You know, Father, I feel somewhat remiss in not having offered any financial support to your church in the years I've known you."

"It's never too late," the older man said cheerfully. "The Church of the Holy Oneness is constantly in need of funds.

For instance, we hope to enlarge the church kitchen so that we may provide food to more of the unfortunate homeless. But at the moment that seems just a dream. I have obtained estimates and find it would cost at least ten thousand dollars to build the kind of facility we need."

Clayton had a fit of coughing, and the Father had to pound him on the back until he calmed enough.

"Of course," Callaway continued blandly, "I realize ten thousand is a large donation for any one individual to make. But perhaps a large New York corporation might be willing to contribute to the welfare of the city's poor and hungry."

"Yes," Clayton said, much relieved, "that makes sense. Would you be willing to accept a ten-thousand-dollar contribution from Starrett Fine Jewelry, Incorporated?"

"Gladly, my son, gladly," Callaway said. "And bless you for your generosity. The donation, of course, would be tax-deductible. And when may I expect the check?"

"I'll have it cut and mailed tomorrow. You should have it by the end of the week. And when do you plan to give mother your recommendation on my divorce?"

Father Callaway smiled benignly. "By the end of the week," he said.

24

Eleanor and Clayton Starrett sat at a round table for eight, and directly across from Clayton was Bob Farber's new wife. She was a petite young woman wearing a strapless gown of silver lamé, but all he could see above the starched tablecloth were the bare top of her bosom, bare shoulders and arms, bare neck, and head topped with a plaited crown of blond hair. It was easy to imagine her sitting there absolutely naked, amiably chatting with her husband, laughing, her sharp white teeth nibbling a shrimp.

He tried not to stare but, uncontrollable, his gaze wandered back. She seemed to him soft, warm, succulent. And beside him sat his hard, cold, bony wife.

He dreamed of the day when he might be seen in public with his new wife, Helene. He would wear her proudly: a badge of honor. Her youth, beauty, and sexuality would prove his manhood and virility. What a conquest Helene would be. What a trophy!

His wife kicked his shin sharply under the table. "You're

191

allowed to blink occasionally, you know," she said in a low, venomous voice, smiling for all the other diners to see. "You keep staring like that and your eyeballs will fall into your soup."

"What are you talking about?" he said, injured.

Eleanor paid him no more attention, for which he was thankful. He sneaked continual peeks at Mrs. Farber and let his fantasies run amok. The candlelight gave her flesh a rosy glow, and he dreamed of Helene, a fireplace, a bear-skin rug.

The remainder of the party was endured only by drinking too much wine. At least, he told himself, he had sense enough not to dance. Eleanor was a miserable dancer, stiff and unrhythmic, and Clayton didn't dare ask Mrs. Farber lest he might suddenly become frenzied, wrestle her to the floor, and then . . . He shook his head. He could, he reflected gloomily, get twenty years for what he was thinking. Just for *thinking* about it.

He put his wineglass aside and rushed out onto the terrace. He stood there, breathing deeply of the cold night air, until his brain cleared and his ardor cooled. Then he was able to think rationally, more or less, and felt frustrated that so much time—perhaps a year!—must elapse before his dreams might be realized.

Eleanor was silent on the ride home, and so was he. They remained silent when they were alone in their suite, and finally this embittered silence convinced him that now was the moment. If he was going to do it, then *do* it. So, as she was removing her jewelry, he said, almost casually, "Eleanor, I want a divorce."

Her reaction was totally unexpected. He had thought she might faint, scream, weep, or at least express disbelief.

192

Instead, she nodded, continued to take off her jewels, and said coolly, "It's Helene Pierce, isn't it?"

"What?" he said, aghast. "What are you talking about?"

She stopped what she was doing and turned to face him. "You're really brainless, Clay—you know that? I knew it before we were married, and nothing you've done since has changed my mind."

"I swear to you," he said hotly, "Helene and I have never—"

"Oh, cut the bullshit," she interrupted in a tone of great disgust. "You've been banging her since the day you met. Do you take me for a complete idiot? I've seen the way you look at her. The same way you looked at Bob Farber's new wife tonight. Is that what gave you the idea, Clay?"

"I'm telling you there's nothing between Helene and me."

"Laughing at her feeble jokes," Eleanor went on relentlessly. "Agreeing with all her stupid opinions. Rushing to help her on with her coat. Any excuse to touch her. There's no fool like an old fool, Clay."

"I'm not old," he shouted at her. "And you're dead wrong about all those things. I was just trying to be a good host."

"Oh sure," his wife jeered. "That's why you made certain you sat next to her every time she came to dinner. Playing a little kneesy, Clay? Listen, don't ever get the idea that the wife is the last to know. The wife is the *first* to know. When her rotten husband starts being extra pleasant and accommodating. When he starts buying clothes too young for him and gets facials. That's you, Clay. You're really a moron if you think I haven't known what's been going on. Sure, you can have a divorce, sonny boy, but it's going to cost you an arm and a leg, now and forever."

"Believe me," he said wrathfully, "whatever it costs, it'll be worth it to dump a sour, dried-up hag like you."

Still she would not weep. "Oh, Helene will marry you," she said, showing her teeth in a mirthless grin. "That greedy bitch has a bottom-line mentality. I give it a year, and then she'll walk. That's *another* alimony check every month, Clay. Then you'll find a new conversation piece— and I do mean *piece*— and do it again, and keep on doing it until you grow up, which will be never. You're a victim of your glands, Clay."

"Just have your attorney contact Arthur Rushkin in the morning," he said stiffly.

"With pleasure," his wife said. "Before I get through with you, you'll be lucky to have fillings in your teeth. Did you tell your mother about this?"

"Yes."

"Poor Olivia," she said. "She's the one I feel sorry for. She's had more than her share of troubles lately. But she's a tough lady; she'll survive. I'm sure she already knew her only son was short-changed in the brains department. Now I'm going to bed, Clay, and I think it would be best if you slept somewhere else."

He was outraged. "Where am I going to go at this time of night?" he demanded.

"You can go to hell," Eleanor spat at him. "You miserable shit!"

25

Turner Pierce paced about Helene's apartment, head lowered, hands clasped behind him.

"My God, you're antsy," Helene said. "Calm down; it's only Sid."

"I have bad vibes about this," he said. "I reminded him we had agreed on no private meetings unless there was an emergency. He said this was an emergency, but he sounded so damned smug. I don't like the way he sounded."

"He's such a scamp," Helene said.

"A *scamp?*" Turner repeated. "Darling, the man is an out-and-out crook—and a slimy crook at that."

"It takes one to know one," she said, and he turned to make certain she was smiling. She was.

He sat down on the couch, took a swallow of his Stolichnaya. "At least we don't promise suckers everlasting life in the holy oneness. Now that's slimy."

"Yes," she said, still smiling, "we do have our standards, don't we. Did I ever tell you Sid has the hots for me?"

"That was obvious in KC. Did he ever make a move on you?"

"Once," she said, not smiling now. "I told him what I'd do to him if he tried anything. He backed off."

Turner glanced at his watch. "If he's not here in ten minutes, I'm splitting. I have a date with Felicia tonight."

"Where are you going?"

"Who said we're going anywhere?" he said.

"Have you figured a way to stall her?"

"I have, but you don't want to know it, do you?"

"Not really."

"What about Clayton?"

"I can handle him," she said. "He's pussy-whipped. All we want is another year—right?"

He nodded. "That should do it."

The phone rang and Helene picked it up. "Yes? That's correct. Send him up, please. Thank you." She hung up. "That was the concierge. Sid's on his way up."

"I'm not looking forward to this," Turner said.

The first thing Father Brian Callaway did when he entered the apartment, even before he removed his hat and coat, was to rip off his clerical collar. "That damn thing is going to cut my throat one of these days," he said.

"We should be so lucky," Helene said, and Sidney Loftus laughed.

"What a kidder you are," he said. "What're you guys drinking?"

"Stoli rocks," Turner said.

"Sounds good to me," Loftus said, rubbing his palms together. "With a splash of water, please."

Helene rose, sighing, and went into the kitchen. Sid sat down heavily on an armchair. The two men looked at each other with wary smiles.

"How's the church doing?" Turner asked.

Loftus flipped a palm back and forth. "Not hellacious but adequate," he said. "The take is good but I've got to live in that shithouse on Twentieth Street, kip in the back room, and ladle out slop to a bunch of crumbums."

"Why don't you move?"

The other man shook his head. "No can do. It's the reverse of a flash front, y'see. Living in that dump proves my spirituality. I couldn't live in a Park Avenue duplex and plead poverty, now could I?"

"Image-building," Turner said.

"You've got it," Sid said, nodding. "Very important in our game, as you well know. Thank you, my dear," he said, taking the glass from Helene. He raised it. "Here's to crime," he toasted. But he was the only one who drank.

"Sid," Turner said, "I've got a meeting to get to. What's this big emergency you mentioned?"

Loftus crossed his knees. He adjusted the crease in his trousers. He leaned back. He took a pigskin case from an inner pocket. He extracted a long cigarillo carefully. He lighted up slowly.

"An impressive performance," Turner said. "Keep it up and I'm going to waltz out of here. Now what's on your mind?"

"Business, business," Sidney said, shaking his head. "With you it's always business. You never take time to smell the flowers. Very well, I'll be brief. You know, of course, that Clayton Starrett is divorcing Eleanor."

"Who told you that?" Helene demanded.

He looked at her, amused. "Olivia," he said. "She tells Father Brian Callaway everything."

"My God," Turner said, "you're not porking the woman, are you?"

"Oh, dear me, no," Loftus said. "I am her confidant, her father confessor. She dotes on me."

"You've got a sweet little scam going there," Turner said.

Sid shrugged. "To each his own," he said. "And Olivia also told me that as soon as Clayton can give his wife the boot, he plans to marry Helene." He turned to her. "Congratulations, my dear," he said. "May all your troubles be little ones."

"Stuff it," she told him.

He smiled and took a swallow of his drink. "Too much water," he said. "Now this is the way I figure it . . . Clayton has told you, Helene, of his impending divorce and has already proposed. I'm sure you've discovered that Clayton is not the brightest kid on the block. He's easily manipulated, and I'm guessing that you'll play him along until his divorce comes through, and then you'll take a walk. Am I correct in my assumptions?"

Helene started to reply, but Turner held up a hand to silence her. "Suppose you are," he said to Loftus. "What's it got to do with you? Where do you come in?"

"Why," the other man said, "it seems to me unjust that only you two should profit from this unique situation. And profit mightily, I may add. After all, I was the one who introduced you to the Starrett family. Surely I deserve a reward."

Turner nodded. "I figured it would be something like that," he said, "you're such a greedy bugger. And if I was to tell you to go take a flying fuck at a rolling doughnut, what would be your reaction, Sid?"

Loftus sighed. "I would have to give the matter serious consideration. It's possible my decision would be that it was my bounden duty, as spiritual advisor to Olivia, to inform her of certain details in the background and history of you two charmers."

"Blackmail," Helene said flatly.

Loftus made a mock shudder. "That's such an ugly word, dearie," he said. "I prefer to think of it as a finder's fee. For helping you aboard the gravy train."

Turner smiled coldly. "You're bluffing, Sid," he stated. "It works both ways. We might find it necessary to tell the Starretts about *your* history."

"Would you really?" Loftus said, beaming. He took another swallow of his vodka. "To save you the trouble, I should tell you that Olivia is already aware of the indiscretions of my past. Not *all* of them, of course, but most. I told her, and she has forgiven me. Y'see, these religious mooches just love repentant sinners. They put their heaviest trust in the lamb who has strayed from the fold and then returned."

Turner said, "I underestimated you, Sid."

"People sometimes do," Loftus said complacently, "and end up paying for it."

"And what do you feel would be a reasonable finder's fee?"

"Oh, I thought fifty grand is a nice round number."

"Fifty thousand!" Helene cried. "Are you insane?"

"I don't believe I'm ready to be committed," Sid said, then laughed at his own wit. "Actually, Helene, it is not an outrageous request, considering what you have taken and will take from Clayton before the divorce is finalized. And I haven't even mentioned your split, Turner, from that lovely finagle at Starrett Fine Jewelry. No, I don't consider fifty thousand unreasonable."

"In cash, I suppose," Turner said bitterly.

"Not necessarily, old boy. A donation to the Church of the Holy Oneness would do the trick. It's tax-deductible, you know."

"Uh-huh," Turner said. "You will allow us a little time to consider your proposal, won't you?"

"Of course," Loftus said heartily. "I didn't expect an immediate answer. I should think a week would be sufficient time to arrive at the only rational decision you can make. Thank you for the refreshment."

He rose and took up his hat, coat, and clerical collar. The Pierces remained seated. Sid nodded at them affably and started to leave. Then he turned at the door.

"Remember," he said with a ghastly smile, "no pain, no gain."

Then he was gone.

"I think I need another drink," Helene said.

"Me too," Turner said. "I'll get them."

She lighted another cigarette while he went into the kitchen. She looked with amazement at the ashtray filled with cigarettes they had both half-smoked and then stubbed out during Sid Loftus' shakedown.

Turner came back with the drinks. They sat close together on the couch and stretched out their long legs.

"You were right," Helene said. "He *is* slimy. Turner, couldn't we tip off the buttons about that phony church of his?"

"Negative," Turner said. "He'd know immediately who had ratted on him and cop a plea by giving them the Starrett Jewelry job. We can't risk that."

"We're not going to pay him, are we?"

"No way," he said. "If we did, it would just be a down payment. He'd bleed us dry."

"So?" she said. "What are our options?"

He turned to stare at her. "Not many," he said. "Only one, in fact. We've worked too hard to split our take with a bastard like Sid."

She nodded. "Could Ramon handle it?" she asked him.

"He could, but I don't want to ask him. First of all, it's a personal thing, and Ramon has no need to know about you and Clayton. Second, it would give him too much of an edge on me. I'm afraid we'll have to handle this ourselves, babe. You willing?"

"Hell, yes!" she said, and he kissed her.

26

Dora Conti figured she'd spend the day on Jewelry Row—West 47th Street between Fifth and Sixth—talking to merchants and salespeople, hoping to find answers to some of the questions nagging her. She was heading for the door when her phone rang, and she went back to answer it. The caller was Gregor Pinchik, the computer maven.

"Hiya, lady," he said. "Listen, I'm in my new place, my hardware is all hooked up, and after I check it out I'll be ready to roll. Probably by tomorrow. Meanwhile I've been making a lot of phone calls, trying to get a line on that Turner and Helene Pierce you gave me."

"Any luck?" she asked.

"Maybe yes, maybe no. There's a hacker in Dallas who's a good friend of mine. I've never met him, but we been talking on computers for years. He's paralyzed and works his hardware with a thing he holds between his teeth. You wouldn't believe how fast he is. Anyway, I asked him about this Turner Pierce, gave him the physical description and all, and he says it sounds like a young hustler who was operating in Dallas almost ten years ago. This guy's name was Thomas Powell, but the initials are the same so I figured it might be our pigeon. What do you think?"

"Could be," Dora said cautiously. "Wrongos who change their name usually stick to the same initials so they don't have to throw away their monogrammed Jockey shorts."

Pinchik laughed. "You're okay, lady," he said.

"What was this Thomas Powell up to?"

"Dallas hackers called him Ma Bell because his specialty was telephone fraud. He started out by developing a cheap whistle that had the same frequency the phone company used to connect long distance calls. You blew the whistle into a pay phone and you could talk to Hong Kong as long as you liked. He sold a lot of those whistles. Then, when the phone company got hip to that and changed their switching procedure, this Thomas Powell started making and selling blue boxes. Those are gadgets that give off tones that bypass the phone company's billing system and let you make free long distance calls. Listen, the guy was talented, no doubt about it."

"Didn't they ever nab him?"

"My pal says he always stayed one step ahead of the law. For instance, he never sold the whistles or blue boxes to the end-user; he always sold to a crooked wholesaler who sold to crooked retailers who sold to the crooked customers. Powell was always layers away from the actual fraud. By the time the cops traced the merchandise back to him, he was gone."

"Where to? Does your friend know?"

"He talked to a couple of local hackers and called me back. One guy says he heard that Thomas Powell took off for Denver when things got too hot for him in Dallas. I have some good contacts in Denver, and as soon as my machinery is up to speed I'm going to try to pick up Ma Bell's trail there. Okay?"

"Of course," Dora said. "It may turn out to be a false alarm, but it's worth following up. Did your Dallas friend say anything about Helene Pierce?"

"Nope. He says this Thomas Powell was a handsome stud with a lot of women on the string, but no one special. And no one in Dallas knew he had a sister; they thought he was a loner."

"Keep after him," Dora said, "and let me know if anything breaks."

"You got it, lady," Pinchik said.

27

The bistro was on 28th Street between Lexington and Third, and nothing about it was attractive. The plate glass window needed a scrub, the rolled-up awning had tatters, and one pane of beveled glass in the scarred door had cracked and was patched with adhesive tape. Inside, it was obvious the designer had striven for intimacy and achieved only gloom.

Sidney Loftus strolled in and looked about curiously. He was wearing a tweed sport jacket and flannel slacks under his trench coat, and the Father Callaway collar was missing. Instead, a silk foulard square was knotted rakishly at his throat. He saw Helene Pierce seated alone in a back booth, lifted a hand in greeting, and sauntered slowly toward her. Only two of the dozen tables in the restaurant were occupied and, except for Helene's, the eight booths were empty.

"Good evening, luv," Sid said lightly. He hung his coat on a wall hook and slid into the booth opposite her. "What an elegant dump. I can't believe you dine here."

"I don't," Helene said. "Probably instant gastritis. But the drinks are big. I'm sticking to Tanqueray vodka."

"Sounds good to me," Loftus said. He signaled a waiter, pointed to Helene's glass, held up two fingers. "I was surprised to hear from you," he said. "I figured Turner might call, but not you."

"I thought we should get together," she said, looking at him directly. "In some place that Turner isn't likely to visit and where you wouldn't be recognized."

"My, my," he said, "that does sound mysterious. Then Turner doesn't know we're meeting?"

"No, he doesn't."

"Uh-huh," Sid said, and didn't speak while the dour, flat-footed waiter served their drinks, placing the glasses on little paper napkins that had a black Scottie printed on the front.

"Charming," Loftus said, holding up the napkin with his fingertips. "Real class. Well, whatever your motives, dearie, I'm happy to have a drink with you without Turner being present. Where is the lad tonight?"

"If you must know," she said, "he's out of town trying to raise fifty thousand bucks: your finder's fee."

Loftus sampled his drink. "Good," he pronounced. "Not quite chilled enough, but good. I can't believe raising fifty grand will be a problem. I'm sure the two of you have the funds available."

"I don't think you fully understand, Sid," Helene said earnestly. "Those 'mighty profits' you mentioned have yet to be realized. I admit the potential is there, but so far the actual receipts have been anemic. Clayton pays my rent and he's given me a few pinhead diamonds, but that's about it. The business at Starrett Fine Jewelry will pay off eventually—no doubt about it—but right now the returns are practically nil. Don't get me wrong, I'm not pleading poverty, but Turner will have to get a loan to come up with the fifty G's. And that means heavy vigorish, of course."

Sid took another sip of his drink and smiled bleakly. "Don't tell me you invited me to haggle over the price, Helene. Haggling is so demeaning, don't you think?"

"No," she said, "no haggling. Turner will come up with the fifty thousand. We don't have much choice, do we?"

"No choice at all," he agreed.

"But Turner expects some of that to come out of my take," she said stonily. "I don't like that. Which is why I wanted to talk to you privately."

"No disrespect intended, luv, but you don't mind if I have the teensiest-weensiest suspicion that Turner may have sent you to set me up."

"Listen to my proposition first," she advised, "and then make up your mind."

"I'm all ears," he said, smiling, and summoned the waiter for another round.

They waited silently while their fresh drinks were brought and the waiter left. Then Helene leaned across the table. She was wearing a V-necked sweater of heavy wool in periwinkle blue, and as she leaned forward the neckline gaped and he could see tawny skin, the softness of her unbound breasts.

"Tell me the truth, Sid," she said, "what do you *really* think of me?"

He tried a smile that failed. "Why, I think you're an extremely attractive young woman. Beautiful, in fact. With all the equipment to make an old man forget his years and dream of pawing up the pea patch."

"You're not an old man, Sid," she said impatiently, "and cut out the physical stuff. You've been around the block twice; what's your personal opinion of who I am and how I operate?"

He started slowly and carefully. "I think you're a very shrewd lady with more than your share of street smarts. I think you have a heavy need for the lush life. Ambitious. Money-hungry. With the morals of an alley cat."

She burst into laughter, tossed her head back; her long hair flung out in a swirl. "You've got me pegged," she said. "I plead guilty."

"There's nothing to feel guilty about," he told her. "You're the female equivalent of Turner, or me, or any other shark in the game. It's just a little unusual to find those characteristics in a woman. But I'm not condemning you. *Au contraire,* sweetie pie."

"As long as you know," she said.

"Know what?" he asked, puzzled.

"What my motives are. I told you I resent the fact that some of your finder's fee is going to come out of my poke. I don't like that. I've worked too long on Clayton Starrett to turn over my take without trying to protect it. I also know you have eyes for me. You proved that in Kansas City."

"So I did," he admitted, "and you gave me the broom."

"You still feel the same way?"

He looked at her approvingly. "Could be. What's on your mind, luv?"

"As long as you know it's not mad, carefree lust."

"That's a laugh," he said.

"It would be strictly a business deal," she said, looking steadily into his eyes. "My chance of getting back some of my contribution to your finder's fee. Shocked?"

"Hardly," he said, returning her stare. "It's in character. You're a tough lady, Helene."

"Tough?" she said. "You know any other way to survive?"

"No," he said, "I don't. So what you're getting at in your oblique way is that you'd like a kickback from what Turner pays me. For favors granted. Have I got it right?"

"You've got it right."

"And what size kickback were you planning to ask for?"

She leaned forward again. The sweater neckline widened. "I haven't even thought of it. I just wanted to try the concept with you. If you turned me down, that's it. If you're willing to play along, then we can work out the details. I'm a reasonable woman."

He laughed. "And I'm a reasonable man. We're two of a kind, we two. It's an interesting idea, Helene. Dangerous but interesting. If Turner ever finds out, we're both dead."

"You think I don't know that? But I'm willing to take the risk. Are you?"

He looked down at his drink, moved it in slow circles over the tabletop. He looked up again at the slim column of her bare throat and caught his breath.

"I might be willing to take a flier," he said. "But then we're faced with the problem of logistics. Specifically, where and when?"

"I can hardly see us checking into the Waldorf, can you?" she said. "Or any other Manhattan hotel or motel. Either of us might be seen and recognized. And it can't be my apartment. I think Clayton is paying off the concierge to keep track of my visitors. I just can't chance it. That only leaves your place."

"My place?" he protested. "It's an armpit."

"I'm sure I've seen worse," she said, then finished her

211

drink. "Let's go there now and clinch the deal. This one will be a freebie to convince you that you're making a smart move."

"It's practically a monk's cell," he warned her.

"That might be fun," she said.

He surrendered completely. "It will be," he assured her.

28

Arthur Rushkin had mentioned casually that after going over the computer printout, he had been "somewhat surprised" by the quantity of gold being traded by Starrett Fine Jewelry. Instead of being surprised, Dora thought grimly, he should have been shocked. But then the attorney hadn't spent a damp day doing research on gold in the public library, and he hadn't schmoozed with the shrewd jewelry merchants on West 47th Street.

The reaction of one of them, a tub of lard in a tight plaid suit, was typical. Dora inquired if the average jewelry store could use the weight of gold Starrett was allegedly selling, and he looked at her as if she had just landed in a flying saucer.

"Absolut imposs," he said in an accent she could not identify. "Total out of the ques, my lovely young miss. Never in a mill years or more."

He then went on to explain in his fractured English that the average jewelry shop made none of the items they stocked, but depended on distributors and wholesalers to keep them supplied. If they did repair work, they might keep a small inventory of gold wire, chains, clasps, settings, etc. But these would be 14- or 18-karat alloys, not the fine gold Dora was talking about.

"Then no jewelry store would need pounds or kilos of the stuff?" she asked.

"Ridic," he said. "Utter ridic. You want to build a Stat of Liber, God bless her soul, of pure gold? With that much you tell me, you could do it. But for a small store, not even grains or ounces of the fine. I speak the trut."

"I believe you," she said hastily, and other proprietors and salespersons she talked to told her the same thing.

So on a bright morning she sat in her hotel suite staring moodily at the mess stacked on the cocktail table: the computer printout, her library research, and her spiral notebooks.

She wondered where further investigation of Starrett's gold trading might lead. She questioned what, if anything, it had to do with the murder of Lewis Starrett and the beneficiaries' claim on his life insurance. That, after all, was her prime concern, and even if the gold trading turned out to be illegal but had nothing to do with Lewis Starrett's death, then she was just spinning her wheels.

She was still pondering her wisest course of action when the phone rang.

"H'lo," she said, almost absently.

"Hi, Red," John Wenden said. "I've got good news for you. I think we can drop the Starrett case."

"*What?*" she cried.

"Because if we just wait long enough," he went on, "everyone connected with it will get knocked off."

"John," she said, "what the hell are you talking about?"

"It just came over the Department wire," he said. "Early this morning, Sidney Loftus, also known as Father Brian Callaway, was found murdered in the back room of the Church of the Holy Oneness on East Twentieth Street."

"Oh my God," Dora breathed.

"There goes your favorite suspect in the Starrett kill," Wenden said. "Sorry about that, Red."

"Was he stabbed?" she asked.

"Now how did you guess that? This case has more knives than Hoffritz. Listen, I don't know any of the details, but I'm on my way there now. Will you be in this afternoon?"

"I'll make it a point to be."

"After I find out what went down, I'll give you a call or maybe stop by for a few minutes."

"Stop by," she urged. "I'll pick up some sandwich makings."

"Sounds good to me," he said. "I'm in a salami mood today."

"You'll get it," she promised.

After replacing the phone, she went back to staring at the stack of papers, not seeing them. Her first reaction to the news of Callaway's death was dread at how the killing might affect Mrs. Olivia Starrett. That poor woman had already suffered through the murders of her husband and a close family friend. Now she would have to endure the "passing" of a man who might have been a swindler but who undoubtedly served as her spiritual advisor and, Dora supposed, provided solace and counseling. Callaway's motives might have been venal, but Dora was convinced he was a comfort to Olivia, something she could not obtain from husband or family.

It was two o'clock before Wenden finally showed up, looking as exhausted and disheveled as ever. He stripped off a tatty mackinaw and flopped onto the couch. "I'm bushed," he announced, "and the day's hardly started."

Wordlessly, Dora brought him a cold can of Bud and popped it for him. He drank almost half without stopping, then took a deep breath.

"Thanks, Red. You're looking mighty perky today."

"I don't feel perky," she said. "What happened?"

"He was stabbed four or five times. Chest, stomach, ribs, abdomen. Then, for good measure, his throat was slit. Someone didn't much like the guy. The place was a butcher shop."

"You think it was one of those dopers or derelicts his church feeds down there?"

"No," the detective said, and stirred uncomfortably. "He was lying naked, faceup on his bed. And he was tied up."

"So he couldn't fight?"

Wenden stared at her. "He was spread-eagled. Ankles and wrists tied to the bedposts with silk scarves. Slipknots. He could have pulled loose. It was a sex scene, Red."

She looked at him, expressionless.

"A lot of guys go for that bondage stuff," John said, shrugging. "I've seen kinkier things than that."

"You think he was gay and picked up some rough trade?"

"That was our first thought, but now we're not so sure. It may have been set up to look that way. The crime scene guys are still working, vacuuming the whole joint. We'll know more when we get their report. Hey, I'm hungry. You promised me a sandwich."

"I'm sorry, John. I got so interested in what you were

saying, I forgot. The sandwiches are already made. Salami on rye with hot mustard. And kosher dills."

"Oh yeah," he said, "I can go for that."

She brought out a platter of sandwiches covered with a damp napkin, and the pickles.

"You're not drinking?" he asked her.

"Maybe a diet cola."

"Will you stop it?" he said, almost angrily. "You've got this complex about being too fat."

"It's not a complex; I know I am."

"I don't think so," he said, and began to wolf down one of the thick salami sandwiches.

"John," Dora said, nibbling, "how do you figure this connects with the Starrett and Guthrie homicides?"

"I don't know that it does," he said, then looked up at her. "Do you?"

"Not really," she confessed. "But knives were used in all three."

"Different knives," he told her. "I can't say for sure until the ME does his thing, but I'd guess that the blade used on Callaway was different from the chef's knife that killed Starrett and the stiletto that finished Guthrie. A lot of shivs in this town, kiddo. The weapon of choice. They don't make noise."

"But all three victims *were* connected," she argued. "They knew each other. All were part of the Starrett circle."

He started on a second sandwich. "It could be a serial killer who just happened to pick three targets who were acquainted. I don't believe that for a minute. Or it could be someone with a grudge against the Starrett family and their friends and associates. So he's picking them off one by one."

"Have you put guards on the Starrett apartment?" she asked worriedly.

"Of course. But you know as well as I do how much good that will do. A determined killer can always find a way. And sooner or later, the guards will have to be withdrawn."

"So you *do* think the same person, or persons, is responsible for all three murders?"

"It's a possibility," he admitted. "Is that what you think?"

"To tell you the truth," she said, "I don't know what the hell is going on."

"You and me both," John said, and sat back, sighing. "That hit the spot. This is probably the only solid food I'll have all day."

"Take the leftover sandwiches with you," she said. "I insist."

"You'll get no argument from me," he said with a sheepish grin. "I can use the calories. Listen, after I leave here, I'm going back to Twentieth Street. Callaway's murder wasn't my squeal, but I want to hang around the edges and see if the guys running it come up with anything."

"Like what?"

"They'll check all the trash baskets, garbage cans, and catch basins in the area to see if they can find the knife. And they'll brace all the neighborhood stores, bars, and restaurants—flashing a photo of the dear, departed Father—to ask if he was in last night, and if so, was he with someone."

"John, that'll take days."

"At least," he agreed. "Maybe weeks. But it's got to be done. Hey, you look sad. What's wrong, Red?"

"I am sad," she said. "You know about what? I'm sad

about Sidney Loftus, aka Father Brian Callaway. I know he was a swindler and con man. I know he was taking Olivia Starrett and other religious saps for every cent he could grab. He was *bad*. But I still feel sorry for him, dying that way."

"That's a luxury I can't afford," John said. "Feeling sorry. I let myself feel and I'm no good to the Department."

"I don't believe that."

"Believe it," he insisted. "I'm like a surgeon. He goes to cut out a cancerous tumor, he can't feel sorry for the patient; it would interfere with his job. All he's interested in is if he's getting out the entire malignancy. He's got to think of the person under his knife as a thing. Meat. He can't be distracted by feeling sad or feeling sorry."

"Is that the way you think of people—as things?"

"Only the bad ones. Sid Loftus was a thing, so I can't feel anything toward him. I don't think of *you* as a thing. You know how I feel about you."

"How?" she challenged.

"All the time," he said, and she laughed.

"You're a bulldog, you are," she said.

"It sounds like a line, doesn't it?" Wenden said. "It's not. It's a very, very serious pitch. I think it would make us both happy. All right, so it would be a temporary happiness. Nothing heavy, nothing eternal. Just a great rush that doesn't hurt anyone. Is that so bad?"

"You don't know," she objected. "That it wouldn't hurt anyone. You can't predict."

"I'm willing to take the risk," he said. "Are you?"

She was silent.

"Think about it," he entreated.

"All right," Dora said, "I will."

29

He said his name was Ramon Schnabl, and no one questioned it or even considered inquiring about his antecedents. He was a serious man, and the few people who had heard him laugh wished they hadn't. He was reputed to be enormously wealthy which, considering the nature of his business, was likely.

He was an extremely short, slender man whose suits were tailored in Rome and his shoes, with an invisible build-up, were the creation of a London cobbler. Everything he wore seemed tiny, tight, and shiny, and it was said that the toilet seats in his Central Park South apartment were custom-made as he might fall through a conventional design.

He was not an albino, exactly, for his eyes were dark and there was a faint flush to his thin cheeks. But he was undeniably pale, hair silver-white, skin milky, and even his knuckles translucent. He favored platinum jewelry and double-breasted white suits that accented his pallidness.

He also wore, indoors and out, deeply tinted glasses as if he could not endure bright light or garish colors.

Turner Pierce thought him a dangerous man, quite possibly psychotic. But Helene thought him a fascinating character. What attracted her, she said, was the contradiction between his diminutive size and the menace he projected. Ramon never threatened, but associates were always aware that the power to hurt was there.

His apartment was as colorless as the man himself. The living room had blank white walls, a floor of black and white tiles set in a checkerboard pattern, black leather furniture with stainless steel frames. Over the cold white marble fireplace was the room's sole decorative touch: the bleached skull of an oryx.

Ramon and Turner sat facing each other in matching clunky armchairs. The host had provided glasses of chilled Évian water. He was both a teetotaler and rigidly anti-smoking. At the moment, his guest was wishing fervently for a cigarette and tumbler of iced Absolut.

"Matters are progressing well," Schnabl said in his dry, uninflected voice. "You agree, my friend?"

"Oh yes," Pierce said. "No problems."

"None?" the other man said. "Then tell me why you appear so troubled."

"Do I?" Turner said, wishing he could peer behind the dark glasses and see the eyes that saw so much. He tried a laugh. "Well, you know they say a man has only two troubles in this world: money and women."

"And which is yours?"

"Not money," Pierce said hastily. "No trouble there at all. I have a personal problem with a woman."

"Oh?" Schnabl said. "Surely not Helene, that dear lady?"

Turner shook his head.

"Then it must be Felicia Starrett, Clayton's sister."

Turner nodded, not questioning how Ramon knew. This little man knew *everything.* "Not a serious problem," he assured Ramon. "But she is inclined to be very emotional, very unpredictable."

"A bad combination, my friend. Vindictive?"

"I'm afraid the possibility is there."

"I thought she was dependent on you for her supply."

"She is," Turner said, "but it isn't working out quite as I had planned. She still wants more."

"More?"

"Me," Pierce said, realizing he was giving up an edge but not seeing any alternative.

"I understand, my friend," Ramon said, totally without sympathy. "You have a management problem."

"Yes," Turner said, "something like that."

"Perhaps stronger medicine is called for."

Pierce looked at him, puzzled. "Such as?"

Ramon regarded him gravely for a moment. Then: "I am introducing a new product line. Large crystals of methamphetamine that can be smoked. On the street it is called 'ice.' I believe it may be the preferred recreation of the 1990s; other products will become declassé. The great benefit of ice is that it produces euphoria that lasts twenty-four hours. It might prove to be the answer to your management problem."

"Thank you," Turner Pierce said humbly.

He met Felicia that night. They dined at Vito's, and he smiled at her blather, laughed at her jokes, and held hands when they strolled back to his apartment. A tumescent moon drifted in a cloudless sky, and the whole night seemed swollen with promise: something impending on the wind, something lurking in the blue shadows, ready to pounce, smirking.

"What a hoot," she chattered on. "Clay divorces Eleanor and marries Helene. And you and I tie the knot. One big, happy family! Right, Turner? Am I right?"

"You're right," he said. "We'll be the fearless foursome."

"Love it," she said, squeezing his hand. "The fearless foursome—that's us. We might even have a pas de quatre some night if we all get high enough. Would you go for that?"

"Why not," he said.

She wouldn't even let him pour brandies, but began removing her clothes the moment she was inside the door. But he was deliberately slow, something spiteful in his teasing. He did enjoy her need and his power, meaning to punish for all the trouble she was causing him. But his cruelties only aroused her the more, and she welcomed the pain as evidence of his passion. This woman, he decided, was demented and so trebly dangerous.

Later, he left her on the bed and went into the kitchen for his cognac. He returned to the bedroom carrying the brandy, a glass pipe, a small packet of crystal chunks. She looked at him with dimmed eyes, then struggled upright.

"What's that?" she asked.

"Something new for you," he said. "It's called ice. The latest thing. You smoke it."

"You, too?"

He held up the brandy. "This is my out," he said. "The pipe is yours."

She inspected the crystals. "Ice," she said. "Like diamonds."

"Exactly like diamonds," he told her. "It's the *in* thing. Everything else is declassé."

That's all she had to hear, being a victim of trendiness, and she packed the pipe with trembling fingers, clutching it tightly while he held a match. She took a deep puff and inhaled deeply with closed eyes.

The rush hit her almost immediately. Her eyes popped open, widened, and she sucked greedily at the pipe.

"Good?" he asked her.

She looked at him with a foolish smile and leaned back against the headboard. She continued to fellate the pipe but slowly now, sipping lazily.

He put a palm to her naked shank and was shocked at how fevered her flesh had become. She was burning up.

The crystals were consumed. Turner took the glass pipe from Felicia's limp fingers and set it aside.

Suddenly she began to laugh, convulsed with merriment. Energized, she rose swiftly from the bed, stood swaying a moment, still heaving with laughter. She rushed into the living room, staggering, banging off the walls, and returned just as quickly, before he could move.

"How do you feel?" he asked curiously.

She looked at him, laughter stopped. She pulled him onto the bed with a strength he could not resist.

"I am the world," she proclaimed.

"Of course you are," he agreed.

"The stars," she said. "Planets. Universe. Everything and all."

"And all," he repeated.

She flopped around and crammed his bare toes into her mouth. He pulled away, and again he felt her incredible heat and saw how flushed her face had become. He put a hand to her breast, and the heavy, tumultuous heartbeat alarmed him.

"Are you all right, Felicia?"

She began to gabble incoherently: unfinished sentences, bits of song, names he didn't recognize, raw obscenities. The jabber ceased as abruptly as it had started. He left her like that and went into the kitchen for another brandy.

She was still at it when he returned to the bedroom. But now her face was contorted, ugly, and she was panting. He sat on the edge of the bed and observed her dispassionately, noting the twitching legs, toes curled. She seemed to be winding tighter and tighter, her entire body caught up in a paroxysm.

Suddenly she shouted, so loudly that he was startled and slopped his brandy. Her body went slack and her eyes slowly opened. She stared at him blankly, not seeing him, and he wondered where she was.

"Felicia," he said, "I'm Turner."

"Turner," she repeated, and soft understanding came back into her eyes.

"You're in my apartment," he told her.

She looked at him with love. "Do you want to kill me?" she asked. "You may, if you like."

30

Mrs. Olivia Starrett, wearing a lacy bed jacket, sat propped upright by pillows, a white wicker tray across her lap. And on the tray, tea service and a small plate of miniature croissants, one half-nibbled away.

"He was such a *dear* man," she said, dabbing at her eyes with a square of cambric. "I would be even more desolated than I am if I wasn't inspired by his teaching. Accept all, he said, and understand that pain and suffering are but a part of the holy oneness. Are you sure you don't want a cup of tea, dear?"

"Thank you, no, Mrs. Starrett," Dora said. She sat alongside the canopied bed in a flowered armchair. "You have certainly had more than your share of grief lately. You have my deepest sympathy."

Olivia reached out to squeeze her hand. "How sweet and understanding you are. The passing of Lewis, Sol Guthrie, and Father Brian were sorrows I thought would destroy me. But then I realized that one cannot mourn forever. Does that sound cruel and heartless?"

"Of course not."

"One must continue to cope with life, the problems of the present, and worries for the future." She picked up the half-eaten croissant and finished it. "You told me you have no children?"

"That's correct."

Mrs. Starrett sighed deeply. "They are a blessing and a burden. Have you heard about Clayton? And Eleanor?"

"Heard about them? No, ma'am, I've heard nothing."

Olivia, alternately dabbing at her eyes and taking teeny bites of a fresh pastry, told Dora of her son's impending divorce.

"Eleanor has already moved out," she said.

Then she spoke of Clayton's plan to marry Helene Pierce.

"Much too young for him, I feel," she said. "But I do *so* want a grandchild. Father Callaway, the last time I saw him, told me I am not being selfish."

"He was right," Dora said. "You're not."

"Still . . ." Olivia said, and looked about vaguely. "Sometimes it is difficult knowing the right thing to do. Young people are so independent these days. They think because you are old you must necessarily be senile."

"You are not old, Mrs. Starrett, and you are certainly not senile."

"Thank you, my dear. You are *such* a comfort. Sit with me a while longer, will you?"

"Of course. As long as you like."

"I could never talk to Lewis. Never. Not about important things. He thought I was just chattering on. And he would grunt. I love Clayton, of course. He is my son. But I can't talk to him either. Clayton is lacking. There is no depth to him. I love depth in people, but Clayton is not a serious man. He floats through life. He has never been a leader. Sometimes he lacks sense. Eleanor knew that when she married him. Perhaps that's *why* she married him."

Dora listened to this rambling with shocked fascination. Shocked because she suddenly realized that Mrs. Olivia Starrett was not a flibbertigibbet, not just a soft, garrulous matron. There was a hard spine of shrewdness in her. Despite her religiosity she saw things clearly. She had depth and had been married to a man who grunted.

"Felicia . . ." Mrs. Starrett maundered on. "So unlucky with men. A pattern there. She has taste in clothes, music, art. But not in men. There her taste deserts her. All her beaux have been unsatisfactory. Weaklings or cads. I could see it. Everyone could see it. But not Felicia. The poor thing. So eager. Too eager. Now she is running after Turner Pierce. Oh yes, I know. A man much younger than she. It is not seemly." Her gaze suddenly sharpened. She stared at Dora sternly. "Do you agree?"

"You're right," Dora said hastily. "It's not seemly."

"You are such a bright, levelheaded young lady."

"Thank you, Mrs. Starrett."

"I wish you'd talk to Felicia."

Dora was startled. "Talk to her?"

"About her life, the way she's wasting it."

"But I'm not a close friend."

"My daughter has no close friends," Olivia said sadly. "Not even me. Perhaps she'll listen to you."

"But what could I possibly say to her?"

"Offer advice. Give her the benefit of your experience. Try to steady her down. Felicia has these wild mood swings. Sometimes she frightens me."

"Mrs. Starrett, she may need professional help. A psychotherapist."

"It may come to that," Olivia said somberly, "but not yet, not yet. Oh, she is such a desperate girl. Desperate! But she will not discuss her problems with me. And she refused to talk to Father Callaway. But you are near her age. Perhaps she will confide in you, and you may be able to help her. Will you try?"

"If you want me to," Dora said doubtfully, "but she may resent my prying into her personal affairs."

"She may, but please try. I know she is unhappy, and this business with Turner Pierce worries me. Felicia has been hurt so many times; I don't want her to be hurt again."

"All right, Mrs. Starrett, I'll try."

"It's my family," the older woman said fiercely, "and I must do everything I can to protect them. Even if I think them stupid or wrong, even if they cause me pain, I must protect my children. You do understand that, don't you?"

"Of course," Dora said, rising. "Thank you for giving me so much of your time. I wanted to express personally my condolences at Father Callaway's passing."

"It was sweet of you, and I appreciate it."

"Mrs. Starrett, did Eleanor leave an address or telephone number where she can be reached?"

"She's staying with friends. Charles has the address and phone number. He'll give them to you."

"Thank you. And I'll try to set up a meeting with Felicia."

Mrs. Starrett turned her head away and stared at the thin winter light at the window. "She didn't come home last night," she said in a whispery voice.

No one awaited Dora in the foyer, so she walked back to

230

the kitchen. Charles and Clara Hawkins were seated at an enameled table, drinking coffee and sharing a plate of what appeared to be oatmeal cookies. Houseman and cook looked up when Dora entered.

"Good afternoon," Dora said briskly."Mrs. Starrett said you could give me the telephone number for Mrs. Eleanor Starrett."

Charles nodded and stood up slowly."I'll fetch it," he said, and left the kitchen. Dora figured he was going to get Olivia's approval before handing over the phone number.

"How are you today, Clara?" she asked brightly.

"Surviving," the woman said, and Dora decided this had to be the most lugubrious couple she had ever met. She wondered if husband and wife ever laughed or even smiled, and she tried to imagine what their sex life must be like. She couldn't.

"Clara," she said, "Detective John Wenden told me you think the eight-inch chef's knife disappeared during the cocktail party on the night Mr. Lewis Starrett was killed. Do you have any idea who might have taken it?"

"No."

"I'm not asking if you know definitely who took it. I don't want you to accuse anyone. I'm just curious about who *might* have taken it."

Clara stared up at her, and Dora saw again that discernible mustache and couldn't understand why in the world this dour woman didn't *do* something about it. A daily shave, for instance.

"I don't name no names," the cook said sullenly.

Dora sighed. "All right," she said, "I'll name the names. You just shake your head no or nod your head yes. Okay?"

Nod.

231

"Was it Clayton Starrett?"

Shake.

"Eleanor Starrett?"

Shake.

"Felicia Starrett?"

Shake.

"Helene Pierce?"

Shake.

"Turner Pierce?"

Shake.

"Father Brian Callaway?"

Nod.

Charles came back into the kitchen, carrying a scrap of paper. He looked at his wife accusingly. "You been shooting off your mouth again?" he demanded.

"She hasn't said a word," Dora told him. "I've been doing all the talking, about what a great chef my husband is."

"She talks too much," he grumbled, and handed over the slip of paper. "That's Mrs. Eleanor's phone number and address. West Side," he added sniffily.

"Thank you, Charles," Dora said. "Now would you get my hat and coat, please; I'm leaving. Nice to see you again, Clara."

"Likewise," Clara said.

Dora hurried back to her hotel, anxious to get to her notebook and record all the details of that surprising conversation with Olivia. Plus what she had learned from Clara's dumb show.

She filled two pages with notes that included all her recollections of what Mrs. Starrett had said and implied about the Clayton-Eleanor-Helene triangle and the

Felicia-Turner relationship. If this entire case was a soap opera, Dora reflected grimly, it had a deadly plot. Too many corpses for laughing.

She went down to the dining room for dinner and ordered a tuna salad, trying to recall if this was her fourth or fifth diet since being assigned to the Starrett claim. Brooding on her futile attempts to lose poundage, she remembered what John Wenden had said about her increasing girth: "More of you to love." What a *nice* man!

She returned to her suite and called him. He wasn't in but she left a message, hoping he might get back to her before midnight. He didn't, so she called Mario. He wasn't home. There was nothing left to do but brush her teeth and go to bed in a grumpy mood, wondering what the hell her men were doing and imagining direful possibilities.

31

It was easy to fake it, with Clayton or any other man, and Helene Pierce had learned to deliver a great performance. She considered herself a "method" actress and her motivation was that growing hoard of unset diamonds.

The dialogue came easily:

"Oh, Clay, you're too much . . . you drive me wild . . . I can't get enough of you . . . Where did you *learn* these things?"

She left him hyperventilating on the rumpled sheets and went into the kitchen to pour fresh drinks from the bottle of Perrier-Jouët he had brought. The guy had good taste, no doubt about it, and there were no moths in his wallet. Helene wanted to play this one very, very carefully and, for once in her life, sacrifice today's pleasure for tomorrow's treasure.

He was sitting up when she returned to the bedroom with the champagne. He was lighting a cigar, but she was even willing to endure that.

"Here you are, hon," she said, handing him the glass.

She lay beside him, leaning to kiss his hairy shoulder. "You are something," she said. "One of these days you'll have to call 911 and have me taken to Intensive Care."

He laughed delightedly, sipped his champagne, puffed his cigar, and owned the world. "I can never get enough of you," he told her. "It's like I've been born again. Oh God, the time I wasted on that bag of bones."

"Eleanor?" she said casually. "What's happening there?"

"Like I told you, she's moved out. My attorney, Arthur Rushkin, doesn't handle divorces but he's put me in touch with a good man, a real pirate who's willing to go to the mat for the last nickel. That's the way things stand now: My guy is talking to her guy. Listen, sweetheart, this is going to take time. Are you willing to wait?"

"After what we just did," she said, looking at him with swimming eyes, "I'll wait forever."

"That's my girl," he said, patting her knee. "Everything will come up roses, you'll see."

He started talking about the way they'd live once they were married. A duplex on the East Side. Cars for each; maybe a Corniche and a Porsche. Live-in servants.

"Younger and more attractive than Charles and Clara," he said.

They'd probably dine out most evenings. Then the theatre, ballet, opera, a few carefully selected charity benefits. A cruise in the winter, of course, and occasional shopping trips to Paris, London, Milan, via the Concorde. They might consider buying a second home, or even a third. Vermont and St. Croix would be nice. World-class interior decorators, naturally. *Architectural Digest* stuff.

As he spun this vision of their future together, Helene

listened intently, realizing that everything he described was possible; he wasn't just blowing smoke. Turner had told her how much Clay was drawing from Starrett Fine Jewelry as salary, annual bonus, dividends, and his share of that deal with Ramon Schnabl.

And Clayton had a million coming in when that claim on his father's insurance was approved. And when his mother shuffled off, he'd be a multi multi. So all his plans for the good life were doable, and she'd be a fool, she decided, to reject it for a more limited tomorrow with Turner.

"How does it sound to you?" Clayton asked, grinning like a little kid who's just inherited a candy store.

"It sounds like paradise," Helene said.

"It will be," he assured her. "You know that old chestnut: 'Stick with me, kid, and you'll be wearing diamonds.' In this case it's true. Which reminds me, I have another chunk of ice for your collection."

"You can give it to me later," she said, taking the cigar from his fingers and putting it aside. "Let's have an encore first. You just lay back and let me do all the work."

When he left her apartment, finally, she had a lovely four-carat trilliant, a D-rated stone that was totally flawless. But before he handed it over, he subjected her to a ten-minute lecture on the four Cs of judging diamonds: color, clarity, cut, and carat weight.

After he was gone, she sprayed the entire apartment with deodorant, trying to get rid of the rancid stink of his cigar. Then she sat down with her fund of diamonds, just playing with them while she pondered her smartest course of action.

Turner was the problem, of course. She had a commitment there, and since the Sid Loftus thing, Turner had an edge that could prove troublesome. But she thought she knew how that could be finessed. She worked out a rough game plan, and as her first move, she phoned Felicia Starrett.

32

He insisted on taking her to a steak joint on West 46th Street.

"It's not a fancy place," he said. "Mostly cops and actors go there. But the food is good, and the prices are right. We'll have a rare sirloin with garlic butter, baked potatoes with sour cream and chives, a salad with blue cheese dressing, and maybe some Bass ale to wash it all down. How does that sound?"

"Oh God," Dora moaned, "there goes my diet."

"Start another one tomorrow," Wenden advised.

It was a smoky tunnel, all stained wood, tarnished brass lamps, and mottled mirrors behind the long bar. The walls were plastered with photos of dead boxers and racehorses, and posters of Broadway shows that had closed decades ago. Even the aproned waiters looked left over from a lost age.

"What have you been up to?" John asked, buttering a heel of pumpernickel.

"Nothing much," Dora said. "I went to see Mrs. Olivia Starrett to tell her how sorry I was about Callaway's death."

"How's she taking it?"

"She was sitting up in bed and looked a little puffy around the gills, but she's coping. She's a tough old lady."

She told the detective some of what she had learned. Some, but not all. Clayton and Eleanor were getting a divorce, and he wanted to marry Helene Pierce. And Felicia Starrett was playing footsie with Turner Pierce.

"Interesting," John said, "but I don't know what it all means—if anything. Do you?"

"Not really. Sounds to me like a game of Musical Chairs."

"Yeah," he said. "You want to hear about the Sid Loftus homicide now or will it spoil your dinner?"

"Nothing's going to spoil my dinner," she said. "I'm famished. If I never see another tuna salad as long as I live, it'll be too soon."

They finished their martinis hastily when the waiter brought big wooden bowls of salad and poured their ales.

"The knife that did him in wasn't like the ones that iced Starrett and Guthrie," Wenden said, going to work on his salad. "It was maybe a three- or three-and-a-half-inch blade. We figure it was a folding pocket knife, a jackknife. There must be jillions of them in the city. The big blade on this one was razor sharp."

"That wasn't in the papers," Dora said.

"We don't tell the media *everything*. Another thing we didn't release was that the crime scene guys and the lab think the perp may have been a woman."

Dora put down her fork and stared at him. "A woman? You're sure?"

"Pretty sure. They vacuumed up a few long hairs and particles of face powder."

"What color hair?"

"Black, but it may have been colored. We sent the hairs to the FBI lab to see if they can definitely ID the color and also what kind of shampoo or hair spray was used, if any."

They were silent while their steaks and baked potatoes were served. Dora looked down at her plate with amazement. "I'll never be able to eat all that."

"Sure you will," Wenden said. "I'm betting on you."

"So it *was* a sex scene?"

"Looks like it started out that way, but that's not how it ended. He hadn't had an ejaculation before he died. Too bad. A loser all around."

Dora ate in silence a few moments, pondering. Then: "Any cigarette butts?"

"Nope," Wenden said. "Just butts from those cigarillos he smoked. But when they took up the floorboards, guess what they found."

"Not Judge Crater?"

"About three grams of high-grade coke."

Dora paused with a forkful of steak half-raised. "You mean he was snorting?"

Wenden nodded. "Recently enough so that there were traces in his urine." He laughed. "What a splendid man of the cloth that old schnorrer was! Does Olivia Starrett still believe in him?"

"She seems to, and I didn't tell her any differently. Not even Callaway's real name or how he died. This steak is something else again, and I'm going to finish every bite."

"I thought you would. It's aged meat. They scrape off the green mold before they broil it."

"I hope you're kidding."

"Sure I am." He sat back and sighed. "Great food, and screw cholesterol. Now I'm going to have coffee and a shot of Bushmills Black, just to put the icing on the cake. How about you?"

"I'll have coffee, but Irish Whiskey is a little raunchy for me."

"Tell you what: Have a half-and-half of Bushmills and Irish Mist on the rocks. You'll love it."

"All right, I'm game. I hope you'll let me pay for all this, John. It'll go on the pad."

"Nope," he said. "It's my turn. You've fed me enough."

"Salami sandwiches," she scoffed. "This is *food.*"

They dawdled over their coffee and postprandial drinks.

"John," she said, "you think Loftus picked up some floozy off the street?"

He shook his head. "No," he said. "I don't see him as a guy who had to rent a hooker. Also, there was loose cash in the back room, credit cards, and some valuable jewelry, including a Starrett wristwatch. A streetwalker would have snaffled the lot. No, I think his playmate was someone he knew. Whoever it was went along with his kinky idea of fun. He couldn't have tied his own wrists to the bedposts."

"And then the party got rough?"

He stared at her. "Doesn't make much sense, does it? But that's the way it looks."

"Did your guys come up with anything at local bars and restaurants?"

"Negative. But as they say in the tabloids, the manhunt is widening."

"Was there any evidence that drugs had been done that night, before he was killed?"

He shook his head again. "The coke we found was in sealed glassine envelopes. There was nothing to indicate coke or anything else had been used. Analysis of his blood showed he had had a few drinks, but he wasn't drunk. How do you like *your* drink?"

She rolled her eyes. "Heavenly. I'd like to fill a bathtub with this stuff, roll around in it, and then drink my way out."

He laughed. "Talk about kinky! More coffee?"

"Maybe a half-cup. You working tonight?"

"No, I'm starting a forty-eighter. And I'm going to sleep all of it away."

"I hope so," Dora said. "You look beat. How do you feel?"

"A hundred percent better than I did two hours ago."

"A rare steak will do that."

"It's really a rare you," he said, looking at her. "You always give me a lift."

He drove her back to the Bedlington and double-parked outside.

"Thanks for a memorable dinner," she said.

"Thanks for sharing the memory."

"You want to come up for a nightcap?" she asked hesitantly.

"I'd love to," he said, "but I'm not going to. I've got a long drive ahead of me, and then I want to hit the sack. Raincheck?"

"Of course."

He turned sideways to face her. He put an arm along the back of her seat, not touching her. But she stiffened and continued to stare straight ahead through the windshield.

"I'll tell you something," he said, his voice sounding rusty. "You may not believe it, but it's the truth. When I first met you—and later, too—I know I pitched you, coming on like a hotrock. I figured a toss in the hay would be nice—why the hell not?"

"John," she said softly.

"No, let me finish. But now it's more than that. I think about you all the time. I dream up excuses to call you or see you, and then I don't do it. You know why? Because I'm ashamed of acting like a schmo by bugging you all the time. And also, I'm afraid of rejection. I've been rejected before and shrugged it off because I didn't give a damn. Now I give a damn. I don't know what I feel about you, I don't know how to label it, but I wasn't lying when I said that just being with you gives me a lift. It's like I'm hooked, and I get a rush every time I see you."

"Maybe it's because we're working together," she said quietly. "People who work in the same office, for instance, or on the same project, develop a special intimacy: shared work and hopes and aims."

"Sure, that's part of it," he agreed. "But I could be a shoe salesman or you could be a telephone operator and I know I'd feel the same way. It's more than just the job. This is something strictly between you and me."

Then she turned to look at him. "Don't think I haven't been aware of it. At first I thought you were just a stud looking for a one-night stand. Wham, bam, thank you, ma'am. But now I think you're telling the truth because my feelings toward you have changed." She laughed nervously. "I can even tell you exactly when it happened: when I suddenly realized I should have bought you a maroon cashmere muffler for Christmas. Nutsy—right? But as I've said many times, I'm married, and as I've said many, many times, happily married."

"And that's the most important thing in your life?"

"It was. Damn you!" she burst out, trying to smile. "You've upset my nice, neat applecart. You're the one who's making me question what really is important to me. I was *sure* before I met you. Now I'm not sure anymore."

They'd never know whether she kissed him first or he kissed her. But they came together on the front seat of that ramshackle car, held each other tightly, clinging like frightened people, and kissed.

He was the first to break away. "I'll take that nightcap now," he said hoarsely.

"No, you won't," Dora said unsteadily. "You'll drive home carefully and grab some Z's. And I'll go up to my bedroom by myself."

"It doesn't make sense," he argued.

"I know," she agreed. "But I need time to figure this out. Good night, darling. Get a good night's sleep."

"Fat chance," he said mournfully, and they kissed just one more time. A quickie.

33

"Hiya, lady. This is Gregor Pinchik."

"Hello, Mr. Pinchik. I'm glad to hear from you again."

"Mr. Pinchik! Hey, you can call me Greg; I won't get sore."

"All right, Greg. And you can call me Dora instead of lady; I won't get sore."

"Sure, I can do that. Listen, this guy you got me tracing, this Turner Pierce—it's really getting interesting."

"You've found out more about him?"

"I'm almost positive it's him. About five years ago or so a hacker shows up in Denver calling himself Theodore Parker. Same initials, T and P—right? Like Thomas Powell in Dallas. But in Denver he's got a wide black mustache just like you described, so I figure it's gotta be him."

"Sounds like it. What was he up to in Denver?"

"Still pulling telephone scams. But now he's selling access codes. Those are the numbers companies issue to their employees so they can call long distance from outside the office and have it billed to the company. Like a salesman on the road can call headquarters and have the charges reversed by punching out his access code."

"How did Theodore Parker get hold of the codes?"

"Oh hell, there are a dozen different ways. You invade a company's computers and pick them up. Or you buy software that dials four-digit numbers in sequence until you hit one that works. Or maybe you steal the salesman's code card. Then you're in like Flynn. It's easier when the company has an 800 number, but you can also get on their lines through their switchboard."

"And he was peddling the codes?"

"That's right. Mostly to college students and soldiers away from home, but also to heavies who made a lot of long-distance calls to places like Bolivia and Colombia and Panama and didn't want to run the risk of having their own phone lines tapped."

"What a world!"

"You can say that again. Anyway, this Theodore Parker had a nice business going. He was even selling the codes to penny-ante crooks who were running what they call 'telephone rooms.' These are places you can go and for a buck or two call anyplace on earth and talk as long as you like. It would all be billed to the company that owned the access codes the crooks bought from Parker."

"Beautiful. And what happened to him?"

"The Denver hackers I contacted told me the gendarmes were getting close, so Theodore Parker skedaddled. For Kansas City. How does that grab you?"

"I love it. Any mention of a woman skedaddling along with him?"

"I struck out there. Everyone says he was a loner, just like in Dallas. Plenty of women, but no one resembling

Helene Pierce the way you described her. That's all I've got so far."

"Greg, I've received your hourly bills and sent them on to the Company. But you didn't list the expense of all the long-distance calls you've been making or your modem time. The Company will pay for that."

"They are. I'm using their access codes."

"You stinker! Did you invade their computers again?"

"Nah. Listen, you can buy a long-distance access code on the street for five or ten bucks. But I didn't even have to spend that. Your Company's access codes are listed on an electronic bulletin board I use. I picked the numbers up from that. Well, I'm going to start on Kansas City now. I'll let you know how I make out."

"Please. As soon as possible."

"Nice talking to you, lady."

Dora hung up smiling and then jotted a précis of Pinchik's information in her notebook. She sat a moment recalling her initial reaction to Turner and Helene Pierce: supercilious people with more aloof pride than they were entitled to. It was comforting to learn that Turner was apparently a two-bit lowlife scrambling to stay one step ahead of the law.

She glanced at her watch, then took a look in the full-length mirror on the bathroom door. She was wearing the one "good" dress she had brought from Hartford: a black silk crepe chemise that wasn't exactly haute couture but did conceal her tubbiness. She fluffed her red hair and vowed, again, that one of these days she was going to *do* something with it. Then she went down to the Bedlington cocktail lounge, hoping Felicia Starrett wouldn't be too late.

Surprisingly, she was already there, sitting at a corner table and sipping daintily from a tall pilsner of beer.

"Surely I'm not late," Dora said.

The woman looked up at her. "What?" she said.

"Have you been waiting long?"

Felicia shook her head. "I'm out of it, Nora."

"Dora. What's wrong? Are you ill?"

No reply. Dora looked at her closely. She was thinner, drawn. The cords in her neck were prominent enough to be plucked. Her nose had become a knuckle, and her stare was unfocused.

Dora went over to the bar and ordered a beer. While she waited, she observed Felicia in the mirror. She was sitting rigidly and when she raised the glass to her lips, her movements were slow, slow, as if she had planned every motion carefully and was dutifully obeying her mind's command.

She was wearing a belted cloth coat, buttoned to the neck although the cocktail lounge was overheated. And she had not removed her soiled kidskin gloves. She was hatless; her long black hair appeared stringy and unwashed.

Dora carried her beer back to the table. "Would you like something to eat?" she asked, taking the chair opposite. "Perhaps a sandwich?"

"What?"

"Are you hungry?"

"No," Felicia said, and looked about vaguely. "Where am I?"

Dora wasn't certain how to handle this. Felicia didn't appear drunk or high on anything else. But certainly she was detached. The woman was floating.

"The cocktail lounge of the Hotel Bedlington," Dora

said. "I'm Dora Conti. Thank you for meeting me for a drink."

"A cigarette," Felicia said.

Dora fished a crumpled pack from her shoulder bag. But when she offered it, Felicia made no move to take a cigarette. Dora put the pack on the table.

"I see you're drinking beer," she said as lightly as she could. "No Chivas Regal today?"

The woman looked at her blankly. She said, "That's for me to know and you to find out."

Dora was shocked by this childish response. "Felicia," she said, "is there anything I can do?"

"About what?"

"Are you feeling all right?"

"I will be." She paused and slowly the focus of her eyes changed until she was actually looking at Dora. "I'm getting married," she said suddenly. "Did you know? Of course not; no one knows. But I'm getting married."

"Why, that's wonderful," Dora said. "Congratulations. Who's the lucky man?"

"I bought him," Felicia said, mouth stretched in an ugly grin. "I bought the lucky man."

Dora drank off half her beer, wondering whether to end this mad conversation as soon as possible or take advantage of this poor woman's derangement. "Turner Pierce?" she asked quietly.

"Oh," Felicia said, "I did tell you. I forgot. You know Turner?"

"We've met. I hope you'll be very happy."

"He knows how to make me happy." She leaned across the table and beckoned with a long forefinger. Dora bent forward to hear. "I'm naked," Felicia said in a low voice.

"Pardon?"

"Under my coat. I haven't a stitch on. Look." She opened two buttons, pulled the neckline apart. Dora saw bare breasts.

"Button up," she said sharply. "Felicia, why on earth aren't you dressed?"

"What's the point? I don't feel like it. I don't have to do anything I don't want to do. And mother can't make me." That bony forefinger beckoned again, and again Dora leaned forward. "Clayton is going to marry Helene. Good. You know why?"

"Why?"

"Because I thought Turner and Helene were making it."

"Felicia! They're brother and sister."

"So? But now it's all right. Turner is mine. I'll never give him up."

She said this so fiercely that Dora was saddened, fearing what might happen to this vulnerable woman. Felicia sat back and looked at her pridefully. "I've moved in with Turner. It's my home now."

"And when will the wedding be?"

The focus of Felicia's eyes flattened, the aimless stare returned. "Soon," she said. "Real soon. I think I better go. Turner worries about me. He doesn't like me to be out by myself. He wants me with him all the time. Every minute."

"That's nice," Dora said not believing a word of all this. "Felicia, please, take care of yourself. And see your mother as often as you can."

"I don't think so. Do you have any money?"

Dora was startled. "I have a little with me."

"Could you give me a twenty for a cab?"

"Of course," Dora said. She took out her wallet and handed over a bill.

Felicia stood up, steadily enough, and unexpectedly proffered her hand. "I've enjoyed our little chat," she said formally. "So nice seeing you, and we must do this again very soon."

"Yes," Dora said.

Felicia turned away, then came back to put an arm across Dora's shoulders and lean close. "I call him the ice-man," she whispered. "Turner. When we're getting it off, I say to him, 'The iceman cometh.' Isn't that hilarious?"

Dora nodded and watched her go, feeling horrified and helpless. An avalanche was beginning to move, and there was no way to stop it.

34

That demented conversation with Felicia Starrett spooked her. But it wasn't only Felicia, Dora acknowledged; the entire case involved befuddled and vexatious characters, all seemingly acting from irrational motives. Their lives were so knotted, ambitions so perverse, plans so Byzantine that she despaired of sorting it all out.

But then, she admitted ruefully, her own life was hardly a model of tidiness. John Wenden's confession—and implied plea—was never totally banished from her thoughts. An analysis of the way she felt about him was proving as frustrating as untangling the Starrett mishmash. She, whose thinking had always been so ordered and linear, seemed to have been infected by the loonies who peopled this case. She had caught their confusion and was as muddled as they.

Almost for self-preservation, she resolutely decided to concentrate her attention on Solomon Guthrie's computer printout and what it might reveal about the perplexing gold trading by Starrett Fine Jewelry, Inc. Now she was dealing with names, addresses, numbers, transactions: all hard data that had none of the wild emotionalism of the Starrett clan and their intimates.

She jotted a page of notes and planned a course of action.

She phoned the car rental agency used by the Company, identified herself, and gave her credit card number. She arranged for a Ford Escort to be brought to the Hotel Bedlington the next morning at 7:00 A.M.

She left wake-up call instructions at the hotel desk.

She was waiting on the sidewalk the following morning when the Escort was delivered. It was dark blue, had recently been washed, and the interior smelled of wild cherry deodorant.

She drove to LaGuardia Airport, parked, and waited twenty minutes before boarding the next Pan Am shuttle. Destination: Logan Airport, Boston.

She had a window seat on the port side of the plane and midway in the flight, above the cloud cover, she waved at the ground. The man seated next to her, reading *The Wall Street Journal,* looked up and asked curiously, "What are you waving at?"

"My husband," Dora said. "In Hartford."

"Oh," the man said.

She waited in line for a cab at Logan, then handed the driver the address she had written down. He read it and turned to look at her. "You sure you want to go there?"

"I'm sure," Dora said. "You can wait for me, then drive me back here."

"If we're alive," he said mournfully.

The address was in Roxbury, on a street that was mostly burned-out buildings and weed-choked lots. But there were three little stores huddled together, awaiting the wrecking ball. One was a bodega, one a candy store cum betting parlor. The third was Felix Brothers Classic Jewelry.

"This is it," the cabdriver said nervously. "If you're not back in five minutes, I'm taking off—if I still have wheels."

"I'm not going anywhere," Dora said.

She got out of the taxi and inspected the jewelry store. Ten feet wide at the most. A plate glass window half-patched with a sheet of tin. Glass so dusty and splattered she could hardly peer within. She saw a few empty display cases, a few chairs, one lying on its side. There was no use trying the door; it was behind a rusty iron grille and secured with an enormous padlock.

A man lounging nearby had watched Dora's actions with lazy interest. He was wearing camouflaged dungarees and a fake fur hat with earflaps that hung loosely.

"I beg your pardon," Dora said, "but could you tell me when the jewelry store is open."

The idler was much amused. "Cost you," he said.

Dora gave him a dollar.

"It ain't never open," the man said.

"Thank you very much," Dora said, and hastily got back in the cab.

"Thank God," the driver said, and gunned away.

She took the next shuttle back to New York. She reclaimed the Ford Escort and drove into Manhattan. She left her car for the Bedlington doorman to park and went up to her suite. She immediately called John Wenden.

"Got a minute?" she asked.

"All my life," he said. "What's up?"

"Listen to this . . ." she said, and related her day's activities. Then: "John, that place isn't even a hole-in-the-wall. It's a falling-down dump. It's never open. No stock and no customers. It's a great big nothing."

"So?"

"Two months ago the Starrett Fine Jewelry branch store in Boston sold Felix Brothers Classic Jewelry more than a million dollars' worth of pure gold."

"Son of a bitch," the detective said.

35

He sat ripping the baguette apart with jerking fingers, rolling the dough into hard little balls and tossing them aside.

"Turner," Helene said, "what *are* you doing?"

He looked down at the mess he had made. "Jesus," he said, "I'm losing it."

He was about to say more, but then the waiter served their veal chops and angelhair pasta. The bartender brought over a chilled bottle of Pinot Grigio and showed the label to Turner. He nodded, and the bottle was uncorked and poured.

"Now calm down and eat your dinner," Helene said.

Turner tried a bite of veal, then pushed his plate away. "I can't make it," he said. "You go ahead. I'll have the wine and maybe a little pasta."

Helene ate steadily, not looking up. "What's she on?" she asked.

"Ramon gave me some new stuff he's distributing. Smokable methamphetamine. Called ice. He said it would be a great high, and it is. Lasts for hours. But Ramon didn't tell me about the crash. Disaster time."

"Then cut her off," Helene advised.

"I can't. You're hooked with the first puff. The stuff is dynamite. I had her move in so I can keep an eye on her. The woman is dangerous—to herself and to me."

Helene looked up frowning. "Dangerous? You mean suicidal?"

"Suicidal, homicidal, depression, hallucinations, delusions—you name it. She can't even talk clearly."

"You've got a problem, son."

"Thanks for telling me," he said bitterly. "I thought I could keep her quietly stoned. That's a laugh. She smokes the stuff and starts climbing walls. That stupid Ramon!"

Helene ate steadily. "If he's stupid," she said, "how come he's so rich?"

"That's where you're wrong," Turner told her. "The richest men I've known have been the dumbest. It has nothing to do with intelligence. The ability to make money is a knack, like juggling or baking a soufflé."

"Uh-huh," Helene said. "Aren't you going to eat your chop?"

"I have no appetite. You want it?"

"About half. Cut it for me."

Obediently, he trimmed the chop on his plate, cut slices of the white meat, and transferred them to her plate.

"Thank you," she said. "So what are you going to do?"

"I don't know," he said fretfully, and went back to rolling balls of bread dough. "I tried to cut her off, and she went wild. Absolutely wild. She threatened me. Can you imagine that? She actually threatened me."

"Threatened you how?"

"Said she'd kill me if I didn't bring her more ice. And believe me, she wasn't kidding."

"You're scared?"

"Damned right I'm scared," he said, gulping his wine. "She's totally off the wall."

"Turner, maybe you better go to Clayton or Olivia and suggest she be put away for treatment."

"And have her tell them where she's been getting the stuff? No way! That would queer everything."

Helene finished her wine, took the bottle from the ice bucket, and refilled Turner's glass and her own. "You want to close up shop and take off?" she said quietly.

"I don't know," he said. "I don't know what to do."

His head was down as he pushed the bread pills around the tablecloth. Helene sat back and regarded him closely. He was right; he *was* losing it. Skin sallow, puffy circles under his eyes, twitchy fingers. And he, who had always been such a dandy, now wore a soiled shirt, tie awkwardly knotted, unpressed jacket. She could almost *smell* his fear.

"How long can you keep her going?" she asked.

"God knows," he said. "I've got to be there when she crashes. If I let her out of the apartment, she might go home, and then we're dead. Helene, you have no idea what that stuff has done to her. She's lost weight, she can't sleep, I've got to bathe her like an invalid. When she's smoking, her body gets so hot I'm afraid to touch her. But when she's high, she just wants to keep going. It lasts for hours, sometimes a whole day. Then she falls apart and wants to kill herself. Or me—if I don't get her out of her funk. Which means more ice."

"Where is she now?"

261

"At my apartment. Locked in. I fed her some downers, hoping she'd sleep it off. I better get back. If she's set fire to the whole place, I won't be a bit surprised. Maybe you're right; maybe we better split. I can't see any way out of this mess."

"Let's think about it," Helene said. "You go on home now. I'll finish my wine, maybe have an espresso, and take a cab home."

"Will you pick up the tab?"

She looked at him. "Sure," she said.

He stood up and tried a smile. "Thanks, sweetie," he said. "I can always depend on you. We'll come out of this okay; you'll see."

"Of course we will," she said.

She sipped her wine slowly, then had an espresso and a small apple tart. She paid the bill and overtipped, asking the waiter to go out onto Lexington Avenue and get her a cab. She was back in her apartment within a half-hour.

She looked up the unlisted number of Ramon Schnabl in her address book. But when she phoned, all she got was an answering machine. When it beeped, she gave her name, phone number, and asked Mr. Schnabl to call her at his convenience.

Then she phoned the Starrett apartment. Charles answered, and she asked if Clayton was there. The houseman said that Mr. Starrett was attending a business dinner that evening but was expected home shortly. Helene asked that he call her whatever time he arrived.

She made herself a cup of instant black coffee and took it to the living room desk. She went over her accounts, adding up her cash on hand and what she might expect from an emergency sale of those unset diamonds. She estimated the total, roughly, at about fifty thousand. That was hardly poverty, but it was very small peanuts indeed compared to her dreams.

She was finishing her coffee when the phone rang, and she let it shrill six times before she picked it up.

"H'lo?" she said in a sleepy voice.

"It's Clay, honey. Did I wake you up?"

"That's all right, Clay. I've only been sleeping a few minutes. It was nothing important. I just wanted to tell you how much I love you and how much I miss you."

"Hey," he said, his voice eager, *"that's* important! Did you really go to sleep so early?"

"There's nothing special on TV, so I thought I'd go to my lonely bed."

"Listen" he said, almost choking, "we can't have you going to a lonely bed. How's about if I pop over for a while? You can always sleep later."

"Well . . ." she said hesitantly, "if you really want to. I'd love to see you, Clay, but you must be tired."

"I'm never *that* tired," he said. "I'll be there in twenty minutes."

She undressed quickly, brushed her teeth, took a quick shower. By the time he arrived, she was scented and wearing a peach-colored silk negligee.

"Oh sweetheart," she said, embracing him tightly, "I'm *so* happy to see you. I know how busy you are, but I was hoping you'd come over tonight. I felt so alone. I really need you."

He stayed for almost two hours. As he was dressing, he took out his wallet and gave her five hundred dollars.

"That's just walking-around money," he told her. "After the divorce comes through and we're married, I'll put you on the store payroll at a thousand a week. We'll call you a styling consultant or something like that. It'll be a no-show job, but if anyone asks we can say you check out competitors' displays and new designs."

"A thousand a week," she repeated. "Thank you, darling. You're so good to me."

After he left, she showered again, poured herself a brandy, and changed the sheets and pillowcases on her bed.

She went back to her accounts, and finished the evening by making a meticulous list of her diamonds and their carat weight. Then she went to bed. She lay awake a few minutes, thinking that Turner should have left money for their dinner. That young man was developing short arms and low pockets. Clayton Starrett was different.

36

Mrs. Eleanor Starrett was unexpectedly gracious on the phone.

"I'm *so* glad you called, *chérie*," she said. "I've never been busier in my life, but I can always find time for *you*."

Dora thought that a bit much, but asked when and where they might meet. Well, Eleanor had an appointment for a massage at Georgio's Salon on East 56th Street at 11:30, and if Dora could meet her there, they'd have time for a nice chitchat.

Dora found her in a curtained back room, lying naked on a padded table and being worked on by a gigantic flaxen-haired masseuse.

"Pull up a chair, darling," Eleanor caroled. "We can talk while Hilda reduces me to a mass of quivering jelly. You really should do something with your hair."

"I know," Dora said.

"Such a gorgeous shade, but it *is* a mess. I'll ask Georgio to handle you personally. The man is *très chic* and does absolutely marvelous things with his magic scissors."

"Maybe some other time," Dora said. "Mrs. Starrett, I want to—"

"Oh, do call me Eleanor. I don't know why, but I feel I've known you for years and years. Dora—isn't it?"

"Yes."

"Well, Dora, when— Oh my God, Hilda, you're breaking my leg! Well, Dora, I'm sure you've heard I'm getting a divorce from Clayton, and that rat has to turn over a list of all his assets, so of course it's very important for me to know when he's getting that million from his father's insurance."

Now Dora could understand her gushy friendliness. "I really can't give you a definite date, Eleanor, but I'm sure it won't be much longer."

"I hope not. I want to hit that schmuck where he lives— and that means his bank account."

"I was sorry to hear about the divorce," Dora said.

"Don't be sorry, sweetie; be glad, because I certainly am. I should have dumped that moron years ago. He is *so* dumb. A dumb rat. Of course Helene Pierce isn't his first playmate. He's been cheating on me since the day we were married. And the idiot thought I didn't know!"

"Why did you put up with it?" Dora asked curiously.

Eleanor raised her head to look at her. "Everyone cheats, luv. It's hardly a capital crime, is it? If it were, there wouldn't be enough electric chairs in the world. There's nothing so terrible about cheating—I've had a few flings myself—but one should try to be discreet, don't you think? And ending a marriage just for the sake of a roll in the hay is definitely *de trop*. I mean, it just isn't done. Except by rat finks like Clayton Starrett. Well, I wish him happiness with his Barbie Doll. She'll take him for whatever he has

266

left after I get through with him. Poor Clay will end up washing windshields at stoplights." She cackled with glee.

"Eleanor, one of the things I wanted to talk to you about was Felicia. I met her yesterday, and she seemed—uh, she seemed ill."

"Ill?" the other woman said with a harsh laugh. "Stoned out of her gourd, you mean. Felicia is a basket case. She really should be under professional care somewhere, but Olivia doesn't know what's going on."

"What *is* going on?"

"Oh, she's doing coke, no doubt about it. I think Turner Pierce turned her on, but if it wasn't him, it would be someone else. Felicia is lost. She's going to get into serious trouble one of these days."

"Why would Turner Pierce want to supply her with drugs?"

"What a child you are! Felicia is hardly poverty-stricken, is she, and Turner has expensive tastes. As I well know. One of those flings I mentioned, I had with Turner. But I soon gave him the broom. A very, *very* grabby young man. Just like his sister."

"I thought you liked the Pierces. At our first meeting you were very complimentary."

"That was when I was a member of the family," Eleanor said bitterly. "Now I can tell the truth, and they can all rot in hell!"

When she left the salon, Dora stood on the sidewalk a few moments, gulping deep breaths. She needed that sense of a world washed clean, everything spotless and shining.

It wasn't Eleanor's vindictiveness toward Clayton that dismayed her; the scorned wife was entitled to that. Nor were the revelations of Felicia's addiction a shock; Dora had guessed that doomed woman was beyond her help—and probably any other Samaritan's.

But what really depressed Dora were Eleanor's blithe comments about cheating. Was she right? Did everyone do it? Was adultery no more serious than a mild flirtation at a cocktail party, and no more reason for marital discord than the toothpaste tube squeezed in the wrong place?

She walked west on 56th Street wondering if she was hopelessly naive, an innocent with no real perception of how the world turned and how people behaved. "What a child you are!" Eleanor had said, and perhaps, Dora acknowledged, she *was* a child, with all her notions of right and wrong the result of her teaching, and not wisdom distilled from experience.

She cut over to 54th Street and continued to plod westward, still brooding. Could she be right and everyone else wrong? It hardly seemed likely. John Wenden had said, "Life is too short to be faithful," and perhaps that was a universal truth that had somehow eluded Dora Conti, happily married and now questioning if her world was ridiculously limited.

She shook off these melancholic musings and looked about her. She stood on the corner of 54th Street and Eighth Avenue. This neighborhood was vastly different from the one she had just left. There was a police station, hemmed in by parked squad cars. Then there was a crowded stretch of tenements, garages, and low-rise commercial buildings.

She dodged traffic, crossed Eighth, and walked west on 54th, watching the numbers and realizing she still had a block or two to go.

When she told John about that empty jewelry shop in Roxbury, the detective had said, "Look, this gold-trading caper is yours. I have my hands full with the three homicides; I can't suddenly start chasing gold bars. Why don't you stick with it and see what you can come up with. I'm here and ready to help. Okay?"

Sure, Dora had told him, that was okay, and she went back to the plan of action she had outlined prior to her Boston trip.

She had the address of the vault of Starrett Fine Jewelry in Brooklyn, but it didn't seem worthwhile to investigate because she had no idea when a shipment of gold might be delivered. It made more sense to check out Starrett's main supplier of gold bullion, an outfit called Stuttgart Precious Metals, Inc., located on West Fifty-fourth Street in Manhattan. According to the computer printout, Stuttgart was the USA subsidiary of Croesus Refineries, Ltd., headquartered in Luxembourg.

Dora had expected to find Stuttgart Precious Metals in a blockhouse of a building, a thick-walled bunker surrounded, perhaps, by a heavy fence topped with razor wire, with armed guards in view. Instead she found a one-story concrete block building with no fence, no guards. It was located just west of Tenth Avenue and looked as if it had been built as a garage, with a small office in front and wide, roll-up doors leading to the main building. There was no sign.

Even more perplexing than the ordinariness of the physical structure was its air of dilapidation. It looked deserted, as if business had dwindled and bankruptcy loomed. A derelict was rooting in the garbage can outside the office door. Looking for gold bars? Dora wondered.

She had eyeballed the building from across the street. Now she marched resolutely up to the office door and pushed her way in. She found herself in a barren, wood-floored room with stained walls carelessly plastered and no chairs or other amenities for potential customers. There was a scarred wooden counter, and behind it, at an equally decrepit desk, a bespectacled, gray-haired lady sat typing steadily. There were no other papers or documents on her desk.

She stopped typing when Dora entered, and looked up. "Yes?" she said in a crackly voice.

"Is this Stuttgart Precious Metals?" Dora asked.

The woman nodded.

Dora had prepared a scenario.

"My husband and I have a small craft shop in Vermont," she said, smiling brightly. "We design and fashion one-of-a-kind jewelry pieces, mostly gold and sterling silver in abstract designs. We've been buying our raw gold and sterling in Boston, but I had to come to New York on business and decided to find out if we could get a better price on metals down here."

The woman shook her head. "We don't sell retail," she said.

"Well, it's not actually retail," Dora said. "After all, we are designers and manufacturers. We sell to some of the best department stores and jewelry shops in the country."

The woman didn't change expression. "How much gold could you use in a month?" she asked. "Ounces? We sell our metals in pounds and kilos. Our gold comes from abroad in bars and ingots. Too much for you, girlie."

"Oh dear," Dora said, "I'm afraid you're right; we wouldn't know what to do with a pound of pure gold. Listen, one other thing, I walked over from Eighth Avenue, and it occurred to me that someday we might consider opening a small workshop and showroom in Manhattan. Does Stuttgart own any other property in the neighborhood?"

"We don't own," the woman said, "we lease."

"Oh dear," Dora said again. "Well, I guess I'll just have to keep looking. Thank you for your time."

The woman nodded and went back to her typing.

Dora was lucky; she caught an empty cab that had just come out of an Eleventh Avenue taxi garage. But traffic was murder, and it took an hour to get back to the Bedlington. She went immediately to her suite and kicked off her shoes. Then she phoned Mike Trevalyan in Hartford.

"Gee, it's good to hear from you," he said. "Having a nice vacation?"

"Come on, Mike, cut the bullshit. I need some help."

"No kidding?" he said. "And I thought you called to wish me Happy Birthday."

"I have two words for you," Dora said, "and they're not Happy Birthday. The computers in our property and casualty department use a data base that covers all commercial properties in our territory—right?"

"Oh-oh," he said. "I know what's coming."

"There's this business on West Fifty-fourth Street in Manhattan called Stuttgart Precious Metals, a subsidiary of an outfit registered in Luxembourg. Stuttgart leases their premises. I'll give you the address, and I need to know who owns the property and anything else you can find out about Stuttgart: the terms of the lease, how long they've occupied the place, and so forth."

"What's this got to do with the Starrett insurance claim?"

"Nothing," Dora said breezily. "I'm just having fun."

271

After he calmed down, she gave him the address of Stutt-gart, and he promised to get back to her as soon as he had something.

"Miss me?" he asked her.

"I sure do," she said warmly. "What's your name again?"

She hung up on his profanity and then, a few minutes later, phoned Mario, and they talked for almost a half-hour. Dora got caught up on local gossip and told Mario how much she missed him and their little house.

"It's the home cooking you miss," he said.

"That, too," she agreed.

"When are you coming back?"

"Soon," she promised. "Have you been behaving your-self?"

"As usual," he said, which wasn't *exactly* what she wanted to hear.

But the talk with her husband cheered her, and she went to bed resolved to forget all about people with sloppy mor-als; nothing could equal the joy of a happy, *faithful* mar-riage.

But sleep did not come easily; her equanimity didn't last, and she found herself questioning again. So she got out of bed to kneel and pray. It was something she hadn't done for a long while, and she thought it was about time.

37

Felicia Starrett was not a stupid woman, but introspection dogged her like a low-grade infection. She was aware—continually aware—that her life lacked some essential ingredient that might make it meaningful, or at least endurable. Her mother never ceased to remind her that a loving mate and a happy marriage would solve all her problems. That advice, Felicia thought wryly, was akin to telling a penniless, starving bum that he really should eat good, nourishing meals.

But it was true, she admitted, that her relations with men had soured her life. She was still in her teens, with the arrogance of youth, when she began to offer money or valuable gifts to men. This pattern continued after she was graduated from Barnard and, in an effort to find the cause of this curious behavior, she read many books of popularized psychology. But none offered clues as to the reason she continually met (or sought?) men who accepted her largesse casually as if it were their due.

273

At various periods of self-analysis she had ascribed different motives for her compulsive generosity. First she thought it was a power ploy: She wanted to dominate men. In fact, she wanted to *own* them, reduce them to the role of paid servitors. Finally she concluded that she gave money because she was unable to give love. She was fearful of commitment, recognized the deficiency, and lavished gifts as a substitute.

But recognizing the cause did nothing to ameliorate her unhappiness. And so she surrendered to addictions: caffeine, nicotine, alcohol, a variety of drugs, and eventually cocaine, in an endless search for the magic potion that would provide the joy life had denied her.

She thought her search had finally succeeded when Turner Pierce provided ice, the smokable methamphetamine. Here was a bliss that turned her into a beautiful creature floating through a world of wonders. The high was like nothing she had ever experienced before.

But there was a heavy price to pay. The crash was horrendous: nausea, incontinence, dreadful hallucinations, fears without name, and frequently violence she could not control. But Turner—the darling!—was always there to minister to her and, when the worst had passed, to provide more of those lovely crystals in a glass pipe, and then she soared again.

She was vaguely aware of vomiting, weight loss, respiratory pain, thundering heartbeat, and heightened body temperature. But she became so intent on achieving that splendid euphoria that she would have paid any price, even life itself, if she might slip away while owning the world.

But death held no lure, for there, always, was Turner,

who had promised to marry her, an act of love that made her happiness more intense. So joyful was she that she was even able to acknowledge the beauty and beneficence of Helene—a woman she had formerly mistrusted—who came once to help Turner bathe her and wash her hair. And also clean up the apartment, which Felicia, during a vicious crash, had almost destroyed, slashing furniture with a carving knife, breaking mirrors, and smashing all those cute china figurines belonging to the landlord.

So she alternated between ecstasy and despair, hardly conscious of time's passage but, in her few semilucid moments, realizing with something like awe that she would soon be a married woman and finally, at last, her life would be meaningful.

38

Dora drove around the block twice, and then around two blocks twice. Finally, three blocks away, she found a parking space she hoped she might be able to occupy, but it took ten minutes of sweaty maneuvering to wedge the Escort against the curb. She locked up and walked back to Gregor Pinchik's building in SoHo. She didn't even want to *think* about the eventual problem of wiggling the Ford out of that cramped space.

The computer maven had the top floor of an ancient commercial building that had recently been renovated. There were new white tiles on the lobby floor, and on the walls were Art Deco lighting fixtures with nymphs cavorting on frosted glass. The original freight elevator—big enough to accommodate a Steinway—had been spruced up with crackled mirrors and framed prints of Man Ray photographs.

Pinchik's loft was illuminated by two giant skylights that revealed a sky as dull as a sidewalk. But there was track lighting to fill the corners, and Brahms played softly from an Aiwa stereo component system that had more knobs, switches, gauges, and controls than a space shuttle.

"How about *this,* lady?" Gregor cried, waving an arm at his equipment.

He gave Dora what he called the "fifty-cent tour," warning her not to trip on the wires and cables snaking across the floor. He displayed, and occasionally demonstrated, a bewildering hodgepodge of computers, monitors, printers, modems, tapes and disks, telephones, fax and answering machines, digital pagers, hand-held electronic calculators, and much, much more.

"I'm a gadget freak," the bearded man admitted cheerfully. "If it's electronic, I gotta have it. A lot of this stuff is junk, but even junk can be fun. Now you sit down over here, and I'll get you caught up on the adventures of our pigeon."

Dora sat in a comfortable swivel chair, and Pinchik perched on a little steel stool that rolled about on casters. He settled in front of a monitor and punched a few buttons with his stubby fingers.

"I put the whole file on one tape," he said. "You know what I collected in Dallas and Denver. Now we'll get to the new things."

Typed lines began to reel off across the screen, and Pinchik leaned closer to read.

"All right," he said, "here's the scoop I got from my hacker pals in KC. Our hero showed up in Kansas City after leaving Denver. Now he's Turner Pierce. Same initials, but who the hell knows if it's his real name."

"Still got the mustache?" Dora asked.

"Still got it. And he's still on the con. The reason the KC

hackers knew so much about him was that he set up what was apparently a legitimate business. Office, secretary, letterheads, advertisements—the whole schmear. He called himself a computer consultant and designer of complete systems for any size business, large or small. He was one of the first in that field in KC, and he made out like gangbusters. First of all, he knew his stuff, and he never tried to sell a client more hardware than he needed. Of course Pierce was probably getting a kickback on the equipment he *did* recommend, but that was small potatoes. He lined up some hefty clients: a bank and its branches, a local college, an insurance company, a chain of retail shoe stores, and a lot of factories, distributors, supermarkets, an entire shopping mall, and so forth."

"So he went legitimate?"

"That's what everyone thought. At first. Then there was a string of computer swindles. The bank took heavy losses in cash, and the shoe stores and distributors lost merchandise delivered and logged in as paid for, though payment was never actually made. And the insurance company found itself paying off claims on policies it had never written."

"Don't tell me, Greg," Dora said. "I can guess."

"You got it," Pinchik said, nodding. "All those victims had computer systems installed by Turner Pierce Associates, Inc. What he was doing was leaving what we call a 'trapdoor' in every system he designed. In its simplest form this would be an access code, maybe just a single word or a six-digit number, that would enable a bandit to get into the system from outside, rummage around in all the records, and clip the business the way he wanted for as much as he wanted."

"And that's what Turner was doing?"

The computer expert shook his shaggy head. "Nope," he said, "he was too smart for that. He followed the same pattern we saw him use in Dallas and Denver. He never did the dirty deed himself, but he sold those trapdoors to guys greedier and dumber than he was. When all those crimes came to light, some of the actual crooks were nabbed and convicted, but Pierce folded his tent and quietly slipped away."

"Greg, some of those guys who were convicted must have tried to plea bargain by giving the prosecutor Turner Pierce's name."

"Sure, they fingered him as the guy who sold them access to the computer systems. But what evidence did the prosecutor have to come down on Pierce? No evidence. Just the accusation of an indicted criminal. There was no case against Pierce that would hold up in court, so he was advised to get out of town."

"And he came to New York."

"That's it," Pinchik agreed, then pressed more buttons on his console. "But I haven't told you the juiciest part yet. Wait a sec." He stood to peer more closely at the screen. "Yeah, here it is. You remember I told you that when Pierce set up his business in Kansas City, he had an office, a secretary, everything seemingly legit."

"I remember."

"The secretary was a tall, luscious lady with the first name of Helene."

"His sister!" Dora cried.

"I guess," Pinchik said. "The description I got matches the one you gave me. And when Turner Pierce lammed out of Kansas City, Helene disappeared at the same time, so I guess she came to New York with him."

"I guess she did," Dora said.

Pinchik sat down again on his little stool and wheeled around to look at her. "But I haven't given you the icing on the cake," he said, his face expressionless. "Before this Helene went to work in Turner Pierce's office, she was a hooker."

Dora stared at him a moment. Then: "You're sure?" she asked huskily.

He nodded. "I got the same data from two different sources, and I think it's for real. She was a hooker all right. But I don't mean she walked the streets or leaned against lampposts. My guys tell me she was more like a call girl, a high-priced call girl. She had some very important men as regular customers, and when a convention came to town, she did okay."

Dora took a deep breath. "Do you mind if I smoke?" she asked.

"Only if you give me one," Pinchik said. "I'm all out."

They lighted up and sat a few moments in silence, staring at the ceiling. "It's a wonderful world," Dora said finally.

"You can say that again," Pinchik said.

"It's a wonderful world," Dora said again, smiling. Then she lowered her gaze to stare at the grizzled man, the gadget freak who could use electronics to strip people naked. "Tell me, Greg: You're a been-around guy, what's your take on Turner Pierce?"

Pinchik regarded the glowing end of his cigarette. "I fell once. I knew it was wrong while I was doing it and, God willing, I'll never fall again. But this Pierce comes across as a natural-born outlaw. He just doesn't give a damn. Look, the guy is smart. When it comes to computers, he may even be close to a wunderkind. If he had gone straight, he might have been a zillionaire by now. But like I said, he just doesn't give a damn. No laws or rules for him. He bulls his way through life, and if someone gets hurt, that's tough shit. Excuse my language, lady."

"I've heard worse."

"Also," Pinchik said, "I think he could be very, very dangerous. Remember that."

"I'll remember," Dora promised.

Pinchik dropped his cigarette butt to the tiled floor and ground it out under his heel. "So now we've got Helene and Turner Pierce in New York. I guess that ends my job—right?"

"No," Dora said, "not yet. Will you get back to your contacts in Kansas City and see if you can find out more about Helene Pierce. Like where and when she was born, why she gave up on being a call girl to team up with her brother—anything you can find out."

"Sure, I can do that. I have a few sources in KC I haven't tapped yet." He laughed suddenly. "And one of the hackers, I know for sure, is into the city's computers. He has access to all their records."

"Why would he want to invade city hall?" Dora asked curiously.

Pinchik shrugged. "Just for the fun of it. Because it's *there*. The same reason people climb Mt. Everest."

"The other thing," Dora said, "is a man named Sidney Loftus. He's dead now, but he died as Father Brian Callaway, a preacher who invented his own religion. I think he was in Kansas City at the same time as the Pierces, and I'd like to find out if they knew each other."

"Okay, let me get a tape recorder, and you give me all you've got on Sidney Loftus, including his physical description, and I'll see what I can dig up."

When Dora returned to her Ford Escort, she discovered the car parked tightly ahead had disappeared, and she had no trouble pulling out and heading uptown. She took this as a good omen: An apparently intractable problem had been solved by chance or a smiling Almighty.

"Thank you, God," she said aloud. "Now see what You can do about clearing up the Starrett mess."

When she arrived back at the Bedlington, there was a message for her at the desk: She was to call Michael Trevalyan in Hartford as soon as possible. She went up to her suite, made herself a cup of tea and opened a fresh package of Pepperidge Farm cookies: Orange Milanos, her favorite. Then she phoned.

"You sure threw me a curveball," Trevalyan said aggrievedly. "That Stuttgart Precious Metals, the dump on West Fifty-fourth Street, I had it looked up by a computer guy in the property and casualty department."

"And?"

"Like you said, Stuttgart leases. The lease was signed about two years ago and runs for five years with an option to renew on the same terms."

"Who owns the building and land?"

"An outfit called Spondex Realty Corporation."

"Never heard of them," Dora said. "Did you?"

"Will you just shut up for a minute," Trevalyan said wrathfully, "and let me finish. The computer whiz in property ran a trace on Spondex and found out it's owned by R. L. Jessup Investments, another corporation. Now the computer guy got interested because it began to smell. You know when there's a paper trail like that, someone's trying to cover up. Anyway, the ownership of the property on West Fifty-fourth was traced back through four corporations and finally came to rest at a holding company that owns real estate in LA and New York, a shipping line, a boutique in Palm Beach, a big coffee plantation in Colombia, a ranch in Wyoming, and God knows what else."

"What's the name of the holding company?"

"It's called Rabl Enterprises, Ltd. And this will kill you: It's registered in Luxembourg. Isn't that where Stuttgart's parent company is registered?"

"You got it, Mike," Dora said. "And it *is* beginning to smell. Who's the owner of Rabl Enterprises?"

"It's set up as a limited corporation. Maybe a dozen shareholders. It's not listed on any exchange. The chairman of the board, president, and chief executive officer is a guy named Ramon Schnabl. I guess that's where they got the name of the holding company: first two letters of his first name and last two letters of his last name. We've gone through all our data bases, but there's nothing on Ramon Schnabl."

"All right, Mike. Thanks for your help. I'll take it from here."

"Does that mean we'll be able to deep-six the Starrett insurance claim?"

"I don't know what it means," Dora said worriedly, "if anything."

"Well, watch your tail, kiddo. That chain of corporate ownership makes me suspect someone may be playing hardball. Don't do anything foolish."

"Why, Mike," Dora said, "you're concerned about me. How sweet!"

"Ahh, go to hell," he said gruffly, and hung up.

Dora rushed to her spiral notebook and jotted down all the names she could recall from that telephone conversation. Then she called Detective John Wenden, but he was in a meeting and not available. She left a message and went back to her notebook, scrawling a condensed version of everything she had learned from Gregor Pinchik that morning. She was still scribbling when the phone rang and she grabbed it up.

"Hiya, Red," Wenden said. "I only got a few minutes. What's happening?"

"I'll make it fast," Dora said, and told him about her visit to Stuttgart Precious Metals on West 54th Street, and how the Company had run a computer search to discover who owned the property and, after following a complex corporate trail, had come up with the name of a holding company registered in Luxembourg.

"Does the name Ramon Schnabl mean anything to you?" Dora asked.

There was no reply.

"John?" Dora said. "Are you there?"

"Listen," Wenden said, his voice suddenly urgent, "do me a favor, will you? Don't do another thing about Starrett's gold trading. Not a thing, you understand? Don't go back to that place on West Fifty-fourth. Don't ask any more questions about it. Don't even mention Starrett's gold trading to *anyone* until I get back to you. Okay? Will you promise to lay off until I call?"

"John, is this important?"

"Is life important? Will you promise not to make a move until you hear from me?"

"All right," Dora said faintly. "If you say so."

"I love you, Red," Wenden said.

39

Despite what Turner had said, Helene Pierce equated wealth with intelligence. Smart people made big money; that was a given. Now, seated in the colorless living room of Ramon Schnabl's minimalist apartment, she stared at his dark glasses and wondered what secrets those cheaters concealed. This little man in his tight, shiny white suit could pass as a Palermo pimp, but he was, she knew, a Croesus who would never be listed in the Forbes 400.

"What a pleasure to see you again, dear," he said in his bloodless voice. "I was surprised—delighted but surprised to hear from you. Does Turner know you're here?"

The question was so sudden and sharp that Helene was startled. "No," she said, "he doesn't. I thought it best not to tell him."

Schnabl nodded. "I certainly shan't," he said, no hint of humor in his tone. "You wish to discuss something concerning Turner?"

"And you," Helene said.

He waited, patient and silent, sipping his chilled Évian water.

"You know, of course," she said, wishing desperately for a cigarette, "that Turner is involved with Felicia Starrett."

"I am aware of their relationship."

"I'm afraid it may be a problem," Helene said.

"A problem? Felicia or Turner?"

"Both. She is totally hooked, and trying to control her is beginning to affect Turner's judgment. And not only his judgment but his personality, even his physical appearance. To put it bluntly, Ramon, the man is falling apart."

"I am extremely sorry to hear that, dear. I wish only the best for Turner, just as I do for you. Are you suggesting that his behavior is becoming somewhat, ah, erratic?"

"It's come to that," Helene said, lifting her chin but never taking her stare away from those tinted glasses. "But I think Felicia is the more immediate danger. She's irrational. She trashed Turner's apartment. And when she crashes, she's completely psychotic."

"What a shame," the little man said, sighing. "The price we pay for our pleasures. Well, this is disquieting news, dear. Have you any suggestions as to how this distressing situation may be remedied?"

Helene took a deep breath. "Did you know Clayton Starrett is getting a divorce?"

"I have heard something to that effect."

"He wants to marry me when his divorce is final."

Schnabl showed no surprise. "I see. And do you wish to marry him?"

"Yes. I mention this personal matter only to convince you that if you should decide to eliminate Turner . . . from your plans," she added quickly. "If you should decide to eliminate Turner from your plans, I wanted you to know that it need not affect the Starrett deal. I can control Clayton."

"And why should I want to, as you say, eliminate Turner?"

"Because he is going through a very bad time with Felicia. It has changed him. He is not the man he was six months ago, or even six weeks ago. He is no longer dependable. And, of course, Felicia represents an even greater threat. There is simply no telling what that insane woman might do. Another factor you may wish to consider: If Turner was out of the picture, you would save his share of the Starrett take. I assure you I have no desire to inherit it. Clayton is making quite enough for the two of us."

"You are not only a lovely woman, dear, but you are wonderfully shrewd. I like that."

Helene started to speak, but Schnabl held up a hand to silence her. He turned his blank stare toward the bleached oryx skull hanging above the cold fireplace. They sat without speaking for a few moments.

"I think not," Ramon said finally, turning his head toward Helene again. "The timing is not right. As you may or may not know, Turner is presently engaged in setting up an operation in New Orleans similar to the Starrett arrangement. It is important to me that this project be completed and brought on-line. Then we have discussed a third organization headquartered in Tucson, Arizona, which is rapidly becoming an important distribution center. No, my dear, I'm afraid I cannot grant your request."

"It wasn't a request," Helene said stonily. "It was merely a suggestion I thought would be to your benefit."

"And yours, too, of course," Schnabl said. "I do appreciate your concern, and I shall certainly keep a close watch on Turner's behavior. If, as you say, he has become undependable, then I may be forced to revise my decision. But for the time being, I intend to take no action. Sorry."

"There's nothing to be sorry about," Helene said. She stood and gathered up hat, gloves, purse, coat. "I just thought you should be aware of the true situation so you might act in your own best interest."

Finally, finally, he smiled: a horrible grimace, a death's-head grin. "We all act in our own best interest, dear. It's the mark of a civilized man. And woman," he added, staring at her.

She cabbed home to her apartment, furious but controlling it because she had already prepared a fallback scenario in case Schnabl couldn't be manipulated. He couldn't, and now she would have to do it herself. She was not daunted by that prospect.

Her spirits rose when the concierge handed her a package that had just been delivered by a messenger from Starrett Fine Jewelry. Helene hugged it to her breast in the elevator; she knew what it contained.

That night she and Clayton were going to attend a charity dinner-dance at the Waldorf, the first time they would be out in public together. Helene had bought a new evening gown: a strapless sheath of lapis-hued sequins. And Clayton had promised to lend her a necklace from Starrett's estate jewelry department.

"Remember, it's only a loan," he had said, "for one night. It has to be returned to the store—unless some woman at the party will kill for it and can come up with the two million five it costs. In which case you get a commission."

"I understand," Helene said.

She tore open the package with trembling hands, lifted the lid of the velvet case, caught her breath. It was a magnificent strand of ten splendid sapphires, each gem set in a pyramid of diamonds, the pyramids linked with 18K gold. Helene guessed the total sapphire weight at about 75 cts. and the diamonds at 50 cts.

She took off jacket and blouse and clasped the necklace about her throat. It was beautifully designed, and lay flat and balanced on her bare skin. She stood before the mirror, turned this way and that, admired the sparkle of the gems, the glow of the gold. This was the kind of adornment for which she was destined. She had always known it. All she had ever needed was a break—and Clayton Starrett was it.

She spent a long time bathing, doing her hair, applying makeup, stepping carefully into the sequined sheath, donning the satin evening pumps. Then she locked that wondrous necklace about her throat and saw in the mirror the woman she had always wanted to be.

She went downstairs carrying a silk trench coat. The stretch limousine was waiting. Clayton was standing alongside on the sidewalk, smoking a cigar. When he saw her, he tried to speak but something caught in his throat. She recognized the longing in his eyes.

"I feel like Cinderella," she said, laughing, "on her way to the ball."

"But midnight will never come," he proclaimed. "Never!"

At the Waldorf, they sat at a table for ten. All the other men seemed to be suppliers to Starrett Fine Jewelry, and they and their wives treated Clayton with the deference a good customer deserved. They were no less ingratiating toward Helene, admiring the necklace, her gown, even the shade of her fingernail polish. She basked.

It was a black-tie affair and, looking about the big dining room, Helene saw nothing but wealth and finery. Flash of jewels. Scent of expensive perfumes. It seemed to be a room without worries, without grief or regrets. This was, she decided, what life should be.

Later, during the dancing, she was introduced to many people: admiring men and sharp-eyed women. She conducted herself demurely, murmured her thanks for compliments, held Clayton's hand and let him exhibit her proudly: his newest and most valuable possession.

The band played "After the Ball" at 2:00 A.M., but it was almost another hour before they had a final glass of champagne, reclaimed their coats, and waited for their limo to be brought around. They returned to Helene's apartment through a soft snowfall that haloed the streetlamps and added the final touch to a fairy-tale evening.

"I'd love to come up," Clayton said huskily, "but I can't. Heavy schedule tomorrow, and besides, I had too much to drink. I better get some sleep."

"Oh Clayton," she said sorrowfully, immensely relieved and gripping his hand tightly, "the first disappointment of a really fabulous night."

"It *was* super, wasn't it? Darling, you were the belle of the ball. I've never heard such praise. All the guys wanted your phone number, of course, but I told them you were taken."

"I am—with you," she said and kissed him fiercely.

"Oh God," he said, almost moaning, "what a life we're going to have!"

"Do you want the necklace now?" she asked.

"No, you keep it till tomorrow. I'll send a messenger around in the morning. Helene, I love you. You know that, don't you?"

She kissed him again as an answer, then went up to her apartment alone, the collar of her trench coat raised to hide the necklace. She undressed swiftly, realizing she would have to shampoo before sleeping to rid her hair of the smell of Clayton's cigars.

She stroked the necklace softly as it lay on her suede skin. It was an enchantment, an amulet that would protect her from failure and bring her nothing but good fortune.

So bewitched was she by this extraordinary treasure that never once did she remember that it would be taken away by a messenger in the morning.

40

Dora Conti was beginning to get a glimmer, just a faint perception of what was going on. She cast Sidney Loftus and the Pierces as the sharks and the Starretts as their wriggling prey. But who was doing what to whom remained murky. Dora even drew a diagram: boxed names linked by straight or squiggly lines. It didn't help.

Then Detective John Wenden called.

"Hey, Red," he said with no preliminary sweet talk, "there's a guy I want you to meet: Terence Ortiz, a detective sergeant. We call him Terrible Terry."

"All right," Dora said, "I'll play straight man: Why do you call him Terrible Terry?"

"He's in Narcotics," Wenden said, "and he shoots people. Listen, can we stop by tonight? Late?"

"How late?"

"Around eight o'clock."

"That's not late," Dora said. "I rarely go to bed before nine."

"Liar!" he said, laughing. "See you tonight."

Terry Ortiz turned out to be a short, wiry man with a droopy black mustache that gave him a melancholic mien. But he was full of ginger and had a habit of snapping his fingers. When he was introduced, he kissed Dora's hand, and the mustache tickled.

"Hey," she said, "would you guys like a beer?"

"The sweetest words of tongue or pen," Ortiz said.

"Except for 'The check is in the mail,'" Wenden said.

"Yeah, except it usually ain't," Ortiz said. "I'll settle for a beer."

He was wearing a black leather biker's jacket and black jeans. When he took off the jacket, Dora saw he was carrying a snub-nosed revolver in a shoulder holster. She brought out cans of beer, a bag of pretzels, and a saucer of hot mustard. They sat around the cocktail table, and Terrible Terry slumped and put his boots up.

"I got maybe an hour," he announced, "and then I gotta split. If I don't get home tonight my old lady is going to split *me.*"

"Where do you live, Sergeant Ortiz?" Dora asked politely.

"Terry," he said. "The East Side barrio—where else? Let's talk business."

"Yeah," John said, "good idea. Red, tell Terry how you came up with the name of Ramon Schnabl."

She explained again how she asked her boss to run a computer check on the ownership of the premises occupied by Stuttgart Precious Metals on West 54th, and eventually the paper trail led to a Luxembourg holding company headed by Schnabl."

"Uh-huh," John said, "and who was the first owner you

turned up—the outfit that leased the place to Stuttgart?"

"Spondex Realty Corporation."

The two detectives looked at each other and laughed.

"What are you guys giggling about?" Dora demanded.

"After you mentioned the name of Ramon Schnabl," Wenden said, "I remembered your telling me about that trip to Boston you made and how the store in Roxbury looked like a deserted dump. So just for the hell of it, I called the Boston PD and asked them to find out who owns the building occupied by Felix Brothers Classic Jewelry. Guess what: It's owned by Spondex Realty Corporation."

Dora smacked her forehead with a palm. "Now why didn't I think to check that out?"

"Because you're an amateur," Wenden said. "Talented and beautiful, but still an amateur."

Dora let that slide by—temporarily. "And who is this Ramon Schnabl," she asked, "and what's his racket?"

"Terry," John said, "that's your department. You tell her."

"Ramon Schnabl is very big in the drug biz," the narc said. "Very, *very* big. The guy runs a supermarket: boo, horse, snow, opium, crack, hash, designer drugs from his own labs—you name it, he's got it. He's also got a vertical organization; he's a grower, shipper, exporter and importer, distributor, wholesaler, and now we think he's setting up his own retail network in New York, New Orleans, and some of his field reps have been spotted in Tucson, Arizona. The guy's a dope tycoon."

"If you know all this," Dora said, "why haven't you destroyed him?"

Terry snapped his fingers. "Don't think we haven't tried. So has the Treasury, the FBI, and the DEA. Every time we think we have him cornered, he weasels out. Witnesses clam up. He doesn't kill rats, he kills their families: wives, children, parents, relatives. Drug dealers are willing to do hard time rather than double-cross Ramon Schnabl. He is not a nice man."

"No," Dora said. "But if he's such a big shot in drugs, what's his interest in precious metals and jewelry stores?"

"Beats me," Wenden said. "I thought about gold smuggling, but that doesn't make sense; gold is available everywhere, and the market sets the price. Also, gold is too heavy to smuggle in bars and ingots. Got any ideas, Terry?"

"*Nada*," Ortiz said, and finished his beer. "I thought maybe he might be bringing in gold bars with the insides hollowed out and stuffed with dope. But that wouldn't work because, like you said, gold is heavy stuff and someone would spot the difference."

"So?" John said. "Where do we go from here?"

"This is too juicy to drop," Ortiz said. "I think maybe I should take a look at Stuttgart Precious Metals. It could be just a front, and instead of gold, their vault is jammed with kilos of happy dust. I'll case the joint, and if it looks halfway doable, maybe we should pull a B and E. John?"

"I'm game," Wenden said.

Ortiz turned suddenly to Dora. "You got wheels?" he asked.

"A rented Ford Escort," she said.

"Lovely. We may ask for a loan."

"If you need a lookout," she said, "I'm willing."

"I love this woman," Terry said to Wenden. "*Love* her." He stood up, pulled on his jacket and a black leather cap. "I'll check out Stuttgart and let you know. Thanks for the refreshments. You coming, John?"

"I think I'll hang around awhile," Wenden said.

The narc raised his hand in benediction. "Bless you, my children," he said. He took two pretzels from the bag and left.

Dora laughed. "He thinks we have a thing going," she said.

"I thought we had," John said. "May I have another beer?"

She brought him a cold can. "John, I didn't want to say anything while Terry was here, but you look awful. You've lost weight, and even the bags under your eyes have bags. Aren't you getting any sleep?"

"Not enough. I have to go for a physical next month, and the doc will probably stick me in Intensive Care."

"I worry about you," she said.

"Do you?" he said with a boyish smile. "That's nice. Listen, enough about me; let's talk about the big enchilada: the three guys who got capped. You hear anything new?"

Dora told him about her conversations with Felicia and Eleanor, and how the former planned to marry Turner Pierce. She told him nothing of what she had learned from Gregor Pinchik and his merry band of hackers.

"You think Felicia is hooked?" Wenden asked.

"Definitely. She should be under treatment right now."

"Where is she getting her supply?"

"Eleanor says Turner Pierce is her candyman. But Eleanor is so bitter about the divorce, I don't know if she's telling the truth."

John shook his head. "We find coke under the floorboards in Father Callaway's pad, Felicia is snorting the stuff, and now Ramon Schnabl, a drug biggie, turns out to have some connection with Starrett's gold trading. Maybe it all fits together, but I don't see it. Do you?"

"Not yet," Dora said. "Do *you* have anything new on the three homicides?"

He brightened. "Yeah—we finally got a break. At least I hope it's a break. Remember I told you we were checking out all the stores, bars, and restaurants in the neighborhood of the Church of the Holy Oneness, to see if Loftus-Callaway had been in the night he was offed. We finally got to a scruffy French restaurant on East Twenty-eighth Street, and an old waiter there says he thinks the good Father was in that night."

"John, it's taken a long time, hasn't it?"

"You think it's an easy job, that you just walk into a joint, flash a photo of the dear departed and ask if he was there at a certain time on a certain date, and then people tell you? It's not that simple, Red. Clerks and bartenders and waiters have so many customers, they forget individual faces. And also, it's hard to find out who was on duty that particular night. And then it turns out that one of the waiters has been fired, or quit for another job, or maybe moved out of the state. And then he's got to be tracked down. Believe me, it's a long, ass-breaking job, and chances are good it'll turn out to be a dead end. But it's got to be done. So as I said, we finally found this restaurant on East Twenty-eighth where a waiter remembers Callaway being in the night he was killed. The reason the waiter remembers him was that the noble padre didn't leave a tip. The moral of that story is: Never stiff a waiter."

"Was Callaway alone or with someone?"

Wenden looked at her admiringly. "You're pretty sharp—you know that? I'm sorry for that crack I made about you being an amateur. But I did say you were a talented and beautiful amateur. That helps, doesn't it?"

"Some," Dora said, but it still rankled. "Who was Callaway with?"

"The waiter says he sat in a booth with a young woman. But the waiter is so old that to him a 'young woman' could be anyone from sixty on down."

"What's your next move?"

"I went to Mrs. Olivia Starrett and got photographs of Eleanor, Felicia, and Helene Pierce. They're color Polaroids taken at a dinner party last Christmas at the Starretts' apartment. I'm having blow-ups made, and I'm going back to that waiter and see if he can pick out one of them as the woman who sat in the booth and had drinks with the recently deceased. It's a long shot, but it's all I've got."

"It sounds good to me," Dora said enthusiastically. "I think you're doing a great job."

"Tell that to my boss," the detective said mournfully. "He thinks I'm dragging my feet. Actually, I'm dragging my tail. Order me to go home, Red, and get some sleep."

"Go home and get some sleep."

"Yeah," he said, "I should. Remember the night you let me crash here?"

"Not tonight, John," Dora said firmly.

"You don't trust me?"

"I don't trust either of us. Besides, you're too bushed even to go through the motions."

"You're right," he said, groaning. "I feel like one of the undead. Well, thanks for everything, Red."

"John, drive carefully."

He stared at her with eyes heavy with weariness. "No decision yet, huh?" he said.

"Not yet."

"But you're thinking about it?"

"All the time," she said, almost angrily.

"Good," he said. "It would work for us, Red, I know it would."

They embraced before he left, hugged tightly, kissed long and lingeringly. Finally Dora pushed him out the door and turned her head away so he wouldn't see the tears brimming.

She cleaned up the pretzel crumbs, still snuffling, a little, and dumped the empty beer cans. She took up her pen and notebook but sat for several moments without scribbling a word. After a while she was able to stop brooding about John Wenden and concentrate on what she had learned from ballsy Terry Ortiz.

She figured he'd probably go ahead with a break-in at Stuttgart Precious Metals, and John would help him, and so would she. She knew what they would find—and it wasn't drugs. But she'd never tell the detectives what she had guessed; it would bruise their masculine egos. Let them go on thinking she was an amateur.

41

Numbers had always fascinated Turner Pierce. He even gave them characteristics: 1 was stalwart, 3 was sensual, 7 was stern, 8 was lascivious. But even without this fanciful imaging, numbers had the power to move the world. Once you understood them and how they worked, you could exploit their power for your own benefit.

But now, in his elegant, number-ordered universe, a totally irrational factor had been introduced. The presence of Felicia Starrett was like the "cracking" of a functioning computer by the invasion of a virus. The software he had designed to program his life was being disrupted by this demented woman.

He was quite aware of what was happening to him. It was as if he had caught Felicia's unreason. His linear logicality was constantly being ruptured by her drug-induced madness, and his reactions were becoming as disordered as her hallucinations and paranoia. He knew his physical appearance was deteriorating and his work for Ramon Schnabl suffering from neglect.

Her speech was becoming increasingly incoherent. She had lost the ability to control her bladder and bowels. Her rages had become more violent. She had lost so much weight that her dry, hot skin was stretched tightly over white knobs of bones. Turner was chained to a convulsive skeleton whose paroxysms became so extreme that he was forced to restrain her with bands of cloth. But even when fettered to the bed, her thrashings were so furious he feared her thin bones might snap.

It was only when she smoked a pipe of ice that these frightening displays of dementia were mollified. But then her body temperature rose so high, her breathing became so labored, her heartbeat so erratic, that he panicked at the thought she might expire in *his* bed, in *his* apartment. His life had not been programmed to handle that eventuality.

He phoned Ramon Schnabl, twice, intending to ask if an antidote existed that might return Felicia to normality. His calls were not returned. He then phoned Helene and, trying not to sound hysterical, asked her to come over and baby-sit "the patient" so he could get out of that smashed and fetid apartment for a while, have a decent dinner, and try to jump-start his brain in the cold night air.

Helene, not questioning, said she'd be there as soon as possible.

"Thank you," Turner Pierce said, not recognizing his own piteous voice.

Felicia Starrett dwelt in a world she did not recognize. It was all new, all different: colors more intense, sounds foreign, smells strange and erotic. She heard herself babbling but could not understand the words. She wasn't aware of who she was or where she was. Her new world was primeval. She remembered a few things in brief moments of lucidity: an aching past and a glorious future when she would marry Turner Pierce and everything would be all right. Forever and ever. She stared about with naked eyes.

Once, in Kansas City, when she had repulsed Sid Loftus, he had said to her, "You're not deep, you're shallow." Then he had added, "But wide." Helene Pierce had never understood what he meant by that. If he was implying that she was incapable of reflecting on the Meaning of Life, he was totally wrong; Helene often had deep thoughts. She was not, after all, a ninny.

Experience had taught her that life was dichotomous. People were either staunch individuals, motivated solely by self-interest, or they were what might be termed communicants who devoted their lives to interactions with families, spouses, friends, lovers, neighborhoods, cities.

It seemed to Helene the choice was easy. Being a communicant demanded sacrifice of time and energy—and life was too brief for that. Being a self-centered separate demanded less sacrifice but more risk. You were on your own, completely. So she began to equate the communicant with timidity and the individual with courage. She had, she told herself, the balls to go it alone. Gamble all, lose all or win all.

Then Turner phoned and asked her to come to his apartment and watch over nutty Felicia while he took a break. Hearing the panic in his voice—she was sensitive to overtones when men spoke—Helene immediately agreed. She recognized at once that it was an opportunity that might not soon occur again.

305

As she prepared to leave, she reviewed the scenario she had devised. It had the virtue of simplicity. It was direct, stark, and she figured it had a fifty-percent chance of success. But her entire life had been a fifty-fifty proposition; she was not daunted by a coin flip.

And so she started out, excited, almost sexually, by what she was about to do.

Turner had the apartment door locked, bolted, chained; it took him a moment to get it open.

"My God," he said in a splintered voice, "am I ever glad to see *you,* babe. Come on in."

Helene tried not to reveal her shock at his appearance: haunted eyes, sunken cheeks, unshaven jaw, uncombed hair. Even his once meticulously groomed mustache had become a scraggly blur. His clothes were soiled and shapeless.

She said nothing about the way he looked but glanced about the disordered apartment with dismay.

"Turner," she said, "you're living in a swamp."

"Tell me about it," he said bitterly. "I've tried to clean up, but then she goes on a rampage again. And I obviously can't hire someone to come in with a raving lunatic in the next room."

"She's in the bedroom?"

He nodded. "I've had to tie her to the bed. It's for her own safety," he added defensively. "And mine."

"How's she doing?"

"At the moment she's sleeping. Or unconscious; I don't know which. She had a pipe this afternoon. If she comes out of it tonight she'll be groggy for a few hours before she crashes. Think you can handle it?"

"Of course," Helene said. "Get yourself cleaned up, go have a good dinner. I'll be here when you get back."

"Thanks, babe," he said throatily. "I don't know what I'd do without you. What's it like out?"

"Absolutely miserable. Snow, sleet, freezing rain. Cold as hell and a wind that just won't quit."

"Maybe I'll run over to Vito's and grab a veal chop and a couple of stiff belts. Make me a new man."

"Sure it will," Helene said.

He went into the bathroom, and a moment later she heard the sound of his electric shaver. She didn't go into the bedroom but made a small effort to straighten up the living room, picking books and magazines from the floor, setting chairs upright, carrying used glasses and plates back to the kitchen. She took a look in the refrigerator. Nothing much in there: two oranges, a package of sliced ham, some cheese going green. There was a bottle of Absolut in the cupboard under the sink, but she didn't touch it. She didn't need Dutch courage.

Turner appeared looking a little better. He had shaved, washed up, put on a fresh shirt, brushed his hair and mustache.

"Two things," he said. "Keep the front door locked and don't, under any circumstances, untie her. She may beg you to turn her loose, but don't do it. You just don't know what she'll do. I'll be back in an hour."

"Take your time," Helene said.

After he left, she bolted the front door and glanced at her watch. Then she went into the bedroom. It was a malodorous place, furry with dust, and overheated. Illumination came from a dim bulb in the dresser lamp. The rug was littered with scraps of torn cloth, newspapers, a few shards of broken glass. And there were great, ugly stains.

Felicia Starrett, eyes closed, lay under a thin cotton sheet despoiled with blotches of yellow and brown. Her breathing was shallow and irregular; occasionally little whimpers escaped from her opened mouth, no louder than a kitten's mewls. Her wrists were bound together with a strip of sheeting. Her ankles were similarly shackled, and a long, wide band of cloth had been run under the bed, the two ends knotted across her waist.

Helene thought she looked in extremis, that her next small breath might be the last. She pulled a straightback chair to the bedside, touched one of those bound claws lightly.

"Felicia," she said softly.

No response.

"Felicia," she repeated and stroked a blemished, shrunken arm. "Felicia, dear, can you hear me?"

Eyelids rose, not slowly but suddenly; her eyes just popped open. Helene leaned closer.

"Felicia," she said gently, "it's Helene. Do you recognize me, darling?"

Eyes swung to her, but the focus was somewhere else.

"Water," Felicia said, trying to lick dry lips.

Helene went back to the kitchen, found a plastic cup, filled it with tap water, brought it to the bedroom. She held it to those parched lips while the fettered woman gulped greedily. She finished it all, turned her head aside and spewed it all over the pillow, bed, floor.

"Never mind," Helene said, controlling her own nausea at the sight, "we'll try again a little later. Is there anything you want, Felicia?"

Rheumy eyes turned to her. "Helene?" the woman asked.

"Of course! I'm Helene, dear, here to help you. How do you feel?"

"I'm sick."

"I know, Felicia, but you're going to be better real soon."

"Where's Turner?"

"He had to go out for a little while, but he'll be back before you know it."

Felicia looked down at her bound hands lying atop the soiled sheet. "Untie me," she said in a scratchy voice.

"Not right now, dear. Maybe when Turner gets back. Would you like to try a little more water now? Maybe an orange would taste good. There's a nice cold orange in the fridge. I'll get it and peel it for you."

She returned to the kitchen again, and, after searching a few moments, found where Turner had hidden the knives: on the top shelf of the cupboard over the range. Helene selected the long, pointed carving knife, the one Felicia had used to slash the furniture. She brought the knife and orange back to the bedroom.

She sat calmly, slowly slicing rind from the orange with the sharp blade, letting the peelings drop to the floor. She was aware that Felicia was watching her every move.

"There we are!" Helene said brightly, holding up the naked orange. "Doesn't that look nice? Would you like a piece right now?"

"Where's Turner?" Felicia repeated.

"He had to go out for a little while," Helene said again, "but he'll be back soon. You love Turner, don't you, darling."

Felicia blinked her eyes, tried to moisten her cracked lips. She attempted to speak, once, twice, and finally croaked, "We're going to get married."

"That's what I wanted to talk to you about," Helene said,

hunching closer. "Now listen to me, dear, and try to understand what I'm saying."

She spoke slowly, distinctly, for almost ten minutes, repeating everything until she was satisfied the other woman had heard and comprehended, even dimly. There was no reaction, no objection. But Felicia's mouth sagged open again, eyelids shut as suddenly as they had opened.

"I'm going now, dear," Helene said. "Turner will be back soon. But let me untie you first."

Rather than attempt to loosen the tight knots, Helene used the carving knife to slice them through. Felicia lay motionless. Helene left the peeled orange and knife on the sheet alongside that flaccid body in its mummy posture.

"I hope you're feeling better real soon, darling," she said lightly. "Do take care of yourself."

Then she went swiftly into the living room, grabbed up hat, coat, purse, and left the apartment. Outside, she bent forward against the wind, the gusts of stinging hail, and walked westward as rapidly as she could.

He had unbelted his trench coat to get at his keys.

When he entered the apartment, it was almost completely dark.

The only illumination was a weak light coming from the bedroom.

He turned to flip on the wall switch.

His coat swung open.

"Helene!" he called. "I'm home!"

The knife went in just below his sternum.

The force of the blow slammed him back against the closed door.

The blade was withdrawn and shoved in again.

Again.

Again.

In shock, body burning, he looked down at the blood blooming from his wounds.

He looked at the naked wraith crouched in front of him.

Dimly he saw her lips drawn tight in a tortured grin.

He glimpsed a matchstick arm working like a piston.

He felt the blade penetrate.

Scorching.

He tried to reach out to stop that fire, but his knees buckled.

He slid slowly downward until he was sitting, legs thrust out, hands clamped across his belly, trying to dam the flood.

She would not stop, but bent over him, stabbing, stabbing.

Even after he was dead, she continued to poke with the knife, in all parts of his body, until she was certain he had ceased to exist.

42

"It's *perfect* weather!" enthused Detective Ortiz. "All the precinct cops will be in the coop, and all the bums will be in cardboard cartons under a bridge somewhere."

"What's the setup, Terry?" Wenden asked.

"There is no setup. No security guards and no alarms that I could spot. The place is Swiss cheese. We go in through the front door. I could pick that lock with a hairpin. Then we're in the office. A back door leads to the warehouse. I got a quick look at that, and there's nothing but a push-bolt as far as I could see. Listen, we'll be in and out of that joint before you can finish whistling 'Dixie.' "

"You got it all straight, Red?" Wenden said. "You drop us at Tenth Avenue and Fifty-fifth. Then drive around the block. Park as close to Stuttgart as you can get. If you have to double-park, that's okay, too. Give us two blasts of your horn if you see something that could be a problem. Okay?"

"A piece of cake," Dora said.

She was driving the Ford Escort. The two detectives,

dressed in black, sat in the back. The windshield wipers were straining, and Dora leaned forward to peer through slanting rain, fierce flurries of sleet.

"If you guys are going to be so quick," she said, "maybe I better keep the motor running. I wouldn't care to stall out and have to call the Triple-A."

"Good idea," Terrible Terry said. "You got a full tank?"

"Of course," Dora said, offended. "This isn't my first criminal enterprise, you know."

"Love this woman," Ortiz said, *"Love* her!"

Traffic was practically nil. No buses. A few cabs. A civilian car now and then. They saw a snowplow heading up Eighth Avenue and a sander moving down Ninth. Dora pulled across Tenth Avenue on 55th Street and stopped.

"Have a good time," she said.

The two cops climbed out of the car.

"Twenty minutes," Ortiz said. "But if we're late, don't panic."

"I never panic," Dora said. "I'll be waiting for you."

She drove slowly around the block, being careful to stop for red lights. She found a parking space almost directly across the street from Stuttgart Precious Metals. She turned to watch the two men come plodding down 54th, bending against the wind but taking a good look around. Dora thought they must be freezing in their leather jackets. They were the only pedestrians, and no vehicles were moving.

She saw them pause, glance about casually, then saunter up to Stuttgart's front door. Both bent over the lock. Ortiz was true to his word; they were inside within a minute. The door closed behind them. Dora turned on the radio. She caught a weather forecast. It didn't sound good: rain and sleet turning to snow. Accumulations of up to two inches expected in the city, four inches in the suburbs. She lighted a cigarette and waited.

Nothing occurred and she was disappointed; a little high drama wouldn't have been amiss. Less than twenty minutes later, the two men came cautiously out of Stuttgart's front door. They paused a moment while Ortiz fiddled with the lock. Dora turned on her lights, and the cops came trotting across the street and climbed into the back of the Escort.

"Jee-*sus!*" Ortiz said. "It was cold in that dump."

Dora opened the glove compartment, took out a brown paper bag, handed it back to them. It contained a pint of California brandy.

"Something to chase the chill," she said.

"Did I tell you I love this woman?" Terrible Terry said to Wenden. "*Love* her!"

They opened the bottle and handed it back and forth as Dora pulled out and started back to the Bedlington.

"Not too fast, not too slow," Wenden warned.

"I know the drill," Dora said crossly. "How did you guys make out?"

"Drive now, talk later," he said.

She didn't offer another word on the trip back to the hotel. The two detectives conversed in low voices in the back, but she paid no attention. She was almost certain she knew what they had found at Stuttgart.

The cops had flashed their potsies and left John's heap in the No Parking zone in front of the hotel. Dora double-parked, cut the engine, lights, and windshield wipers. The snow was beginning, but it was a fat, lazy fall; the flakes looked like feathers in the streetlight's glare.

She turned sideways, looked back at them. "Find any drugs?" she asked.

"Not a gram," Ortiz said.

"Gold bars?"

Both detectives laughed.

"Oh yeah," John said, "we found stacks of gold bars. As a matter of fact, we even took shavings from one of them with my handy-dandy Boy Scout knife. Want to see?"

He dug a hand into his jacket pocket, then stuck an open palm forward for Dora's inspection. She saw what she expected to see: thin curls of a dull pewterish metal.

"What the hell is that?" she asked, all innocence.

"Lead," John said. "Starrett Fine Jewelry has been dealing in lead bars."

"Shit!" Terry said disgustedly. "You'd think a high-class outfit like Starrett would have the decency to coat their lead bars with genuine gold. But no, those bars were *painted*, with five-and-dime gilt. Can you believe it?"

"I don't get it," Dora said, willing to give them their moment of triumph. "Why are Starrett and Ramon Schnabl schlepping gold-painted lead bars all over the country?"

"It's a be-*yooti*-ful scam," John said. "Here's how we figure it works: Cash from Schnabl's drug deals is carried by courier to cities where Starrett has branch stores and delivered to the managers. They buy gold from Starrett in New York and pay with the drug money. Starrett headquarters, in turn, transfers the money electronically to their overseas gold suppliers, all owned by Schnabl."

"But there is actually no gold at all," Dora said. "Just lead bars they keep moving back and forth to get apparently legal documentation in the form of bills of lading, shipping invoices, warehouse receipts, and so forth."

"You've got it, Red," Wenden said. "The whole thing is just a scheme to launder drug money, get it out of the country in what appear to be legitimate business transactions."

"But what's the reason for Felix Brothers Classic Jewelry in Boston," Dora asked, "and all those other little jewelry shops?"

"Fronts," Ortiz said. "Set up by Schnabl so, on paper, the Starrett branch stores can show they have legit customers for all that gold they're buying from New York. And maybe some of those holes-in-the-wall are also banks for local drug deals."

Dora thought a moment. "Clayton Starrett must be in on it."

"You better believe it," John said. "Up to his eyeballs. And the branch managers hired a couple of years ago. And probably the guy running Starrett's Brooklyn vault. They're all involved and getting a piece of the action. Solomon Guthrie was too honest to turn. But he knew something was going on that wasn't kosher, so he got whacked. By Schnabl's hatchets."

Dora shook her head. "You've got to admit it's slick. I wonder who dreamed it up."

Wenden said, "My leading candidate is Turner Pierce, the computer genius. It would need computers to keep track of purchases, sales, expenses, and then come up with a bottom line every week or so."

"If it really was Turner Pierce," Dora said slowly, "you think his sister knew about it?"

"Helene? Of course she knew. Had to. And she's going to marry Clayton Starrett, isn't she? That keeps the fraud a family secret; no outsiders allowed."

"John," Ortiz said, "we'll have to bring the *federales* in on this."

Wenden slumped. "Say it ain't so, Terry."

"It is so. This caper is interstate and international with the electronic movement of big money. It's going to take an army of bank examiners, lawyers, accountants, and computer experts to sort it out and make a case. We just don't have enough warm bodies. We'll have to notify Treasury, the DEA and FBI."

"Aw, shit," Wenden said, "I guess you're right. But make sure that Red here gets the credit." He smiled and leaned forward to pat Dora's arm. "There wouldn't be any case at all if she hadn't started snooping."

"There's enough glory to go around," Dora said. "What's your next move, John?"

"Go back to the office, alert the Feds, and start the wheels turning. But before they get their act together, maybe I'll look up Turner Pierce and have a cozy little chat."

"I think I'll come along," Terry said. "If we lean hard on him, he might rat on Ramon Schnabl. I want to see that bastardo in Leavenworth, playing Pick-Up-the-Soap in the shower."

"I know why Guthrie was capped," Wenden continued, "but I'd like to find out why Lewis Starrett and Sid Loftus were put down. It all connects somehow to the gold trading plot and laundering of drug money."

Dora made no response.

"Listen," Terrible Terry Ortiz said to her, "maybe I never see you again, which is a big sorrow for me. I just want you to know you are one lovely lady, and it was a pleasure to make your acquaintance." He leaned forward to kiss her hand. "And take care of *mi amigo*," he added, jerking a thumb toward Wenden. "He deserves a break."

Dora nodded, but said nothing as they climbed out of the

Ford, got into John's clunker, and drove away. She maneuvered her car into the spot they had just vacated in the No Parking zone. Then she went into the Bedlington, told the night clerk what she had done, and asked if the doorman would take care of the Escort when he came on duty.

The clerk assured her that her car was okay right where it was and handed her two messages, both from Gregor Pinchik. Please call him as soon as possible, at any hour of the day or night. But it was then close to 2:30 in the morning, and all Dora wanted was to hit the sack and grab some Z's.

Upstairs, she made herself a warm milk. She sipped it slowly while she reflected on the night's events and how they might or might not affect the insurance claim she was supposed to be investigating. She felt like someone in search of honey who finds herself enveloped in a swarm of buzzing and ferocious bees. But she could not flee; that would be unprofessional.

She wondered if she stuck to this case, to all her assignments, because of the raw human emotions they revealed. Perhaps her own personal life was so staid and commonplace that she needed to share the excitement of other people's travails, just as poor Felicia Starrett needed a periodic fix. And maybe that, after all, was why the possibility of an affair with John Wenden had not been instantly and automatically rejected. She yearned for something grand in her life, something that might shake her up, even if it left her frustrated and tormented.

She felt a terrible temptation to dare.

43

Dora had intended to sleep late, but when the phone jangled her awake she glanced at the bedside clock and saw it was only 8:00 A.M.

"H'lo?" she said drowsily.

"Good morning, lady. Gregor Pinchik here. Listen, something came up I think you should know about. Can you come down here right away?"

She groaned. "In this weather?"

"What weather?" he said. "The sky is blue, the sun is shining, and all the avenues have been scraped."

"You can't come here, Greg?" she asked hopefully.

"Nope. There's something on the screen you've got to see."

"All right," she said. "Give me an hour."

She brushed her teeth, combed the snarls out of her hair, and pulled on sweater and tweed skirt. Shouldering her big bag, she rushed out. Remembering the parking problem on her previous visit to SoHo, she decided to leave the Escort wherever it was and take a cab downtown.

Pinchik had been right: It was a brilliant morning, crystal clear, and what snow remained was rapidly turning to slush as the sun warmed. Traffic was mercifully light, and she was seated in Pinchik's loft a little after nine o'clock. Greg provided coffee and buttered bagels, for which Dora was grateful.

"You eat and I'll talk," he said. "I got some interesting stuff. There are no secrets anymore. Privacy is obsolete—did you know that? Anyway, first of all, that lowlife you told me about, Sidney Loftus: He was involved in a lot of shady deals and used a half-dozen phony names."

"I know," Dora said. "The Company has him on Red Alert because he was running an insurance swindle. What I wanted to know was whether Loftus knew Turner and Helene Pierce in Kansas City."

"Sure he did," Pinchik said. "As a matter of fact, he steered a few clients to Pierce for his computer consulting service—for a commission, of course. One of the clients he landed for Pierce was a guy who owned a string of bars, fast-food joints, and hot-pillow motels. Now get this! It later turned out this same guy was dealing dope. After he was indicted, the KC papers called him a kingpin in the Midwest drug trade. That's the kind of riffraff Loftus and the Pierces were associating with. Nice people, huh, lady?"

"Not exactly pillars of society," she agreed. "Did you get any reports that Loftus and the Pierces were using drugs themselves?"

He shook his head. "I got nothing on that, but the stuff was easily available to them if they wanted it. Now about Helene Pierce and her history before she showed up as a hooker. She came from a little farm town in Kansas and moved to the big city after high school, hoping to become a rich and famous movie star. She had the looks, I guess, but not the talent. She did some modeling for catalogues and such, and then she drifted into the party circuit, and before long she had her own plush apartment and was on call."

Dora sighed. "Hardly a unique story."

Pinchik stared at her. "I saved the best for last. Her real name is Helene Thomson."

Dora returned his stare. "I don't understand, Greg. Her brother's name is Turner Pierce. Different fathers? Adopted? Or what?"

"Lady," he said softly, "they're not brother and sister. They're husband and wife. Turner Pierce married Helene Thomson. They're still married, as far as I know."

Dora took a deep breath. "You're absolutely sure about this, Greg?"

"I told you I know a KC hacker who's cracked city hall. Take a look at this."

He switched on one of his computers, worked the keyboard, and brought up a document on the display panel. He gestured and Dora leaned forward to look. It was a reproduction of a marriage license issued four years previously to Helene Thomson and Turner Pierce.

Dora reached out to pat the computer. "Deus ex machina," she said.

"Nah," said Pinchik, "it's an Apple."

She cabbed home, thoughts awhirl, wondering where her primary duty lay. Warn Felicia? Inform Olivia? Tell Clayton? Or keep her mouth shut and let those loopy people solve their own problems or strangle on their craziness. One person, she decided, who *had* to know was Detective John Wenden. If he and Terry Ortiz were going to brace Turner Pierce, knowing of his "secret" marriage to Helene might be of use.

Her taxi was heading north on Park Avenue, had crossed

34th Street, when it suddenly slowed. Dora craned to look ahead and saw a tangle of parked police cars, fire engines, and ambulances spilling out of a side street. A uniformed officer was directing single-lane traffic around the jam of official vehicles.

"Something happened," her cabbie said. "Cop cars *and* fire engines. Maybe it was a bombing. We haven't had one of those for a couple of days."

"That's nice," Dora said.

The moment she was back in her hotel suite she phoned Wenden. He wasn't in, so she left a message asking him to call her as soon as possible; it was *extremely* important.

Then, faced with the task of entering Gregor Pinchik's revelations in her notebook, she said aloud, "The hell with it," kicked off her shoes and got into bed, fully clothed, for a pre-noon nap. She had never done that before, and it was a treat.

But a short one. For the second time that day she was awakened from a sweet sleep by the shrilling phone.

"John," Wenden said. "What's *extremely* important?"

"I've got to tell—" she started.

"Wait a minute," he interrupted. "There's something I've got to tell *you*. I'm calling from a drugstore on Lex. I've just come from Turner Pierce's apartment in Murray Hill. He's dead as the proverbial doornail. Stabbed many, many times—and I do mean *many*. There goes my cozy little chat. I told you if we waited long enough everyone in this case would get whacked out."

"In Murray Hill?" Dora said. "I went by in a cab. There were fire engines."

"Yeah," he said, "that's how Pierce was found. Felicia Starrett iced him last night and then, this morning, set the

324

place on fire. Neighbors smelled smoke and called in the alarm."

"Is Felicia alive?"

"If you can call it that. She was naked and looked like last week's corpse. And so zonked out on drugs that she couldn't do anything but dribble."

"Are you sure she killed him?"

"Red! She was still gripping the knife, so hard that we had to pry her fingers loose. They took her to Bellevue. Maybe when she gets detoxed she'll be able to tell us what happened. Listen, I've got to run."

"Wait!" Dora cried. "I didn't tell you what I called about. Turner and Helene Pierce weren't brother and sister; they were married."

"What?" he yelled. "Are you positive?"

"Absolutely. I saw a copy of their marriage license. John, do me a favor. Even if it looks certain that Felicia stabbed Turner, check out Helene's whereabouts last night. Okay?"

"Yeah," he said tensely, "I better do that. Thanks for the tip, Red. I'll get back to you later today."

"When?" she demanded.

"Look, I've got a million things to do. I don't know when I'll get a break."

"Sooner or later you've got to eat," she argued, "or you'll end up in Bellevue with Felicia. John, I'll stay in all day. You call me when you have time, stop over, and we'll grab a bite in the cocktail lounge downstairs. It'll give us a chance to compare notes."

"That makes sense," he said. "You'll hear from me."

Dora spent the afternoon scribbling in her notebook, happy that she wouldn't be making many more notes. The tangled skein was unraveling, and what she didn't know, she could guess. She even dragged out that nonsensical diagram she had drawn with the names of all the involved characters in boxes connected by straight or squiggly lines. But now the connections seemed clear to her, and infinitely sad. She wondered if all humans are born with an innate capacity to screw up their lives.

John called a little after five o'clock, said he was going to shove his job for an hour, and didn't care if the entire island of Manhattan slid into the Upper Bay while he was off duty. Dora brushed her hair and went down to the cocktail lounge. She took the table which she and Felicia Starrett had occupied during their first meeting.

But when Wenden entered, he went directly to the bar and asked for a shot of rye. He tossed it down, then ordered a bottle of beer and brought it over to Dora's table.

"You'd think I'd be used to seeing clunks, wouldn't you?" he said angrily. "I'm not. But at least I don't upchuck anymore. My God, Red, I can't tell you how bad it was. Not only the remains but also that madwoman. And the apartment—a shithouse!"

"John, you're wired," Dora said, putting a hand on his arm. "Sip your beer and try to settle down. I'll order club sandwiches. All right?"

"Whatever."

He seemed to be operating on pure adrenaline, and she wondered if he might collapse when the rush faded.

"You were right," he said, speaking rapidly and gulping his beer. "I checked with the concierge at Helene's apartment house. She left the place last night about eight o'clock and didn't return until two in the morning. The guy said she was soaked through and looked like she had been walking in the storm. I don't know what that means—do you?"

"That she was at Turner's apartment last night. Will you dust the knife handle for prints?"

"What good will that do? I told you we had to twist it out of Felicia's hand. If there were other prints on it, they'd be smeared to nothing."

"Then check cups and glasses," Dora urged. "I'm sure you'll find Helene's prints."

"So what? She'll claim they were made weeks ago during a visit."

"Then vacuum the place," Dora said desperately. "You may find some long hairs—just like the ones you found in the room where Sidney Loftus was killed."

Wenden glared at her. "Are you trying to tell me that Helene knifed Turner Pierce?"

"No," Dora said, "I don't believe that. But I do think she went there last night."

"What for?"

"To tell Felicia that she was the wife of the man Felicia hoped to marry. She knew what condition that poor woman was in and figured to push her over the edge. Helene may not have actually stabbed Turner, but she guided the knife. She wanted her husband dead."

John took a deep breath, blew it out, and slumped in his chair, suddenly slack and relaxed. "You may be right," he said quietly, "but it's not illegal for a wife to tell another woman that her lover is already hitched."

Then they were silent while their fat club sandwiches were served. John stared at his.

"I'm not sure I can handle that," he said. "My stomach is still churning."

"Try," Dora pleaded. "You need it. You look like death warmed over."

He took a small bite, chewed determinedly, and swallowed. He waited a moment, then smiled and nodded.

"I'm going to be okay," he said. "Tastes good. About those hairs found in the back room of the Church of the Holy Oneness—you're probably right about Helene being there on the murder night. I took the photographs over to that waiter at the Twenty-eighth Street restaurant, and he definitely identified Helene as being the woman Loftus was with the night he was blanked. But that's all circumstantial, Red. A waiter's ID and a couple of hairs—we'd never get a conviction out of that."

"You mean," Dora demanded hotly, "she's going to go free?"

Wenden nodded. "Unless we can come up with something more than we've got. Besides, I'm not so sure Helene did it. I still think the Lewis Starrett, Sol Guthrie, and Sid Loftus homicides were all related and connected somehow to the laundering of drug money."

Dora ignored her sandwich. "Detective Wenden," she said as calmly as she could, "you're full of you-know-what."

"All right," he said equably, "you tell me what you think went down."

"There were four homicides," Dora began. "Four deaths. Four different killers. And four different motives.

"One: Lewis Starrett was murdered by Sidney Loftus, then using the name of Father Brian Callaway. His motive? Eleanor Starrett told me in our first meeting. I put it in my report but didn't see the significance until my boss in Hartford caught it. Lewis had ordered his wife not to give another penny to Callaway's phony church, and Olivia was the good Father's heaviest contributor. No way was that swindler going to lose his richest sucker. So he offed Lewis with the chef's knife taken from the Starrett apartment on the night of the cocktail party. He knew Lewis's death would leave Olivia an even wealthier woman.

"Two: The murder of Solomon Guthrie. You're right about that one; Sol sensed something was fishy about Starrett's gold trading, probably made a fuss about it to Clayton, and took his suspicions to Arthur Rushkin, the attorney. When Clayton, Turner Pierce, and Ramon Schnabl heard about that, they got rid of the threat to their operation by getting rid of Guthrie. I imagine Schnabl provided the hit men; it had all the marks of a professional contract kill.

"Three: Sidney Loftus. This is the iffiest one of the lot, and I admit my ideas are mostly guesswork. Sid Loftus and the Pierces were buddy-buddy in Kansas City, and he had to know they were married. But in New York he had his church scam going and they were clipping the Starretts, so all the sharks were making a nice buck and no one rocked the boat. But then Clayton announced he was going to get a divorce and marry Helene. Loftus saw the chance for a profitable shakedown and put the bite on the Pierces. They weren't about to sit still for blackmail and decided to eliminate their old pal Sidney. Helene made a date with him, maybe promising sex, and put him down in the back room of his fake tabernacle.

"Four: the stabbing of Turner Pierce. I've already told you how I think that went. Turner was going nuts trying to keep Felicia under control with drugs—probably supplied by Ramon Schnabl—and Helene figured who needs Turner? With her hubby out of the picture she really could marry Clayton Starrett with all the goodies that promised. So she egged on Felicia to do the dirty work for her. I think that's the way it happened. One of the reasons I'm sure Helene did it is that I just don't like the woman."

Dora finished, sat back, and waited for Wenden's critique.

"Are you going to eat your sandwich?" he asked.

"Half of it," she said. "You want the other half?"

He nodded, and she lifted it carefully to his plate. They both began chomping.

"I like your ideas," John said. "Everything you say makes sense. If you're right, the Lewis Starrett file is closed because the killer, Sid Loftus, is dead. As for nailing the guys who aced Guthrie, I don't think there's much chance of that unless someone rats on Schnabl, which I don't see happening. And as for Loftus's murder, I'm just as convinced as you are that Helene is the perp, but right now there's not enough evidence to charge her, let alone indict and convict. And maybe she did trigger the stabbing of Turner by Felicia but, as I told you, what she did might have been wicked and immoral but it wasn't illegal. Felicia will get treatment for her drug addiction, and I doubt if she'll do time for an act committed when she was, as her lawyer will claim, temporarily insane while under the influence of dope supplied by the man she killed after learning he had betrayed her. So, as far as I can see, there were four brutal killings, and no one is going to spend a day in jail for any one of them."

"What happened to justice?" Dora cried.

"The law is one thing," Wenden said with a strained smile, "and justice is another. Unless you believe in divine retribution. And if you do, there's a bridge in Brooklyn you may be interested in buying."

"I hate it!" Dora burst out. "Just hate it!"

"The guilty not being punished?" John said. "I have to live with it. Every day."

They had finished their sandwiches and now sat back, gripping empty beer glasses, looking at each other.

"I suppose this just about winds it up for you," John said.

Dora nodded. "I have things to do tomorrow. Then I'll probably take off early Friday morning."

"Back to Hartford?"

"Uh-huh. I think I'll drive home. I can turn in the Escort up there."

"Can we have dinner tomorrow night?"

"Sure," she said. "I'd like that."

"When I called you from Lexington Avenue this afternoon I spotted an Italian restaurant. There was a menu in the window, and it looked okay. The place is called Vito's. Want to try it?"

"I'm game for anything," Dora said.

"I hope so," Wenden said.

44

Attorney Arthur Rushkin came from his inner office to greet her with a beamy smile, looking spiffy in houndstooth jacket and suede waistcoat, a butterfly bow tie flaring under his suety chin.

"Mrs. Conti!" he boomed, shaking her hand. "How nice to see you again. I was hoping you'd stop by."

"I'm leaving tomorrow morning," she told him, "and felt I owed you a report."

He took her anorak and hung it away. Then he ushered her into his private office and got her settled in the armchair alongside his antique partners' desk. He lowered his bulk into the leather swivel chair.

"Mr. Rushkin," Dora said, "I assume you're aware of what's been going on the last few days."

He nodded. "Sadly, I am. Starrett Fine Jewelry and all its branches have been closed. Temporarily, I hope. After that dreadful business in Murray Hill—aren't the tabloids having a field day?—Felicia is receiving medical treatment. The last I heard is that she will survive, but recovery will be a long and arduous process. And expensive, I might add."

"And Clayton?"

The attorney twisted his face into a wry grimace. "My godson? He has not yet been charged, but it's only a matter of time. At the moment he is being questioned by representatives of the U.S. Attorney's office. I can't represent Clayton—there would be a potential conflict of interest there—but I've been able to obtain for him the services of an extremely capable criminal defense attorney. On his advice, Clayton is answering all questions completely and honestly. He can't do much less; the authorities have already seized Starrett's business records, including those dealing with the fraudulent gold trading."

"Do you think Clayton will go to prison, Mr. Rushkin?"

The lawyer linked fingers across his thick midsection and sighed deeply. "I'm afraid so. But if he continues to cooperate, his punishment may be more lenient than you might think. The authorities are not interested in Clayton Starrett so much as they are in Ramon Schnabl, the drug dealer. If Clay helps them put Schnabl behind bars, I think they'll be inclined to settle for a light sentence and a heavy fine. I do believe a deal will be made."

"I intend to see Mrs. Olivia Starrett before I leave. How is she taking all this? Have you spoken to her?"

"I have indeed, and the woman's resilience is amazing. She'll be all right. Mrs. Conti, I have a fairly complete understanding of how the gold trading was jiggered, but I have less knowledge of the homicides it spawned. Can you enlighten me?"

Dora repeated the explanation of the four killings she

had given Wenden. The lawyer listened intently, and when she finished he sighed again and shook his great head so sharply that his jowls wobbled.

"Of course a lot of that is supposition," Dora pointed out. "Some of it can never be proved."

"But I suspect you're right," Rushkin said. "It's a depressing example of chronic greed. That's the disease; violence is a symptom."

"What makes me furious," Dora said, "is that Detective John Wenden doesn't think there's much chance of Helene Pierce going to jail for what she did."

"Policemen have a tendency to be gloomy," the attorney said with a wintry smile. "Quite understandable." Then he leaned across the desk toward Dora. "Let me tell you something, Mrs. Conti. The law is like the Lord: It giveth and it taketh away. In re Helene Pierce, I think it quite likely that the prosecutors may feel she had guilty knowledge. In other words, she was fully cognizant of the gold trading fraud—indeed she profited from it—but did not inform the proper authorities as required. I believe Clayton will testify as to her involvement."

"Are you sure?" Dora asked anxiously.

Rushkin laughed. "Congreve wrote of the fury of a woman scorned. I assure you, Mrs. Conti, a scorned woman's virulence can be matched by the bitterness of a middle-aged man who realizes he has been played for a fool, a patsy, by a piece of fluff half his age. Oh yes, I think Clayton will be more than willing to testify against Helene Pierce. And if the guilty-knowledge ploy doesn't hold up in court, the government has another arrow in its quiver. I'm sure the IRS will be interested in learning if Helene declared all those gifts of money and diamonds that Clayton gave her. In addition, the idiot bought her co-op and was paying the maintenance by check. That left a paper trail the IRS will be happy to follow. No, I don't believe Helene Pierce will cha-cha her way to freedom."

"That makes me feel better," Dora said. She rose and slung her shoulder bag. "I hope you no longer feel guilty about Solomon Guthrie. You gave me his computer print-out, and eventually that led to the solution."

The attorney was suddenly somber, his meaty features sagging. "I am not entirely free from regret, but at my age I can't expect to be. Mrs. Conti, thank you for all your efforts on my behalf and on behalf of Starrett Fine Jewelry. I intend to write to your employer expressing my deep appreciation of your excellent work as strongly as I can."

Dora smiled shyly. "You don't have to do that, Mr. Rush-kin."

"I know I don't *have* to," he said, "but I *want* to. If you ever tire of your job and decide to relocate to New York, please let me know. I can promise you that your investigative talents will be well rewarded here."

"Thank you, sir," she said. "I'll keep it in mind."

Out on Fifth Avenue, in a frigid drizzle, she wondered why she was grinning and walking with a bouncy step. Then she realized it was because her professional performance had been praised and she had been offered a job. That did wonders for the old ego and supplied confidence for the meeting with Mike Trevalyan in Hartford the following day. That tête-à-tête, she knew, would be a brannigan.

Just for the hell of it, she walked over to Park Avenue. As Rushkin had said, the flagship store of Starrett Fine Jewelry was shuttered. The display windows were stripped of gems, and a sign proclaimed: CLOSED UNTIL FURTHER

NOTICE. But Dora was amused to note it didn't deter a mink-swathed matron who was shading her eyes to peer within and furiously rattling the knob of the locked door.

She bused up Madison Avenue, then walked over to the Starrett apartment on Fifth. Charles, looking as funereal as ever, let her enter and left her standing in the foyer while he shuffled away to announce her arrival.

Mrs. Olivia Starrett was sharing the chubby love seat with a diminutive man swaddled in a voluminous white djellaba. He popped to his feet when Dora entered, his robe swung briefly open, and she caught a quick glimpse of skinny shins half-covered with black socks suspended from old-fashioned garters.

"Dora!" Olivia said. "I'm *so* happy to see you, dear. I want you to meet the Maharishi Ziggy Gupta, a very wise man who is teaching me the spiritual truths of the Sacred Harmony."

The little man grinned and bobbed his head at Dora. She nodded in return.

"Pliz," he said, "forgive my language, but I am mostly happy to be making your—your—" He turned to Olivia for help.

"Acquaintance," she suggested.

"Yiss," the Maharishi said. "Your acquaintance."

Dora smiled and nodded again. "Mrs. Starrett," she said, "I just wanted to stop by to offer my sympathy. I know the events of the past few days must be a terrible burden. Is there anything I can do to help?"

"How sweet of you," Olivia said. "But with Ziggy's instruction I am learning to endure. Think of life as a great symphony, and all of us are but individual notes. To know the Sacred Harmony we must contribute our personal sorrows and joys so that the holy music rises to heaven and is pleasing to God."

"Iss so," the guru said, grinning. "For He is the Great Conductor who leads us with His stick."

"Baton," Olivia said. "I can't tell you what a comfort the Maharishi has been to me. He has come from Bombay to bring America his inspiring message of hope and redemption. We were just discussing how we might set up a school in New York, The Academy of the Sacred Harmony, so more pilgrims may achieve spiritual tranquillity by learning how each of us can add to the symphonic universe."

"Yes," Dora said, dazed. "Well, I must be going. I'm happy to see you in good spirits, Mrs. Starrett."

"I am contributing my note," Olivia said with a beatific smile. "To the chords that shall become part of the exalted rhapsody. Did I say that right, Ziggy?"

"Eggsactly," he said, grinning.

Dora fled, found her parka in the foyer closet, and left that apartment. She refused to laugh at Olivia's hopeless hope. That long-suffering woman was entitled to any solace she could find.

When she exited from the elevator, she saw Eleanor Starrett come striding across the lobby, gripping a furled umbrella as if she'd like to wring its neck. She spotted Dora, rushed up, squeezed her arm tightly.

"Did you just see Olivia?" she demanded.

Dora nodded.

"Is she up and about?"

"She's doing fine."

"Thank God!" Eleanor cried. "She's got to give me some money. Did you hear about Clayton?"

"Yes, I heard."

"They can fry that moron in the electric chair for all I care," Eleanor said angrily, "but what about *me?* My lawyer says the government will claim there was a pattern of racketeering, and if he's convicted Clay will be subject to RICO penalties. Do you know what that means? I'll tell you what it means—that they can take everything he's got: money, cars, real estate, jewelry, the fillings in his teeth. So where does that leave *me?* What kind of a settlement am I going to get if the government strips that imbecile down to his Jockey shorts? You know what it makes me? A bag lady rooting in garbage cans for my *déjeuner.*"

Dora stared at her in astonishment, then noted the Starrett pearl choker at her throat, the Starrett gold brooch on her lapel, the Starrett tennis bracelet of two-carat diamonds, the several Starrett rings of emeralds, sapphires, rubies.

"Boohoo," Dora said mockingly, turned, and walked away.

45

She took special pains with her grooming that evening, brushing her hair until it gleamed, snugging on her "good" dress, adding the bracelet Mario had given her for Christmas. Finally she dabbed on a wee drop of Obsession—and wondered why she was tarting herself up. She hadn't been so nervous since her first prom, and breaking a fingernail did nothing to calm her down.

Wenden had wanted to pick her up at the hotel, but not knowing how their dinner-date might end, Dora thought it wiser to have her own transportation. So she drove over to Vito's in the Escort—and then had to park two blocks away and walk back.

John was already there, seated at a small bar just inside the door. He, too, had obviously made efforts to spruce up. His suit was pressed, shoes shined, shirt fresh, tie unstained, and he even had a clean white handkerchief tucked into his breast pocket. Dora thought he looked quite handsome.

They had extra-dry martinis at the bar, then carried refills to the back of the dining room. The detective was on his best behavior, anxious that she was satisfied with their table, holding the chair for her, asking if the room was too cold. Too hot? Too bright? Too noisy?

"John," she said, smiling, "it's just fine. I like it, I really do."

The waiter brought menus, and with no hesitation they both ordered broiled veal chops, pasta with *salsa piccante,* and a salad of arugula and endive. The wine list was left at Wenden's elbow, but Dora said she'd settle for a glass.

"Or two," she said. "I've got to get up early, and I have a long drive ahead of me. John, what's happening with Clayton Starrett?"

"Singing like a birdie," he said. "Ortiz thinks we're really going to nail Ramon Schnabl this time. He's already been charged, but he's out on bond. The judge made him turn in his passport, but Terry is keeping an eye on him just in case."

"What about Helene Pierce?"

"She came in voluntarily for questioning and wouldn't even admit she was at Turner's apartment the night he was offed. I'd love to get a few of her hairs to see if they match up with the ones we found at the Loftus scene, but I don't know how to do it."

"Does she have a cleaning woman?"

Wenden looked at her. "I don't know. Why?"

"Maybe a cleaning woman could get you a few hairs from Helene's brush."

He laughed. "Your brain never stops clicking, does it, Red. Well, it's worth a try. Ah, here's our salad. Wine now?"

"A glass of white with the salad," Dora said, "and a glass of red with the veal. And that's it. Definitely."

They started on their salads, along with chunks of hot garlic toast from a napkined basket. They were both hungry and didn't talk much while they were eating. John did say, "You look very attractive tonight," and Dora said, "Thank you. So do you," and they both laughed and reached for more garlic toast.

The veal chops were just the way they wanted them: charred black on the outside; white, moist, and tender inside.

The pasta sauce was a little more *piccante* than they had expected, but the red wine arrived in time to cool their palates. Dora attacked her food with fierce determination, and Wenden was anything but picky. They finished and sat back, staring with bemusement at the denuded chop bones.

"Think we could get in the *Guinness Book of World Records*?" John asked. "Fastest time for demolishing double veal chops."

"A scrumptious meal," Dora said.

"Dessert?"

"No, no, and no!" she said. "It's diet time again."

Wenden said nothing. She was conscious that he was staring at her, but she would not, could not raise her eyes to his. But she was aware that the lightheartedness of the evening was waning.

John consulted the wine list, then summoned their waiter.

"A bottle of Mumm's Cordon Rouge, please," he said. "As cold as you can make it."

Then Dora looked at him. "Hey," she said, "why the celebration?"

"Not a celebration," Wenden said. "A wake. The answer is no, isn't it, Red?"

She nodded. "You're a good detective."

"It's a downer," he said. "I imagined you had a thing for me."

She reached out to cover his hand with hers. "I love you, John," she said quietly. "I truly do. But I also love my husband."

"I'm not sure," he said, trying to smile, "but that may be illegal."

His reply, even in jest, angered her. "Can't I love two men at the same time? Why not? Men can love two or more women at the same time, and frequently do. What am I—a second-class citizen?"

He held up his palms in surrender. But then the waiter brought their chilled champagne and glasses. They were silent while he went through the ceremony of uncorking the bottle. He poured a bit into John's glass and waited expectantly. But John handed it to Dora.

"You first," he said.

She sampled it. "Just right," she proclaimed.

The waiter filled their flutes, left the bottle in a bucket of ice, and departed. They raised their glasses to each other in a silent toast.

Dora said slowly, "I wish I could explain to you the way I feel in a clear, logical way, but I can't. Because this is something that's got nothing to do with logic. It's a mishmash of emotions and fears and upbringing and education and God knows what else."

"But the bottom line is no," he said.

"That's right," Dora said decisively. "I'm not going to bed with you. But you've got to believe me; I do love you."

They both smiled sadly.

"Look at us," Dora said. "Me, an overweight housewife. You, a burned-out cop. I wish I could understand it, but I can't."

"It happens," John said. "Do you have to understand it? Can't you just accept it?"

"I do accept it," she said. "The love part. Not the infidelity. It's not so much wanting to be faithful to Mario, it's wanting to be faithful to myself. Does that make sense?"

"No," he said, and filled their glasses again.

"Listen," Dora said, almost desperately, "let me take a stab at it. I'm a Catholic. I went to a parochial school. My husband is a Catholic. But neither of us has been to confession for I don't remember how long. Our Catholic friends don't go either. So I don't *think* fear of sin has anything to do with it. But maybe, deep down inside me, it does because of the way I was raised, and I'm just not conscious of it."

"All right," Wenden said, "assuming it's not fear of sin, then what *is* it?"

"It's a lot of things," she said, "and I'm sure you'll laugh at all of them. Look at the people we've been involved with: the Starrett crew and their pals. All of them cheating like mad. You've got to admit they're a scurvy lot; they give adultery a bad name. They make it so *vulgar.* Someone once said morality is a luxury few can afford. Well, *I* can afford it, even if it costs me.

"That's one thing. Another is that it scares me. It really does. I said I love you, and that's the truth. But what if we get it off together, and I like it. Then we drift apart, for whatever reason, and I say to myself, 'Hey, that wasn't so bad. As a matter of fact, it was *fun.* I think I'll find myself another lover.' Then I'm on my way to bimbo-land. It could happen, John."

"What you're saying is that you don't trust yourself."

"You're exactly right; I don't trust myself. I don't dare take the chance. If that makes me a coward, then I'm a coward."

"Or smart," he said with a twisty grin. "Well, Red, I guess you've been doing a lot of heavy thinking about this, and that's kind of a compliment to me. But did you also think about how you might feel tomorrow, next week, next year, ten years from now? No regrets?"

She leaned across the table to stroke his cheek. "You shaved for me," she said. "How nice! Let me tell you something, John. It's like you're driving along a highway. You know where you're going. Then you see a side road leading away. It looks great. All leafy. Beautiful. You're tempted to turn off and explore it. Find out where it goes. But you don't. And maybe you think of that side road a lot in the years to come. Regret is too strong a word, but the curiosity is there. You may never stop wondering where that road led."

He reached for the champagne bottle and poured what was left into their glasses.

"That's what will happen to me," Dora said. "What will happen to you?"

"Nothing," he said. "Which is what usually happens to me. Oh, I'll survive. I've been unhappy before, and I'll be unhappy again. You've been unhappy, haven't you?"

"Yeah," Dora said. "Like right now. Listen, John, why don't you come up to Hartford and visit with us for a weekend—or as long as you like. We've got an extra bedroom."

He stared at her. "I don't think that would be so smart, Red—do you?"

"No," Dora said miserably, "I don't."

John lifted the champagne bottle and tried to pour. It was empty, and he shoved it, neck down, into the melted ice.

"The bubbles are gone," he said.

46

She returned to Hartford the following morning and went directly to the office. She composed her final report on her word processor. Then Dora filled out the forms all claims adjusters were required to submit. She dumped all her papers on the desk of Mike Trevalyan's secretary and went back to her cubicle. She put her feet up on her desk, drank a diet cola, and smoked too many cigarettes.

The summons didn't come until late in the afternoon, and when she walked into Trevalyan's cluttered office, she knew the shit was going to hit the fan; he had two cigars going at once.

"You're approving the claim?" he shouted at her. "You're actually *approving* it?"

"Of course," she said calmly. "None of the beneficiaries had a thing to do with the murder of Lewis Starrett. You want to fight it? You want a lawsuit? Be my guest."

"And look at this!" he howled, waving a fistful of her expense account vouchers. "What the hell were you doing—buying food and booze for every cop in New York?"

"If you read my report," Dora said, "you know what I was doing: helping to break up a fraud for laundering drug money and helping to solve four homicides. Aren't you happy to see a little justice done?"

"Screw justice!" Mike said wrathfully. "All I know is that this is going to cost the Company three million smackers. And what do you think the Accounting Department is going to say when I submit those humongous bills from your so-called computer expert, that Gregor Pinchik. They'll have my balls for hiring that guy."

"Oh Mike, don't be so cheap. Gregor provided the key to the whole case. Look, you want to come out of this smelling like a rose?"

He looked at her suspiciously. "What the hell are you talking about?"

"Pinchik didn't bill for his long-distance calls or modem time because he used our telephone access codes. They were on an electronic bulletin board he subscribes to. But he admitted he's been into our computers and rummaged around. If he can do it, then any smart hacker can do it. Persuade the Company to hire Pinchik as a consultant, to upgrade our computer security with state-of-the-art safeguards. If we don't do it, it's just a matter of time before we start paying out claims to some larcenous hacker who's invaded our records."

Trevalyan thought about that a moment. "Yeah," he said finally, "you got a point there, kiddo. Listen, how about us going out for some food and talking about what I should put in my memo to the brass."

"No, thanks," she said. "I want to get home to Mario."

"You just want one of his gourmet dinners," Mike said grumpily.

Dora smiled serenely. "There's a lot to be said for home cooking."